MW00512041

Wow! What an a[…] good and evil in this world. A riveting mystery with Jesus in control as He always has been, is today, and forever will be! Mrs. Hill brings her characters to such life … you'll wish you could call them on the phone to catch up on what is happening now in their lives.

Molly Gregory
Homemaker, Ozark, Alabama

Following C. J.'s life in this story is an amazing journey for any reader. Everyday people can relate to the story and see how God's grace can save any heart. Mrs. Robin Hill is a beautiful person and a beautiful author who has shown yet another example of the amazing love of Jesus. The Poinsettia Cross is an excellent read for anyone and will challenge your heart and your faith to bigger levels. Let's hope there is more to come from this talented writer!

Lisa Shirley
Teacher, Midland City Elementary
School, Dothan, Alabama

The Poinsettia Cross is a Christian mystery novel that will take readers through the many turns in the life of the central character, C. J. Taylor. Robin is able to develop the story of a troubled young man who finds that amnesia is the least of his troubles. While searching for answers to his many questions, C. J. must first deal with his own rebellion against God. Throughout the book, Robin has woven a thread of God's love and forgiveness for those whose lives are less than perfect.

I count it a joy to have known Robin and her husband Jim for several years. I am constantly amazed at the many talents of this wife of a Southern Baptist Minister. I hope there will be many more writings from the pen of this gifted lady.

Johnny Anderson
Minster of Music, Ridgecrest Baptist
Church, Ozark, Alabama

The Poinsettia Cross

To Gary,
Thank you for all you do for those who come to [illegible]
[illegible]
Romans 10:13

The Poinsettia Cross

A Novel of Hope and Courage

Suffering from amnesia, can C. J. Taylor figure out who he is–and whose he is–before it's too late?

ROBIN D. HILL

Tate Publishing & *Enterprises*

The Poinsettia Cross

Copyright © 2009 by Robin D. Hill. All rights reserved.

No part of this publication may be reproduced, stored in a retrieval system or transmitted in any way by any means, electronic, mechanical, photocopy, recording or otherwise without the prior permission of the author except as provided by USA copyright law.

Scripture quotations are taken from the Holy Bible, King James Version, Cambridge, 1769. Used by permission. All rights reserved.

The opinions expressed by the author are not necessarily those of Tate Publishing, LLC.

Published by Tate Publishing & Enterprises, LLC
127 E. Trade Center Terrace | Mustang, Oklahoma 73064 USA
1.888.361.9473 | www.tatepublishing.com

Tate Publishing is committed to excellence in the publishing industry. The company reflects the philosophy established by the founders, based on Psalm 68:11,
"The Lord gave the word and great was the company of those who published it."

Book design copyright © 2009 by Tate Publishing, LLC. All rights reserved.
Cover and Interior design by Stefanie Rooney

Published in the United States of America

ISBN: 978-1-60604-835-1
1. Fiction, Religious
2. Fiction, Mystery & Detective, General
08.12.16

Dedication

First and foremost, I want to dedicate this work to my Lord and Savior, Jesus Christ. Without his absolutely divine intervention and countless means of encouragement, it would never have been possible. I love you, Lord!

Acknowledgements

To the love of my life, my wonderful honey, my greatest fan, Jim, whose gracious patience continuously prods me along. Without your love and encouragement, I would never have completed the task. And your encouragement for me means everything in the world! I love you!

To Brandon and Robin Marie, to Austin and Cierra—you have always brought me great joy. I love you all more than you can ever possibly know.

To Mom, Dad, Greg, Tina, and Toni, and to all of my extended family—I want to thank you for encouraging me as well. I love you all ... *much!*

And least I forget my greatest friends in the world, Gail, Geoff, Cookie, Terry, and to all of my awesome friends at church—how can I ever thank all of you enough for being there for me every time I needed a friend? I love you!

Foreword

It's like a dream come true. My wife of over thirty-two years now has prayed over and toiled over every paragraph of this book. Several years ago, Robin asked God to allow her to do something to share His love with a wider audience than our personal circle of influence. God promised her that one day, this book would be published, and today, you hold in your hand the fulfillment of that promise. One joy of her life is to share His love in this way.

One of Robin's spiritual gifts is that of giving. In her case, it should be called the gift of sacrifice. She has sacrificed a career to be a stay-at-home mom and raise our children. As the wife of a career Air Force veteran, she has sacrificed to stand beside me. Now as a pastor's wife of nearly twenty years, she continues to selflessly give of herself in more ways than I can explain. Through her love for our Lord, she has sacrificed her life to enable this pastor to minister to the multitudes. Now she is able to share her love for Jesus through what I pray will be a blessing to you, the reader.

Mystery, adventure, and God's love often go hand-in-hand. That love is revealed through C. J.'s life. Robin will have you laughing and crying. She will also challenge you to see God's love in action. I pray that you will enjoy the book and understand a little bit more about God's grace and love.

Jim Hill

Husband, US Air Force (Retired) Veteran, Senior Pastor, Ridgecrest Baptist Church, Ozark, Alabama

Prologue

Filling a corner of the living room, a huge Christmas tree reached up and tickled the ceiling. It had been decorated in a most non-traditional fashion: white lights, homemade bows, and matching ribbon garland. And rather than the traditional ornaments, the tree was filled with a myriad of artificial poinsettias and red berry sprays. The fake poinsettias boasted a display of non-traditional colors, from blues and purples to golds, silvers, and pinks. But the flowers that drew the most attention were the burgundy ones. Year after year, Rhea Richardson had fashioned them into a cross formation on the front of the tree and used berry sprays to mimic droplets of blood that pooled at the foot of the cross.

The poinsettia cross had become a conversation piece, a real favorite—not an expectation, but somehow perfectly suited to the home of a Southern Baptist pastor and his family. But while the floral cross had become a favorite to most of those who laid eyes on it, it wasn't suited to everyone. Year after year, Cory would voice his personal opinion. "Crosses are Easter things, aren't they? Whatever happened to Santa Clause and Rudolph? Where's the sleigh, the candy canes, and the ornaments?"

This year, there would be no complaining. This year, the house had fallen sadly silent.

Chapter 1

Breathe ... got to ... breathe ...

Kicking and flailing his arms, he gasped for air when his head finally broke the surface of the water. He looked up into the vast blackness but saw nothing. Yet he could feel drops of rain falling down onto his face. The water felt cold. Just to breathe was taking an amazing amount of energy, energy he no longer had. His mind raced. Visions of bloodthirsty sharks and stinging jellyfish invaded his head. He felt as though he'd been cast in some sort of horror movie. He could only hope he hadn't been stranded in the middle of the Gulf of Mexico.

He licked his lips, expecting to taste salty water, but the water wasn't salty at all. Viciously weak, he kicked his bare feet until his toes finally reached the slimy bottom. Thankful, he crawled his way out of the water and fell flat on his face onto the mushy ground at the edge, his unconscious body lying very still in the cold December rain.

•

Time disappeared. The rain let up. He felt cold and stiff,

his muscles almost unmovable, his mouth, parched and dry. Darkness had invaded his mind as though it were an infamous London fog. Opening his swollen eyelids had been a terrific struggle, shifting them even more so. He picked up his throbbing head, and in the sky, he finally caught a glimpse of pale blue. Over to his left, he saw a faint light in the distance. His lungs tight, his body cold beyond shivering, he forced himself to stand and slowly staggered through ankle-deep mud toward the light.

Time seemed to drag before he reached a rusty wire fence separating the pasture from a narrow dirt road. The light was closer now, but to get to it, he was forced to scale the antique fence. The numbness in his feet made finding a foothold nearly impossible. But as he topped the fence, it disintegrated under his meager one hundred forty-pound frame, and once again, he fell crashing to the ground. It took several minutes before he could catch his breath and build up enough energy to stand again.

Light ... get to ... light. He looked toward the light and was surprised to find it had multiplied. As the early morning sky was growing brighter and brighter, he could see the light was coming from a house. Whoever lived there must be up and stirring. He stumbled many times as he made his way toward the house. But when he approached the porch, he collapsed to his knees. From inside the house, he could faintly hear people arguing. He gazed down at the steps leading up to the porch and crawled until he could go no farther. He laid his head on the third step and closed his eyes just as the sun came peeking over the horizon.

Chapter 2

Monday, December 5

In the bedroom he shared with his missus, Zachary Taylor shut the door, pulled one of the top drawers out of the dresser, and felt around above its empty space. When he found the large manila envelope he'd been looking for, he carefully pulled it from its hiding place. The outside of the envelope contained an Ozark, Alabama postmark but no return address. He quickly opened it, removed the contents, and studied it very closely. And then with a grin, Mr. Taylor returned the contents to the envelope, quickly slid it back into its hiding place, and returned the drawer into the dresser.

•

Get your fishin' pole! You got one! You got one! Hurry!

The stranger tossed fitfully from side to side, disturbed by the childish voice in his dream. Dazed, he opened his eyes and found the room cast in total darkness; a darkness so thick, his aching eyes could not negotiate it. He closed them hard and opened them again, straining to see until they felt as though they would pure burst out of his head—but still there was nothing. He slowly sat up and felt around, searching for a light without any luck.

His head ached. His skin felt dry and itchy. Like his skin, his head too felt itchy. When he reached up to scratch, he found his hair matted to his head and grotesquely stiff with what felt like caked mud through the ends. His mouth and throat felt as though they'd been stuffed with cotton. His feet were still bare and caked with patches of dried mud. On his body, he found chains wrapped around his neck, his wrists, and his waist. He knew something wasn't right, although he felt surprisingly free to move.

As he continued to feel around, he found he was sitting on top of a twin-sized bed, a waterbed, with drawers underneath. It also had a bookshelf-style headboard that was apparently cluttered with hoards of junk. And he still could not find a single light source.

Although he felt warm, dry, and basically comfortable, he felt trapped by the darkness. And then suddenly, outside the door, he could hear voices yelling.

"That ain't fair! Why do you let C. J. sleep all the time?" the first voice hollered.

"Don't you dare question me!" the other voice hollered back.

The yelling went on for several more seconds and became louder and louder until it finally ended with a smack and a loud crash. A moment later, he heard a door slam and heavy feet stomping down a set of creaky stairs. He picked up his head, noticed a strip of light shining in from around the door, and breathed a sigh of relief. "Well, what do you know. I'm not blind after all," he whispered to himself. Then nonchalantly, he looked up when something from the ceiling glistened in the faint light. "Aah!" he suddenly hollered. In a split second, he rolled himself over, jumped out of the bed, and crouched down in a corner, his eyes wild with terror and his head buzzing relentlessly. A moment later, another door flew open and a woman with dark, shoulder-length hair wearing a thick, green bathrobe came rushing up a short flight of stairs into his room with a small brood of children following her. She groped along the wall until she found a hidden light switch and the room was finally bathed in dull light.

"Ow!" he cried when the sudden light set his eyes on fire and made his head feel as though a sledge hammer had just come crashing down between his ears. He grabbed his head, covered his eyes, and waited until he could begin to open them a little at a time. And with a heavy scowl on his face, he looked up and gawked at the ceiling just above the headboard of the bed.

Her brow furrowed, the woman asked, "C. J. Taylor, what in the world is the matter with you? Why are you sitting on the floor?" She found him in the corner and tried to follow his line of sight. There, hanging from the ceiling on fishing line, she found a twelve-inch long vinyl black widow spider. "Good grief! This place is a *mess!*" she cried as she snatched the toy from the ceiling, threw it down onto the floor, and stomped it until it burst. "If you don't like it, why'd you put it up there in the first place?" she cried when she snatched it up and threw it at him.

Unable to utter a sound, his wild eyes gawking, C. J. gasped, instinctively jerked the dead toy out of his lap, and flung it across the floor. It took him a few seconds before he could release that humongous gulp of oxygen-deprived air from his lungs. And shaking, trying to rub cold chills out of his arms, he found himself silently gazing at the rest of the utterly chaotic room.

Awkwardly long and narrow, the unusual slope of the ceiling, the shallow walls, and the flight of stairs up from the door told him that the room had to be in the attic of the house. The hardwood floor and the particleboard furniture sat cluttered under piles of dirty clothes, scattered books, and tossed magazines. Over in the opposite corner, he found a broken electric guitar. An untold number of wadded-up paper bags from McDonalds, Taco Bell, and Sonic lay scattered all over the room, along with their half-empty cup counterparts. About a dozen empty pizza boxes lay twisted and crushed—and the LEGO bricks! C. J. could not believe the LEGO bricks. Thousands of them! Creatures and vehicles, space ships and robots in varying degrees of completion scattered from one end of the room to the other.

Amazed, C. J. looked up and found the walls and ceiling had been plastered with poster upon poster of longhaired rock stars wearing all black clothing and thick, grotesque makeup. He could not find a single window for all the posters, which explained the absence of natural outside light. And the single, low-wattage light bulb that hung from the center of the ceiling explained the dullness.

C. J. brought his hand up to rub the burning sensation from his eyes when all of a sudden, something else caught his attention. He threw his hands out and glared at them in utter horror when he found a coating of black polish covering his fingernails.

The woman came to him, snatched his right hand up, and dropped it again after she studied it for a single moment. "What *is* your problem today? You put that trash on there yourself! And if it's *finally* bothering you, then you'll have to use polish remover to get it off! Now breakfast is ready. Let's go."

Wide-eyed, C. J. stared hard at the ugly polish, and at the chains, and at the condition of the dirty, black clothing he found himself surrounded by, and he slowly shook his head. "What is this place? Why are you keeping me chained up like this?"

"Son, what are you talking about?" she asked, and when he pulled the chain out from his neck, she rolled her blue eyes and pointed to one of the characters on one of the many posters. The particular young man in the poster emulated evil and death with his gothic get-up; dark clothing and painted face, spiked hair and blackened fingernail. And chains: shiny, heavy, and too many to be counted. "*You're* the one who insists on copying these fruitcakes. You call that trash *jewelry*."

C. J. pulled on the chain that was wrapped around his wrist. "How do I get this junk off?"

"Well, I suppose you take it *off* the same way you put it *on*," his mother complained when she came to him, knelt down, and shoved the gross hair back away from his forehead.

Out of pure instinct, he jerked his head back. "What are you doing?"

"Hold still! When you came home the other day, we found you on the front porch, wet, muddy, and sleeping off a drunk. We also found a huge lump on your forehead. I'm just checking it out. It almost sounds like something or someone has finally knocked some sense into your head. And if that's the case, then when I meet that someone, I'll be sure to thank him. Now, get yourself up out of that corner and get a shower."

"Why don't I remember anything? Why don't I remember you? I take it you're my mother, right?"

She sighed when she remembered the grotesque condition they'd found him in. "I don't know, son. It could be we should have taken you to the doctor instead of dragging you up here to bed. But—" She stood to her feet and headed for the stairs that led to the door. "We didn't do that because this is *not* by any means the first time you've come crawling home looking, acting, and smelling like you've been wallowing in a pigsty. Go get a shower. You have a *job,* remember?"

"*I* … have a *job?*"

Again, she rolled her eyes. "And to think you wanted to move into your own place! Good grief! You're going to be twenty-two years old soon. By now, you ought to at the very least be responsible enough to get yourself out of bed on the days you're on duty. But no. You're so lazy, you'll *never* make it without your momma to get you motivated. I guess that's one pipe dream you can give up.

"It's Monday morning. You've had the whole weekend to sleep it off, now get up and get moving. You've got less than an hour before your father leaves."

C. J.'s face turned bright red. "Look, lady, I don't know what your angle is, but I've had enough of this joke. I already told you I don't know who you are! I don't—"

The woman interrupted him when she leaned toward the door and hollered, "Zachary Taylor, I could use your assistance ... *immediately,* please!"

It was only seconds later when a stern-faced, muscular man of about fifty-some years of age came up the stairway into the room. His salt-and-pepper hair had been cut short, and he wore black dress pants and a navy-blue long-sleeved uniform shirt. The insignia on the front of his shirt made him look important. "Boy, it's about time!" the man cried. "What was it *this* time? Hmm? Was it weed, coke, or was it booze and crack? How many more times do you think you can pull this stunt and get away with it? Huh?"

C. J. glared up at the stranger with a look of absolute confusion. "I don't get it." He yanked the chain from his neck and laid it in a heap on the floor beside him. "I don't remember you either. Why?"

With a look of arrogance that no man could duplicate, Mr. Taylor said, "I don't know and I don't care. Maybe that knock on your noggin finally did us a favor." And then he got down in C. J.'s face and said, "Now you look here, mister. Don't you dare forget this one thing. Part of having some sense about you means doing what you're told, understand? If your mother told you to jump off the Empire State Building, I'd expect you to jump. If she told you to get a shower, I'd expect you to get that shower immediately, and if not then, sooner. You don't question her. You just do it. Do you understand now?"

Unable to determine exactly what to think or how to respond, C. J. finally determined that his best chance would be to play along in their little game. "Well, *Dad,* it seems I'm having a little bit of a recollection problem today. So, why don't you remind me of what kind of job I have? Do I have to dress like *this?*" he asked while pulling on the dirty black T-shirt he was wearing. "Or do I get to dress more impressive ... like *you,* for instance?"

For an instant, the man turned and glanced awkwardly at his wife, mouthed some incomprehensible thing, and then turned back again. "Your uniforms are hanging in your closet where your mother usually keeps them. And apparently you've lost your car again, so you'll be riding in with me. We'll be leaving in about thirty minutes."

To C. J., nothing felt right; from his painted fingernails and oversized clothing to the evil-looking junk room, and from the joke they called "jewelry" to that weird glance between the people who considered themselves his parents. He felt awkwardly out of place like an oak tree growing in the middle of a pine forest. Surely this was right. Surely these people weren't out of their minds. But why could he not remember?

Nothing about this place looked even slightly familiar, not to mention holding a job. "Uniforms ... riding in together ... obviously you and I work for the same company. And while we're on the way to wherever we're supposed to be going, would you mind reminding me of my duties? What are you, anyway?" he asked while studying his father's name badge. "A police officer, a fireman? Whom do you work for?"

The man didn't have time to get anything out of his mouth before his wife broke the tension. "C. J., do you want some breakfast or don't you?"

"No, ma'am. I'll just get my shower and get ready to go. I now have about twenty-nine minutes and forty-seven seconds left out of my thirty-minute allowance. That should be just enough time to scrape this slime off my skin. I would appreciate it, though, if you could show me where to find the stuff to clean this trash off my fingers."

"Fine. Suit yourself," the woman said as she stood up and began picking up some of the scattered clothes. "The polish remover and cotton balls are under the bathroom sink."

C. J. angled his eyes around Mr. Taylor and studied the woman and her three children. The youngest child, a painfully thin, pale-faced girl of about five wearing pink bunny slippers and a pink housecoat, came to him and held out her hand. "C. J., why do you use fingernail polish that's black? Mine is red, see."

He gently took her frail little hand and studied her fingers. "Your polish looks very nice, a whole lot better than mine does." And then he noticed her fair complexion, her long dark hair, and her sparkling pale-blue eyes—very much a duplicate of her mother. He glanced up and noticed that the young boy had the same rich chocolate hair as his mother but he, like the elder boy, had eyes of brown, like their father.

He turned back to the little girl and whispered, "Boys aren't supposed to use fingernail polish on their fingernails, are they?"

"No, but *you* did."

"Julia, that's enough," her mother interrupted. "Go on to your room and get ready for school."

The shy little girl pulled her hand away from C. J. and whispered, "Yes, ma'am," as she headed for the stairs.

The other young child, a boy of about seven, came to him and spoke with a terrible lisp. "C. J., today is the 'sow-and-tell day at 'cool. You p'womised you would 'tum wiss' me so I 'tould 'sow you to my f'winds."

"Dylan!" the woman cried. "I *already* told you you were *not* taking your brother in to your class for show-and-tell! Your friends do not need to see him like this. Now, get yourself out of here, and get ready for school!"

"But he *p'womised!*" the boy cried.

C. J. shook his head and whispered, "Uh … I'm sorry … *Dylan.* But *Mom* said—"

Suddenly, he was interrupted when the woman turned, pointed to the door, and hollered, "*Dylan … out!*" The little boy stomped down the stairs whimpering.

C. J. glanced up at the third child, the tall, lanky teenager. The boy's hair had been dyed black, was much longer than that of his mother's, and stood straight up in the most gruesome set of ten-inch spikes he'd ever seen. Like his own, the boy's clothing also resembled that of the characters in the posters: baggy black jeans, black T-shirt, and chains. When their eyes locked, C. J. noticed a nasty bruise on the left side of his face. Without a word, the boy backed himself down the stairs and out of the room, and C. J. jumped when he heard a door slam further down the hallway. A moment later, music—loud music—began vibrating the very foundation of the house.

As if she didn't notice the music at all, the woman finished picking up the clothes, headed over toward the door, and hollered, "Bo Taylor, if you do that again, I'll make the other side of your face match!" Like he could really hear her idle threat over the pounding bass. And when she turned back toward C. J., she hollered, "And as for you, mister, last chance! Get yourself up out of that corner and go get your shower! The bathroom is out this door and to the left. You'll find everything you need in there."

His mind racing, his brow furrowed, C. J. slowly stood to his feet, yanked another chain from his wrist, and dropped it loudly onto the only bare place on the floor. "Now, correct me if I'm wrong, but shouldn't I already *know* where the bathroom is?"

Mrs. Taylor shook her finger in his face and hollered, "I warned you, mister, no more games!"

He simply shrugged his shoulders. "Who said this was a game?"

"*Go!*"

"Yes, ma'am!"

Chapter 3

As C. J. watched the warm mud-colored water swirl around the drain, he could not remember a single time when a shower had felt so relaxing. The pounding ache that had shot through his head earlier seemed to be washing away along with the mud. He could only hope the smeared face paint he'd found on his face when he looked in the mirror wouldn't leave a stain on his skin.

Out of the shower, while he was combing his wet hair, he stood gazing at his image in the bathroom mirror, wondering whom it was that was staring back at him. Feeling awkwardly out of place, he searched for differences between himself and his younger siblings. Yet, other than to Bo, the more obvious differences were subtle at best. Oh, his eyes might have been a darker shade of blue than his little sister's, and his dark hair might have had more red highlights than Dylan's, but there was nothing major to speak of.

As he pulled on the uniform pants, his mind raced to a far away place; a place he could not quite grasp. When he pulled the belt tight and buckled it, he felt a deep sense of longing; a longing to go home. But where was home? Surely this wasn't it—was it?

Suddenly, his mind was jolted back to reality when his mother knocked on the door. "C. J., open the door and grab this toothbrush." Immediately he glanced down at the cup full of used toothbrushes and suddenly it dawned on him. "Which one is supposed to be mine?" he asked through the door. *Yuck.*

"I have a new one for you! Just come and get it!"

When he opened the door, she had already busied herself shoving folded towels into a linen closet just outside. And when she handed him the new toothbrush that was still in the package, he gently took it out of her hand and said, "Thank you. I, uh, I was wondering—"

"I know! I know!" she interrupted. She rolled her eyes and mockingly added, "You *can't* remember!"

Disappointed that the woman obviously refused to believe him, C. J. sighed. "No ma'am. I *didn't,*" he said as he pulled his uniform shirt off the hanger, slipped it on, and began buttoning it. "What I was wondering is what do I have to do to have this uniform made to fit me? Either it's expanding while it's hanging in the closet, or I'm shrinking. I don't know which."

Mrs. Taylor glanced over the baggy shirt and then noticed a couple puckers in the waistband of his pants. "Listen, bud, the next time you go on one of those ridiculous binges, you'd better eat something so you won't lose so much weight. And as for the uniform, when you get to the station, ask your father to have Mr. Westbrook procure a smaller one for you."

With his gaze lowered to the floor, C. J. simply whispered, "Yes, ma'am."

In all her magnificent anger, the woman had come across as genuine. Surely it wouldn't be she who was losing her mind. Perhaps she had spoken the truth. Perhaps his lapse of memory truly had been caused by his abuse of drugs, alcohol, or whatever foreign chemicals he'd chosen to ingest. Perhaps—

"C. J., take this with you," the woman said as Zach and C. J. were heading for the door. She had come carrying a travel mug and practically forced it into her son's hand.

When he momentarily removed the lid, C. J. found the mug full of steaming hot chocolate. Perhaps had he been given a choice, he might have chosen coffee that morning. With his mind still groggy from the mind-blowing weekend, it sure seemed like coffee would do the trick.

It was when the woman came to him, turned his face up, and looked him square in the eye that she said, "And you make sure you drink *all* of it," that a burning sensation suddenly ignited deep in the pit of his stomach.

"It'll help get your day started," she added.

"Yes, ma'am."

•

When he slid into the passenger seat of his father's old Ford pickup, C. J. asked, "So, are you going to—" Suddenly his attention was stolen away when his father backed out of the driveway onto the dirt road. There, directly across from the house, was the fenced-in cow pasture, and in the center of the pasture was an acre-sized watering hole. The ground was uneven, dropping into a downhill slope with the far end rising up a steep embankment and leveling off near the roadside. The watering hole sat down in the bottom. As he looked, C. J. noticed that a couple different areas of the fencing appeared to have recently been replaced, and any footprints he might have left behind would have already been made obscure between the driving rain and the herd of grazing cattle.

Several awkward moments passed before Zach asked, "Am I going to what?"

"Oh, uh, you know … tell me about what you do," C. J. answered. "And about what *I* do. And about what I'm supposed to call you while we're there." He looked down and read the patch on his sleeve. "I can see we're in the fire department … right? And you're obviously somebody important."

Mr. Taylor slowly nodded.

"Well—" C. J. asked while straining his groggy mind to make mental pictures of every street sign, every stop sign, and every turn.

"Well, what?"

"Well, is that it? Do we just throw a little water on a fire, or is there something more to this uniform?"

"We're fire rescue, okay? You can call me Chief. And since you'll be sticking with me from now on, you'll be getting the hang of it again in no time. Does that answer your question?"

C. J. thought long and hard for several tense moments. "Shouldn't I have had the hang of it at least *once* in order to get it *again?*"

"Maybe your mother was right. We should have taken you to the doctor."

"But you didn't. And now I don't remember things. You know, it doesn't take a rocket scientist to know that my coming to work with this loss of memory, especially in fire rescue, will only cause tension."

Zach never took his eyes off the traffic. But he sighed loudly. "That's exactly why you'll be working with me. Take this as a warning. After last Friday, the crews don't want you back. They'll balk at the very sight of you. This is something you've brought on yourself, especially with that ridiculous costume mess."

In spite of the tinge of defensiveness that was beginning to well up inside of him, C. J. finished the last sip of the hot chocolate and set the mug in the seat beside him. "There. This mess is gone, just like she insisted. Now I don't remember last Friday so why don't you tell me what happened?"

Only a moment later Zach pulled into the station parking lot and stopped the truck. With his left hand readied on the door handle, he cut his eyes toward his son but could not look him in the eye. "Later," was all he could muster.

•

The Taylors hadn't yet reached the entrance before they were met by the changing of the guard, A-shifters heading in, C-shifters heading out. Each man was carrying something in his hands; lunch boxes, coats, etc. "Is *that* C. J.?" one man asked.

Zach nodded hesitantly, and to C. J.'s surprise, his father's words rang true to the nth-degree. He could not believe he was witnessing so many grown men act like such spoiled rotten children. As soon as they laid eyes on him, their heads dropped, their shoulders fell. And the complaining. It was unreal.

Taylor's face turned blood red, and the veins in his neck began to bulge like balloons. "Then C-shifters, *go home!* The kid'll be working on A-shift and with *me* and *me* only! That means *none* of you have anything to worry about, do you?"

One of the A-shift colleagues, a big man by the name of Frank White, stomped his size thirteen foot down and slung his lunchbox across the parking lot, casting sandwich bags and containers in an arc across the pavement. He pointed to Zach's face and hollered, "Taylor, I *told* you that if you brung that kid back here again, even if he *was* cleaned up, that we was all walkin' out! That kid's an accident waitin' to happen!"

Others of the A-shift who had already arrived heard the pandemonium and came rushing to check it out. And C. J. took note that their reaction seemed worse than that of the other group: more than likely because he was expected to work with these.

"He's a *curse*—" this Frank guy continued, "—a *death* trap!"

One of the A-shifters, a young, dark-skinned man, came right up to C. J.'s face, poked him on his chest, and said, "Mister Taylor, after what you did for us last Friday, you can go on home. We don't need you."

His jaw tense and his teeth clamped tightly shut, C. J. backed away and glared over at his father.

Zach threw his hands up in the air and hollered, "Back off, Danny! Now, C. J. here has had a little accident. He got himself knocked in the head."

"Oh, sure, like a knock on *that* head is gonna make a difference!" Danny cried.

"Get him out of here!" another hollered.

And then several of the men began to laugh when Jason Cruz, the A-shift clown whose ancestors had come all the way from Mexico, cried, "You mean you *finally* figured out who was boss around your house?"

"That's enough!" Taylor yelled. "C. J.'s having some trouble remembering things. So he's gonna need—"

"*No way!*" Jason interrupted. "How could *the evil one* ever forget to put his false face on, to spike that hair, or put that *dog* chain around his neck?"

"Open your eyes, Cruz!" Zach hollered.

Standing in the back of the snickering crowd, Shane Westbrook allowed his eyes to roam back and forth from the boss to the son. Oh, sure, he'd heard Zach's explanation, but he would not be so easily convinced after his mind raced back to last Friday.

•

Friday, December 2

The weather had been miserably cold and foggy. There had been an apartment fire—children playing with matches and a candle. Frank had come out of the apartment carrying an injured little girl of about seven years of age. When he passed by C. J., and when the little girl glanced up and caught a glimpse of C. J.'s heavily painted face and gruesomely spiked dark hair, terror filled her eyes. She reached up and clung tightly to Frank's neck, and she began screaming, "*No!* I didn't mean to do it! It was an accident! Don't let him get me! He'll make me *die* cause I was bad! Don't let him get me!"

Frank had tried to reassure her that C. J.'s costume was only makeup, but the little girl would not be comforted. Moments later, she went into cardiac arrest and later died in spite of all the efforts to save her.

The A-shift had grown tremendously weary. As soon as the crew had returned to the station, Shane headed for the showers. But when he passed by Zach's office door, he stopped dead in his tracks when he overheard his boss yelling from inside. "Get your junk out of that locker, get yourself to the house, and get rid of the trash! *If* you are not finished cleaning yourself up by the time I get home, you'll be dead meat! You understand? I've been embarrassed by you for the *last* time!" And then all of a sudden, Zach's office door came flying open and C. J. came flying across the room, landing on his backside against the cinder block wall on the other side of the day room.

Being the only witness, Shane rushed over to his partner to help him to his feet. He might have asked what it was all about, but he already knew the answer. The little girl's death was being blamed on C. J.'s freaky appearance. Shane reached his hand out to help his partner to his feet and asked, "Are you all right?"

C. J.'s face shone blood red, even under the black face paint. But he said nothing as he ignored Shane's offer of help and pulled himself to his feet.

For three long, grueling months, not only had the boy's appearance caused trouble in the field, it had caused great dissention among the crew as well. And his refusal of an explanation only added fuel to the fire. Having been partnered with the kid since his first day, Shane had taken all the flack he could tolerate. The men had laughed and teased, making wise cracks at every opportunity. But the little girl's death became the final straw, the one that broke the camel's back. Shane's blood pressure instantly skyrocketed. "You know what, C. J.? I'm *done* with you! *Get out!*"

All of a sudden, C. J. exploded, knocked his partner out of the way, and headed for the door.

"And *don't* come back," Shane hollered after him, "until you clean yourself up!"

•

Yes, Friday had been a really tough day. "That little girl is *dead* because of him! I tell ya, the kid's a *curse!*" Frank again hollered. "He's a *death* trap! Get him out of here!"

C. J. became flabbergasted when his father retorted by saying, "Then let the curse be on me and on my kid! If anyone is supposed to die because of this curse, it'll be us and no one else!"

"*Curse ... die ...* are you out of your mind?" C. J. cried. "I'm outta here!"

Taylor turned and pointed to his son. "*You! Shut* your mouth!"

What C. J. witnessed next nearly cracked him up. The crew, the whole lot of them, turned to each other, shrugged their shoulders, and said things like, "Works for me," "Have it your way," and "Can we go home now?" It was as if once Zach "accepted" the curse, all of a sudden, they were free. And without another word, they disappeared, each man heading in his own direction. All but Shane, that is.

With a look of absolute confusion written all over his face, C. J. turned to his father and asked, "What just happened here?"

"Ah, some of these quacks still believe in the tooth fairy. All I did was—"

"—remove them from the *curse,*" the boy interrupted. "*My* curse. Is that what this last Friday thing is all about?"

"I said we'll discuss it later," his father replied.

Mr. Westbrook was a tall man and of slender build. Wearing the same blue uniform, he blended with the crowd with his short, sandy blond hair and hazel green eyes. And when the rest of the crew had gone on about their business, Shane came up to C. J. and stared strangely at him.

"Don't tell me. You want rid of me too, don't you?" C. J. asked the stranger with a smirk.

Before Shane could respond, Zach said, "Forget it, Westbrook. I meant what I said. He's staying, but he'll be with me from now on. You are hereby officially relieved of the burden."

C. J. took it as a slam. He shook his head and said, "Thanks, Dad. I appreciate you too." And then he glanced up at Shane. "And I suppose I'm supposed to know who you are too, right?"

"Chief," Shane began while keeping his eye on C. J., "now, you know I don't follow any of that *stupid-stitious* stuff. And as you can see, most of the rest of them don't either. And, yeah, C. J., you probably *should* know who I am."

"Well, Mister West—whatever your name is—would you mind explaining to me what I did last Friday that was so bad? Because *I* don't remember, and *he* ain't talkin'."

"He's *still* with me," Zach interjected. "He's caused enough dissention."

Shane sighed deeply but kept a wary eye on the boy. "Now, Chief, I won't argue with you there. Friday was a bomb," he said with sarcasm. "C. J., I know I told you not to come back until you cleaned yourself up. I see you took me up on my advice. Wise choice."

Silent, C. J. stood there as though being chastised like a disobedient child.

Watching C. J. like a hawk, Shane stared at him with expectation written all over his face.

"Man, I'd sure appreciate it if you would stop sizing me up!" C. J. finally hollered.

"Yeah? And *I'd* appreciate it if you would apologize! You owe me at least that much!" Shane hollered back.

To be honest, C. J. didn't know what to say. Although he felt sure he didn't deserve the chastisement, he couldn't remember enough of anything to even muster an apology. Besides, how could he apologize for the antics of somebody he didn't know? "For what?" he asked.

Disgusted, Shane rolled his eyes, sighed heavily, and turned toward the door. "Forget it, C. J. Just get yourself inside."

"Just tell me where to go."

Shane shook his head and pointed to the door that led to the day room. "Right there. You'll probably have to kick Jason out of your place … as usual."

"Who's Jason?"

"Jason, the clown," he answered. "The 'who's boss in your house' thing. Don't tell me you've already forgotten that too!"

"Oh. That was Jason."

"Yeah!"

Leading C. J. into the day room, Shane came around him and sat himself down at a table.

All of a sudden, C. J. jumped when someone came up from behind and smacked him on his back. "Well, if it isn't Freakazoid, back for another mind-blowing episode!

"Hey, kid, you clean up well," the bald guy said when he came around him and looked him in the eye. "Wait. I don't remember your eyes being *dark* blue. For some reason, I thought they were more—ah, forget it," he said as he finally brushed him off and walked away.

Shane glanced up and tipped his head toward the bald guy. "Taylor, whatever brain-function lapse you got goin' on, it's for sure Jason there will kick it back into high gear in no time."

C. J. nodded with a smirk, studying the man with a hint of suspicion. "Yeah. Thanks for the warning."

Jason dropped himself down into the burgundy recliner over near the corner. "Ain't never seen it, but I always suspected you Taylors had some Hollyweird in ya. Unfortunately, though, in this business, a purdy face ain't gonna pay one red cent more than an ugly one will. It won't put out fires, won't save lives—should'a kept the ugly."

Again, Shane glanced up. "Speaking of looks, C. J., are you willing to get yourself fitted for a new uniform? That thing you're wearing is looking real bad."

When C. J. nodded, Shane nearly fell out of his chair. "*What?*"

With a weird look on his face, C. J. studied him in silence.

"Come with me, then."

"Don't you think I'll bring you some sort of *bad* luck?" C. J. asked as he glanced over at Frank who had made himself practically obscure by finding a place in the corner opposite of Jason.

Shane turned and headed for the door with C. J. following at a distance. "I don't need *stupid-stition,*" Shane added. "I've got Jesus."

"Oh, great! A religious fanatic. That's *all* I need!" C. J. cried. He stopped and began rubbing his temples. The headache had suddenly returned with a vengeance.

To C. J.'s surprise, Shane simply smiled back at him. "I sure am, and I'm proud of it. You ought to try it sometime."

"Fat chance that's gonna happen."

Chapter 4

The new uniform felt a whole lot more comfortable than the old one, but when C. J. came out of the locker room into the day room, he slid his hands down into his pants pockets and just stood there surveying the room. A long wooden table with its bench-style seats filled the center while a menagerie of couches and chairs lined the outer walls. The A-shift crew sat randomly scattered throughout, either reading books and magazines or playing board games. It was the type of scene C. J. had expected until his eyes drifted over to the back right corner. Directly in the corner, the scrawny, shaven-headed Jason Cruz sat sideways in the burgundy recliner with one leg dangling over the arm. He was busy flipping through the pages of a car magazine. But what took C. J. by surprise was what sat next to Jason's recliner. It was an antique upright piano with a black lacquer finish. C. J. could see it had not been cared for. The outer veneer was warped near the bottom and several of the keys were missing their ivory tops.

"What's that doing here?" he asked out of pure curiosity.

"What?" Jason asked. The smallest man on the crew, Jason protected his reputation as shift clown.

"The piano."

"That piece of junk has been sitting there for about twenty years! Don't tell me you don't remember it, either."

What could he say? Fact was, he didn't remember it. He let his eyes drift from face to curious face. The tension had become so thick, he could have cut it with a knife until one of the older veterans said, "About twenty years ago, we put a fire out in some old lady's house. She didn't want the piano afterwards because we got it wet. That's why it's warped. And it's probably rusty all over the inside, too. No one here has ever tried to play it. Does that answer your question?"

"Uh . . . yeah. Thanks."

"Hey, Cee'j," Jason called, trying to blend his initials into a one-syllable name. "How'd you get knocked in the head anyway? Did your daddy finally smack you with that 2 x 4? He's been telling us he was gonna do it. So, what happened?"

Sitting at the table playing a game of checkers with Danny, Shane turned to C. J. and said, "Fact is, we're all more than a little curious. You went from being a complete freak last week to being—"

"—to being Mr. Hollyweird *this* week," Jason interrupted.

"Yeah! What's the deal here?" Danny asked. "What's going on with you?"

C. J. shrugged his shoulders. He hadn't seen Zach come in and stand behind him. "I don't know what day it was, but it was raining … and cold. Before that … I don't know. I don't remember anything."

Jason snapped his fingers and asked, "Ah, you mean your daddy didn't get to smack you after all?"

C. J. turned his gaze down to the white linoleum floor, rubbed his temples, and sighed. "He didn't—" He hesitated and jumped when all of a sudden, Zach took his arm from behind and snatched him around.

"Get yourself inside my office."

"What'd I do?" C. J. hollered.

"Just *do* it!"

"What office?"

Zach raised his hand and pointed to the heavy glass door just beyond the right side of his son's head. "Go!"

Without another word, C. J. followed the directions, went into the office, and dropped down into a chair opposite his father's desk. Zach followed him and sat in his chair behind the desk. "I warned you!"

"What did I say wrong?"

"You just need to keep quiet!"

"About what? I was only trying to tell them that you *didn't* hit me! What's *wrong* with that?"

"Keep this loss of memory thing to yourself!"

"*How?* It's pretty stinkin' obvious, don't you think?"

Zach scratched his head and thought long and hard. "It's a *personal* issue, and we leave our *personal* stuff at home."

"*Personal* … for whom? *You* or *me?* Fact is, *Dad,* you just plain don't believe me, do you?"

The man stared at him, and when he didn't answer, C. J. got up from the chair. "I'm outta here."

Taylor jumped up from his chair. "*Sit down!* I *told* you they were going to be tough! I *warned* you!"

C. J. turned around. "So you did. So you did. But I'm not the only one suffering with a memory loss, am I? You forgot one tiny little tidbit of information, didn't you?"

"What are you talking about?"

"What's this about a *dead* kid?"

When Zach rolled his eyes in disgust, C. J. saw something he did not like—something not completely believable, although he couldn't put his finger on it.

"Give me a break!" Zach cried. "How could you forget?"

C. J. thought for a long moment, and then sighed and got up. "Well, if it's true, then I *definitely* have no business being here. Take me home ... please."

Zach refused to budge. "I'll take you home at six-o'clock tomorrow morning, and not a minute before. Until then, you'll—"

The shrill station alarm instantly broke Zach's concentration, and he slammed his fist down onto the desk. "Let's go!"

C. J.'s brow furrowed. "Go where?"

"That sound means we have a call! Now, you *stay* on my shirttail, you understand?"

The boy rolled his eyes and then nodded.

"Good. Now, let's go!"

Chapter 5

When the fire rescue team of Shane, Zach, and C. J. reached the house, a woman in her mid-seventies came rushing out to meet them. "It's his heart! I just know it's his heart! *Please* hurry!"

Inside, they found a male victim lying on the living room floor. He was not breathing nor did he have a pulse.

Shane immediately sprang into action pulling leads and paddles from the portable defibrillator, and IV equipment from the kit. "C. J., you begin chest compressions while I get him wired." But when C. J. froze, Shane glanced up. "C. J.! I *need* your help, here!"

Wide-eyed and turning pale, the boy cried, "I *don't* know how! What am I supposed to do?"

Chief Taylor, standing back taking information from the victim's wife and quickly scribbling it down on a clipboard, overheard his son's panic. And in a panic of his own, he excused himself, dropped the clipboard, and came up behind the boy. He grabbed the back of his shirt and snatched him backwards. "Get out of the way!" he hollered. He dropped to his knees beside the victim and performed CPR on the man; after a few minutes, he was just able to bring him back.

Later, back in Zach's office, tensions skyrocketed. Taylor got in C. J.'s face and hollered, "That man would have *died* had I not been there! What's *wrong* with you?"

Red-faced, C. J. hollered back. "*Me!* What do you mean what's wrong with *me?* Had that man died, it would have been *your* fault because you're *not* listening to me! *That's* what's wrong! You forced me into a position you know I can't handle! I know *nothing* about this job! I *don't* belong here!"

His father dropped himself down into the chair behind his desk, mopped beads of sweat from his brow, and asked, "Oh? And just where *do* you belong?"

C. J. came over to the desk, slammed his fists down, and yelled, "I *don't* know! But it's *not* here! Take me home! *Now,* please."

Taylor glanced down at his watch. "This is a twenty-four hour shift. It's just ten-thirty. You have exactly nineteen hours and thirty minutes left."

The boy shook his head and turned toward the door. "Never mind. I'll walk."

Zach jumped up and came around the desk with lightning speed. He snatched C. J.'s arm and spun him around. "You're *not* going anywhere! Get back in here!"

C. J. managed to yank his arm out of Zach's hand. "*Get* your hands off me, Taylor! You can't stop me!" And he turned and walked out.

With more sweat beading up on his forehead and his hands balled up into tight fists, Zach stopped himself just outside his office door and watched the boy until he was out of sight. And when he turned back around, he found the rest of the crew gawking.

"Chief, you usually go after him," Jason offered.

"Ah, let him go. He won't get far. He's penniless and on foot. It's cold out there and it looks like rain. How long do you think it'll be before he wimps out and turns back?"

•

Early Tuesday morning, December 6

The rest of the shift dragged by with an eerie yet not totally unusual quietness. By quitting time the following morning, the sun was only beginning to brighten the sky. It had rained overnight, leaving the city lights glistening in the early darkness. Shane thought nothing more of the shift's events. Just par for the course. Every time C. J. had come on duty, tempers flared. Why should this shift have been any different?

But things *were* different.

As he flipped on his turn signal to make the final left-hand turn onto his street, something just over on the right-hand corner caught his eye. There, sitting on the ground underneath a street light, was C. J. Shane dropped his head, shook it, and would have driven by as though he hadn't seen him. But something inside him made him feel compelled to pull his gray Civic over against the curb. The last thing he wanted in life was to be seen in his own private territory with a suspected druggie. But, in spite of his personal paranoia, he stopped, reached across his car, opened the passenger door, and asked, "Taylor, what do you think you're doing?"

The boy was trying to hide his shivering. "Why? Do you live around here or something?"

"Now, you know I do!"

With a scowl on his face, C. J. shook his head. "No, sir, I *didn't* know. I'm sorry, okay?"

"Just get in and let me take you home."

The boy leaned back on his hands. "Westbrook, isn't it?"

"Cut the junk, C. J.! You know full well who I am!"

"Yeah? Well, I hate to do this to you and the others, Mr. Westbrook, but I'm not going back to that station. You're just going to have to squirt those little fires and pump those *still* hearts without me."

With his jaw tightly clenched, and his teeth ground hard against one another, Shane watched him for a moment. "And why should this time be different from any of the rest?"

The boy rolled his eyes. "Thanks," he answered with sarcasm.

"Oh, come on!" Shane cried, his blood pressure skyrocketing. "You might as well face it. You may have changed on the outside, but you know you've been a quitter from the start! You've wimped out of more than one rescue. Now, get in the car and let me take you home!"

"*Home?* To *that* dungeon? I don't *think* so! Have you *seen* those people? They're *weird!*"

Shane sighed heavily and had to agree. But he also knew C. J. "Give me a break. Like *you're* not?"

C. J. instinctively glanced down at his now clean, very normal fingernails. "No, sir. I'm not."

Skeptical, Shane answered, "Yeah, right. You must be freezing. And I'd almost be willing to bet you haven't eaten anything yet either. So, get in the car."

C. J.'s face again turned dark red, and he jumped to his feet. "Why can't you people believe me? And what do you care whether I'm freezing or hungry or whatever? From the sounds of things, I'm not worth shooting!"

"And where are your gang member friends when you need 'em, huh?"

"I don't have any friends like that!"

"With your lousy attitude, I *can't imagine* why you don't have any friends. Like that or like any other for that matter!" Shane hollered. "That's the way it is with dope head gang members, isn't it? You spend all your time in hideaways, always trying to protect some miserable piece of property. But why should any of them care about *you,* as long as they got their dope?" And then he sighed and became shocked when he heard himself saying, "Now, this is your last chance. If you won't let me take you home, then at least let me get you off the street. I'll even let you come on to my apartment until we get this thing—" *Whoa, there! What am I thinking? C. J. Taylor … in* my *apartment?* he thought. Wide-eyed, he found himself glancing at his face in the rearview mirror, wondering if the word sucker had been stamped in bold bright letters across his forehead. It was as if the words came out all on their own. And then he punched the seat, sighed a heavy sigh, and said, "You can at least get warm and dry. And I can have your dad come and get you."

Skeptical, C. J. asked, "Did Taylor send you?"

"I *just* told you that I live over here, remember? Now, get in! You can't stay out here. There's a cold front coming through. The temperature is supposed to drop to the upper thirties today. You'll die from exposure."

The boy turned, wrapped his arms around himself, and began to walk on up the road. "Like somebody really cares. I'll find my own way home."

Shane faced a tough decision: pull the door shut, yell, "Have it your way," and drive on; or keep after him until his opponent conceded. He knew full well that in his confused state of mind, the kid would freeze to death before he could ever make it home, especially considering he was already heading in the wrong direction. Shane dropped his head, sighed heavily again, and breathed a silent prayer with the answer already tugging hard at his heart. When he looked up again, C. J. was already half a block up the street, and he wasn't looking back. Shane slowly drove up to him, his passenger door waving in the wind. "Aren't you going the wrong way?"

"So. What's it to you?"

"Give me a break! Let me at least get you inside before you freeze to death!"

At the moment, things weren't looking too good for C. J. The air felt so bitter cold that he felt his bones rattling. His body shook and ached, in particular his rib cage. Starving, thirsty, and drop-dead tired, he longed for some kind of friend, even if the friendship was a strained one. For a moment, he thought, *What if this guy's a fruitcake like the rest of them?* But in spite of his concerns, he slid himself into the passenger seat, shut the door, and then asked, "Are you going to make me go home?"

"You're plenty old enough to make your own decisions, but spending the night out in this weather was not a good one, okay?"

C. J. leaned forward and glanced up through the windshield at the dark sky. "The night. It sticks around a long time, doesn't it?"

"Uh ... yeah. It usually does this late in the year."

With the door finally shut, the inside of the car was warming up very nicely. C. J. leaned back and sucked in a deep gulp of air. "Mr. Westbrook, I know all this mess sounds like I've totally lost my mind, and I probably have, I don't know. But I'm out here because—" He sighed deeply. "Somewhere along the way yesterday, I must have missed a street sign. My memory ... it isn't working the same. I mean ... they live on a dirt road called Opossum Ridge. And then we turned onto Garden City Road, and then onto ... oh, I don't know. I got distracted or something. I lost it after Garden City."

Shane slammed his fist against the steering wheel. "Your parents have been living on Opossum Ridge since long before you were born! You've lived there *all* of your life. How can you *suddenly* forget?"

His defenses slowly lowering, C. J. dropped his head into his hands. "I'm cold and wet. I'm starving, and I'm drop-dead tired. My head is splitting, and I *can't* remember how to get home. Nothing about this place is familiar. For all it matters, I don't know what city we're in, nor do I know the state. I remember nothing. How can I possibly go from what you say I used to be … to *this* … with no recollection at all?" He then reached over and took hold of the door handle. "Mr. Westbrook, I don't have a clue as to what's going on, but I know I'm in serious trouble here. And if you're not willing to believe me, then let me go. I won't hold it against you."

Oh, how easy it would have been just to let him go. To keep him meant having to answer too many unwelcome questions. But Shane fought the urge, sucked in a deep breath, and said, "Just stay put. But I've got to tell you, Mr. Taylor, I'm not thoroughly convinced. You're going to have to give me some time to work on the belief part."

Without a word, C. J. stared blankly ahead until out of the corner of his eye, he caught a glimpse of a folded newspaper lying down on the floor next to his feet and reached down to pick it up.

"That paper won't do you any good. It's at least two weeks old," Mr. Westbrook offered. "I admit, I'm not so good at keeping the car clean."

C. J. scanned the title on the front page. "*The Crestview News Leader.* Is that the name of this place? Crestview?"

His brow furrowed, something inside Shane's chest shattered, and he knew it was a God-thing. C. J.'s amnesia was not only genuine, there was an unmistakable lostness in his voice. "Yes, Prince Hollywood. We're in a town called Crestview. The state is Florida," he answered.

The boy closed his eyes and rubbed his temples in a circular motion. "What part of Florida is that?"

"We're in the northwest—the panhandle," Mr. Westbrook offered as he pulled the car away from the curb. "We're about fifty-some miles east of Pensacola."

"Okay. At least I have an idea of where that is."

Two minutes later, Shane pulled the car into the parking lot right in front of his upstairs apartment, parked, and then turned and watched his ward. C. J.'s brow was furrowed as if his imaginary headache was a reality. He squinted his eyes as if he was having trouble focusing. And when he began rubbing his eyes, Shane became concerned. "Let's get inside. I'll make a pot of coffee, okay?"

"That sounds warm. Thank you."

The modest, no-frills apartment proved bland at best. Its matte white walls boasted nothing spectacular. Over along the right wall of the small living room sat a gray couch with a coffee table in front and an end table at this end. Across from the couch, over in the left-hand corner, a small thirteen-inch TV sat on a round, three-legged table. Just beyond the end of the couch, a computer sprawled across the small dinette table in what might have been considered a dining nook. And over to the left, the nook opened up into a kitchen that was barely wide enough for one person to turn around in, let alone two. But it was complete with all the amenities, including a stacked washer and dryer unit.

While Shane worked at spooning coffee grounds into the basket of the coffee maker, C. J. wrapped himself in a heavy comforter and sat down on the couch.

"Hey, didn't you see a doctor after you got smacked?" Shane asked while he punched the on switch.

"You probably won't believe this either, but ... I ... woke up ... early yesterday morning ... and my whole life was gone. They claimed I'd been there for a couple days and that when I came home, I was either drunk, or drugged, or something. I found myself in this ... this devil worshipper's bedroom. The room was hideous. I looked hideous. It made me gag until I could get in the shower to scrape it all off. There was no doctor."

Shane came in from around the corner of the kitchen and stared over at the boy. "You know, you just ain't right. Let me see your head."

"No, I'm okay."

"Let me see!"

C. J. sighed as he pushed his wet hair back away from his forehead. "Go ahead. Look. You'd think I would have had some soreness right there after getting hit like he said I did, but I have no soreness at all. It's more like just a purple stain from that ridiculous paint I found on my face."

Shane studied the bruise and used his thumb to

press in on it. And when C. J. didn't complain, he asked, "No pain, huh?"

"None at all. Just a nagging headache."

Mr. Westbrook turned. "Well, you might be right about the paint. You'd been using it for a long time. But I'm just a paramedic, not a doctor." He took two clean cups from a dish drainer near the sink. "You like your coffee black, don't you?"

"Black? Uh, no. I'd rather have it with two spoons of sugar and about five heaping spoons of artificial creamer."

"What? That's not coffee!"

With a slight grin, C. J. said, "You ought to try it sometime. It's pretty good that way."

Shane laughed as he sat the full cups down on the coffee table and then went and got the sugar, the creamer, and a spoon. "Here. Fix it the way you want it."

Lost in thought, C. J. wrapped his cold hands around the warm cup and stared down into it. "Did I really used to drink this stuff black?"

"Yeah. And like a baby drinks milk."

C. J. brought the cup up to his nose and took a deep breath. "Mmm … it smells good." And then he took a sip and screwed up his face. "Yuck! How can you drink it black like that?" he asked as he began dumping sugar and creamer into the cup.

Dumbfounded and wide-eyed, Mr. Westbrook pulled a kitchen chair over and sat down across from him. "Okay. So … other than you're usual fighting with your father, this mess is too crazy for it to be a put on. Now, what can we do about it?"

The boy threw his left hand up. "Oh, no. I'm not even remotely interested in going back to whatever I apparently used to be, if that's what you're asking."

With a grin, Shane shook his head and said, "Actually, no, that's not what I was asking. But it does sound like you're going to have to start over. Obviously, to stick with this job, and to keep your father happy, you're going to need a crash course in CPR. I have a manual here that you can study. I'll make us some bacon, eggs, and maybe some grits, and after we eat, you get busy reading."

"You're not going to call him to come get me?"

"C. J., I've been with the department for twenty-one years this past September. And I'm sure you don't remember calling me boring and lifeless, which you have done many times, but first and foremost, I'm a devout Christian. I live my life in a way that I believe honors God. I won't offer you drugs, alcohol, or even cigarettes.

"I'm forty years old and proud to boast that I am still a virgin. I'll be getting married to the love of my life, another proud forty-year old virgin, next June. It's sad to me, but yes, that would make us a rarity these days. But the fact is I've grown too old to care about the opinions of others. Now, knowing all this about me, are you ready to go home?"

Leaning back on the couch with his hands wrapped around the coffee cup, C. J. glanced up at his new friend. "What about C. J… I mean, what about *me?* What was I? I mean, you say I was heavy into drugs or drinking—"

Knowing the kid's shaky state of mind, Shane again faced a crucial decision. Although he could not remember a single time the boy had ever taken a pill or sipped on a drink in front of him, C. J. Taylor appeared to be a most vile, promiscuous creature. But how could he lay that perception on the boy's shoulders now? "I think you've been through enough for one day. I'm going to go make us that breakfast, okay?"

With a half smile, C. J. said, "Well, that answered that question, didn't it?"

Shane felt humbled. "Yeah. It never looked too good."

"The costume?"

"Yeah. The costume."

C. J. sighed, sat his coffee cup down on the table, and said, "Well, I can't speak for yesterday. I can't remember yesterday. But today, I find you an island in the storm."

Taken aback, Shane smiled. "I never thought I'd ever hear myself say this, especially to you, but thank you. That's the best compliment you've paid to me … ever."

Red-faced, C. J. grinned. "Now, about that manual. … "

It wasn't long before Shane had breakfast finished, but when he brought a plate in to his company, C. J. lay curled up in a ball and was fast asleep, the first-aid manual lying on the couch just in front of his chest. Shane left the plate of bacon, eggs, and grits on the table next to the coffee cup. But while he stood there and watched his ward as he slept, an idea came to him. After obtaining a paper towel and a plastic bag from a kitchen cabinet, he used the paper towel to gently pick up C. J.'s empty coffee cup and placed it in the plastic bag. He then found some notebook paper, quickly scribbled a note, and taped it to the door as he quietly let himself out.

•

"Where is my son?" Mrs. Taylor asked when her husband appeared at the door alone.

The house had become pleasantly silent. The younger children had already left for school and the breakfast dishes had already been washed.

Zach found the morning newspaper lying on a table near his recliner and he snatched it up.

Mrs. Taylor snapped at him with a kitchen towel. "You promised me you'd watch over him!"

Mr. Taylor dropped himself down into his easy chair and flipped his newspaper open. "Yeah? Well the kid got ticked about something stupid and took off."

In a moment of panic, she rushed over and yanked the newspaper from his hands. "What do you mean he took off?"

"I meant what I said! He took off!"

"And you let him go? What's the matter with you?"

"Now Roxanne honey, I *told* you that if this was going to work, we were going to have to make sure things were as normal as possible. So what if he gets uptight? He's going to have to deal with it on his own."

Mrs. Taylor crumpled the newspaper and tossed it into his lap. "Where is he?"

"How should I know?"

"You bonehead! It's not like he knows this place! Not to mention he's *got* to take his medicine! I'm going after him."

Zach began pulling the creases out of his newspaper. "Roxanne, leave the kid alone! He'll find his way back because dogs usually do."

"You sure are mighty trusting for someone whose very life is on the line."

"All for you my dear. All for you."

•

Deanna Clark of the Crestview Police Department was beautiful, even in uniform. Her perfect shape and flowing blonde hair—Shane's heart skipped a beat every time he laid eyes on her.

She was just getting off work when Shane drove up and met her in the parking lot. He wrapped his arms around her, kissed her, and said, "Hi, baby. Have a good night?"

Surprised to see him, Deanna asked, "This isn't Friday already, is it?"

Shane shook his head. "No, but I've got a favor to ask." He went and pulled the bag with the coffee cup from his car and handed it to her. "I know this is a long shot, but I need you to see if you can lift any prints off this cup and then run them for me."

"Why? What's going on?"

"Call it a hunch. I'll explain while we work."

It didn't take long. "Most of the prints are smudged," Deanna said, "but I was able to lift a good partial."

"Good. Let's run it on the computer and see what we come up with."

While the computer screen flashed in the background, Deanna asked, "Are you going to tell me whom they're supposed to belong to or not?"

Shane could not take his gaze off the computer screen. In only a moment, it flashed the words *match found.* Deanna turned around, tapped a key or two, and the screen flashed up C. J.'s face along with all his peculiarities. Deanna had not yet met the infamous Taylor, but she'd heard all the gory details. So when she saw the picture, she giggled to herself, bounced her pencil-thin eyebrows a couple times, and said, "Ooo! Nice face!"

"Hey!"

Deanna laughed. "I was just kidding!" And then it suddenly hit her. "Wait! No, I'm *not* kidding. I thought you told me he was a freakazoid."

"He was! That's why I'm here."

Deanna nodded. "Oh. I get it. Key word, *was.*"

Disappointed, Shane studied the computer. "Exactly." The face on the screen was definitely that of the kid on the couch. "I've only ever seen him in that ridiculous costume, and I wondered what his face is supposed to look like without the … wait. What color are his eyes?"

Deanna glanced down at the screen and said, "Dark blue, like crystals. Why?"

"I never paid a whole lot of attention, but I guess for some reason, I always thought his eyes were a light shade of blue."

"It's too bad he wouldn't let anybody see this side of him. He sure could be an awesome-looking character if he ever decided to turn his life around."

Shane read every word the computer program had to offer on the boy, and although he seemed a bit disappointed, he was not surprised by a single word. C. J. was well known all over the police department as a public nuisance but only in the looks department. Amazingly, he had no record. "Strange, isn't it? Seems like that turn around is heading our way full speed ahead."

Her brow furrowed, Deanna asked, "What do you mean?"

Just then, a pair of uniformed officers came past the room and noticed the computer. "Ah. Taylor's kid. Is there something going on with him that we here in this department need to know?"

After Deanna introduced them as Al Vargas and Billy Rayford, Shane glanced up at Vargas and answered, "No, sir. C. J. is sleeping it off right now. He's inside, he's safe, and out of trouble ... at least for the time being."

Officer Vargas nodded. "Well, if he causes any trouble, you let us know, okay?" And then slowly and strangely methodical, the men walked away.

Alone again, Deanna looked up at her sweetheart. "He's safe, huh? Where?"

"This might be hard to believe, but he's on my

couch. After I left work this morning, I found him wondering the streets aimlessly. I had to take him in because God himself told me to. But C. J. was out even before I could give him something to eat."

Surprised, Deanna cried, "And you left him there ... *alone?*"

Shane sighed. "Something is really not all right with him, and I thought I might have an answer for him. But after seeing that computer, I see it was probably just my imagination. Even so, though, in his present state of mind, I don't believe he's a problem. In fact, let's you and me go to the store together and get him a few things ... things like his own toothbrush, his own comb, maybe a pair of pants and a shirt. You know. Just stuff."

Deanna turned away from the computer. "Do you know his sizes?"

"Ah, how hard can it be to buy something for a five-foot-nine-and-a-half-inch bean pole with no hips?"

The engaged couple walked out of the police station arm-in-arm, convinced they had read everything there was to know about C. J. Taylor. But the computer screen held one more secret, a small insignificant icon at the very bottom left corner of the screen.

Chapter 6

With the electricity knocked out by an unusual late-season thunderstorm, the night had grown dark and unnervingly dreary.

His path lit only by a dimming flashlight, he slowly made his way across the backyard toward the white tin-sided toolshed. But a sudden flash interrupted his mission when the dim light of his flashlight glistened off the swinging blade of a large knife.

•

Later, Tuesday morning, December 6

C. J. nearly jumped out of his skin. The first-aid manual went flying across the room. In a moment, Shane came rushing in and instinctively flipped on a light switch. His heart pounding in his throat, he cried, "Taylor, what's up?"

Sweating profusely, his wild eyes searching the blank ceiling, C. J. asked, "Where am I?"

"You're in my apartment, on my couch, staring at my ceiling. You dozed off a couple hours ago. And when you didn't wake up right away, I—" He stopped when he noticed the terrified gaze in the boy's eyes. "C. J., what is it? What are you looking at?"

C. J. shifted his terrified glare over toward his new friend. "Where'd it go?"

"Where'd what go?"

"The knife! Where'd the knife go?"

His brow furrowed, Shane came to him, shook him, and said, "Hey, wake up, you dopehead. You're just dreaming."

C. J. sucked in a deep gulp of air and pushed himself up on the couch. "Dreaming?" he repeated as if lost in a daze.

Shane turned and headed for the kitchen counter. "I sure hope that's all it was. You about scared the life out of me."

C. J. rubbed the sleep out of his eyes and could not understand why he ached all over: his neck, his back, and his rib cage. Even his hands felt stiff. "You mind if I go wash my face?"

"Be my guest. And by the way, after you fell asleep this morning, I ran out, met Deanna, and we went shopping. We got you a couple things. They're on the table there in front of you."

There, on the coffee table, C. J. found a toothbrush, some toothpaste, and other necessary items. Over to the right, he noticed a burgundy, long-sleeved shirt and a pair of khaki pants folded neatly and lying on the corner. "This is nice, but … why? And who's Deanna?"

Shane came in from the kitchen. "First, Deanna's my girl. She's unavailable so forget it. And second, because it's going to be mighty tough living down your previous reputation. Hopefully, this will start you on the road to a new beginning. Now, how about some coffee?"

"Oh. Yeah, sure. Coffee sounds great," C. J. answered as he wobbled to his feet. But his legs instantly turned to jelly and he dropped back down onto the couch.

"What's the matter?"

C. J. rubbed his aching temples. "Must have been that religious coffee you gave me earlier."

Shane snickered. "Hmm ... maybe then what you need is some religious peanut butter and ... wait a minute." He hesitated when he caught a glimpse of something on the back of the boy's shirt. "What's that on your back?"

Confused, C. J. pulled his shirt around and looked down. The navy blue shirt looked and felt wet and somewhat sticky. And when he pulled his hand away, it came back deep red—covered in blood. "What'd you do to me?" he cried.

Instantly, Mr. Westbrook became irritated. "Oh yeah, right. I bring you in, feed you, let you drink some of my coffee, and give you a place to sleep just so I can stab you in the back. Come on, C. J., I hope you have a little more faith in me than that."

"I'm sorry," C. J. whispered. "I don't—"

Shane didn't let him finish. He came over, pulled C. J.'s shirt up, and found a blood-soaked bandage on the left side of his rib cage and a very odd looking, six-inch long scar just inches below it. "Whoa! Don't tell me you didn't know about this wound. And what's with this scar?"

"Wound? Scar? I have a birthmark over there somewhere. Is that what you're talking about?"

"You call that scar-looking thing a birthmark?"

"Yeah. It's been there as long as I can remember. Why?"

After he pulled the boy's shirt back down again, Shane said, "You're going to a doctor, that's why."

C. J. had grown terribly weak. His face had grown pale. But he pulled away. "Oh, no. I don't need some quack. If you don't mind taking me home now, I'll be all right."

There was a good amount of blood on the boy's shirt, on the comforter, and soaked into the couch cushion. And when Shane glanced up into his face, C. J.'s eyes began to roll up into his head. Shane instinctively pressed the palm of his hand against C. J.'s forehead. "You're burning up, and you're going to a doctor. Now, it's either go voluntarily, or I call one of the guys to come and get you. Let's see," he started as he picked up his phone receiver and punched the number nine, "*Frank* should be on duty today—" He punched the number one. "I'm sure he wouldn't be too happy if he knew it was just you." He reached down to punch the number one again, but with a heavy sigh, C. J. stopped his hand.

"I'm not as dense as you might like to think I am. I don't have blond roots. I was given the miserable privilege of meeting Frank yesterday when we A-shifters were coming on duty. The B-shifters would be on duty today."

"Uh huh."

"Nice try."

"Can't blame a guy for tryin', can you? Let's go."

•

Lying curled up onto his right side on a gurney in the ER, C. J. patiently waited while his head x-rays were read by the resident radiologist. His wound had already been taped together with strips and covered with a clean, white bandage. Although his guardian friend was sitting in a chair near the gurney, the room was quiet. C. J. dozed off for a few moments, but he hadn't slept long when he awoke with a start, looking as though he'd seen a ghost.

"Hey, what's up?" Shane asked when he saw the frightened look in the boy's eyes.

"Where am I?"

Mr. Westbrook thought the answer ridiculously simple, but something else caught his attention. C. J. was not looking at him. His eyes were intensely focused on the wall, and he moved his index finger as though he was reaching up to touch something. "Where do you think you are?" Shane asked.

"It's a picture. It ... it's ... Jesus ... and ... he's carrying a lamb. But ... it's dark. There's nobody—"

Just then, Doctor Roger Stevens entered the room carrying a large manila x-ray folder. "Well, Mr. Taylor, you were right about that painless bruise on your—"

He hesitated when he noticed the faraway look in C. J.'s eyes. "Mr. Taylor?"

His brow furrowed in absolute confusion, C. J. rubbed his temples while he strained his brain. "My head is killing me. Can I go home?"

Dr. Stevens said, "Sure you can, but wouldn't you like to hear my diagnosis first?"

"Duh. That *is* why I came in, isn't it?"

"Well, isn't it?"

"I'm sorry. Yes, sir, it is."

"Mr. Taylor, I'm afraid your dopehead reputation precedes you. You're coming down off a drug-induced high. That's why the headache and weird visions."

"Wait. I don't take drugs."

Shane didn't feel surprised by the doctor's diagnosis. "C. J., I believe you do, or at least you used to."

"You've got to be kidding me!" C. J. cried while rubbing the back of his neck.

"No, sir," the doctor continued. "I'm not kidding. You have a high level of barbiturates in your blood, and the headache won't go away until the drugs wear off. The CT scan shows the reason you don't feel any pain from that place on your forehead is because there is no bruise. That purple mark is only a stain that will fade in time … possibly from the make-up. I don't really know. But there's no concussion, and you haven't got any brain thing going on.

"As for the wound on your rib cage: it's probably two or even three days old by now, and it's already been stitched. But apparently, during your nightmare, you tossed in your sleep just enough to tear a small section of it open again. And now there's an infection in it. That's why the fever."

"Why didn't I notice it when I came to yesterday? I mean, I took a shower. I've changed clothes, but I never felt it. There was no pain. I never saw it. Why?"

Dr. Stevens looked over his glasses. "It's a deep flesh wound, Mr. Taylor. Novocain, waterproof bandages, and the fact that it's on the backside of your rib cage ... there are any number of reasons why you wouldn't have seen or felt it."

Curious, Shane directed the doctor's attention to the scar. "Can you tell where it came from? Our friend here can't seem to remember that one either."

"Mr. Westbrook, I told you it was just a birthmark!" C. J. insisted. "It's been there all my life."

The doctor examined it momentarily. "No, that's no birthmark. It's a classic surgical scar, an old one, quite possibly from your childhood."

"*Surgery?*"

"Could have been anything, an accident, a kidney issue. Without further examination, it would be difficult to determine the nature of it now."

Shane thought for a moment and glanced over at the middle-aged doctor. "Doc, is it possible that the fresh wound on his back could have been made by a knife?" The idea didn't seem so far-fetched given the boy's nightmare added to his reputation.

The doctor slowly nodded and pushed up the glasses that sat precariously on the end of his nose. "It most definitely could have been. But don't get it confused. The wound is not a puncture wound, which means he was not stabbed. I believe it was made by either a swinging knife blade or a sharp piece of glass or metal, and since there are drugs involved, wounds like this are to be documented, photographed, and reported to the police. So you might as well plan to hang around for a little while. The call has already been made."

"But... I can't *tell* the police anything because I don't *remember* anything!"

"Take it easy, Taylor," Shane warned. "They're the good guys, remember? They'll take any information you can give them, like maybe *who* threw the knife."

"Mr. Westbrook, it was *just* a nightmare. There wasn't anybody there. The knife wasn't real. It couldn't have been."

The doctor patted him on his back. "I can admit you to a rehab where you can get yourself cleaned up from the dope."

"But, you don't understand! I'm *not* a user! I don't remember—"

Stevens sighed and turned toward the door, making it sickeningly obvious that he didn't believe his patient. "Then I'll prescribe some aspirin for the fever and antibiotics for the infection. And then you can go home and sleep it off. Now, I've got to go take care of some patients who are really sick. I'm sure you understand."

After the doctor made his exit, C. J. looked up at Shane. "Isn't this just great? The man doesn't believe me. He might as well have called me an addict with a gang-related war wound."

Shane got down in the young man's face. "Listen, Taylor, I never actually saw you take any kind of medicine, let alone drugs. And I don't have a clue as to what's going on with you now—why the sudden flip-flop. But by all your previous accounts, that's exactly what everyone in this city thinks about you, okay? Don't be alarmed or dumbfounded by their attitude toward your reputation."

"If this is a new beginning, how in the world am I ever going to live down the old reputation?"

Shane sat down in the chair next to the wall. "Relax. How does anyone eat an elephant?"

"One bite at a time, I suppose."

"Right. Now listen. I may kick myself for this later on, but you can stay at my apartment ... that is, as long as you don't invite your friends to come and tear the place down."

"Friends you don't have to worry about. If there were any, I wouldn't remember them. But what about Taylor ... I mean, my *dad* ... are you going to tell him where I am?"

"Don't you think your parents have a right to know?"

C. J. thought for a moment. "You tell me. *Should* they know? You seem to know my dad better than I do. Do you think he's capable of swinging a knife at me?"

Shane knew the Taylors had been a dysfunctional family of sorts, but even so, he couldn't imagine it. "Hmm ... now, that's a hard one. I can't answer it because I don't know. But I suppose it's possible that anyone could have swung that knife. I've heard you have some pretty shady friends."

Just then, Officers Vargas and Rayford came strolling through the door.

Chapter 7

Thursday, December 8

The fire department's schedule had been broken into three shifts with twenty-four solid hours on duty and forty-eight hours down time in between. That down time, like all good things, must come to an end.

Although C. J. had remained tucked safely away in the apartment, his situation weighed heavily on Shane's mind. Wondering what he'd gotten himself into by taking the kid's side, he found himself slightly unnerved, suddenly keenly aware, and strangely suspect of his surroundings. At the station, in the parking lot, he recognized each A-shifter's personal vehicle; and then inside, all of the fire trucks remained parked in their usual places. It appeared there had not been a call that morning.

As he made his way toward the locker room to put away his wallet and car keys, questions raced through his mind. *How could a head injury be faked while the resulting amnesia seemed very real? Why the sudden yet un-recollected conversion from the pauper to the prince?* And the most disturbing question. *Just who did throw that knife?* Knowing the Chief's hotheaded nature, it would be highly probable he knew something, but if that were the case, he wasn't talking.

Shane had never actually seen the kid take a drink, pop a pill, nor had he met any one of his elusive friends. Come to think of it, he couldn't be certain any of the above was factual. Any one of them could have easily pulled off a stunt like that for any number of reasons. But for all it was worth, it could be that the boy's dope-saturated mind had finally slipped a cog and joined the schizoid crowd. Other than the deal with the knife, a split personality would perfectly explain the obvious. But in all honesty, although he did not know the answer, Shane did know that the problem was very real.

Standing at his locker, totally lost in thought, Shane nearly jumped out of his skin when he went to shut the locker door and found Jason standing there. "Boo!" Jason cried, with a Cheshire cat grin.

His heart suddenly pounding, his legs weak, Shane cried, "Whoa! Cruz, I ought to … what are you doing? Why do you insist on scaring me like that?"

"Scare *you?* You ain't never been afraid of me before! You ain't never jumped before! Got a guilty conscious, do ya?"

Shane rolled his eyes. "*No,* I don't have a guilty conscious! You caught me off guard, that's all! So what's the deal here?"

"Heap Big Chief sent me to fetch ya."

Sucking in a deep gulp of air, Shane said, "I figured he would, and now you've fetched me. Now you can go back to your doghouse and chew your bone."

"Rrruff!"

Shane could only wag his head at Jason's nauseating childishness. That boy had only been with the department for a few months. One would think that even so, he would have grown up by now.

Sitting at his desk in the office, Taylor looked up and met Shane's gaze. "Seen C. J. lately?"

Mr. Westbrook resisted the urge to tear in to the man. Instead, he studied him while a prayer filled his mind. *Lord, what do I tell him? Did he throw the knife or didn't he?*

"Chief, why are you asking *me?*"

If conviction didn't kill, the anger in Taylor's piercing brown eyes might. "Why? I'll tell you why!" He leaned forward and glared into Shane's eyes. "Because I know you've got him hiding out at your place! That's why! What do you think you're going to do with him? Why, I could have you charged with kidnapping!"

For a long, tense moment, the color washed from Shane's face. *Okay, Lord! You've got my attention! What do I say?* "You know what, Chief? I could ask you the same thing. *You're* the one who let him leave here! *You're* the one who refused to go after him, knowing full well he's not in his right mind! *If* C. J. was a child, and he's not by any means, but if he were, I could have you charged with child endangerment. I found him wandering the streets: no car, no jacket. He'd been out there all night long, lost, confused, and not even remotely interested in finding his way home. Now, why don't you tell me? What are *you* doing with him?"

With an evil hiss in his laughter, Taylor said, "He finally gets rid of the false face, and all of a sudden, you side with him. Make sense out of that one."

"Tell me about the knot on his head. A 2x4 or a shoe?"

Taylor's arrogance came across like fingernails on a chalkboard. "That would be considered assault, now, wouldn't it, Mr. Westbrook?"

"Yes, sir, I'm afraid it would," Shane answered, his teeth clenched in anger. *Lord, are you hearing this guy? Do I dare mention the knife wound?*

All along, Shane had been the calm one: the one to smooth things over when Zach and C. J. had their disagreements. Zach was boss. He was the Dad. He was always right. C. J. was just the rebellious, non-compliant kid. But the tables had turned, and all of a sudden, Shane realized just which of the two had finally fallen off his rocker.

•

Back at Shane's apartment, the low, steady drone of the clothes dryer filled the room. The aroma of fresh coffee permeated the air. Wrapped in a navy blue bath towel, with his hair dripping wet, C. J. stood gazing at his reflection in the bathroom mirror. His mind felt like mush, his brain fried. No amount of straining could force him to recall any part of his life before regaining consciousness in the watering hole.

He leaned over the sink and rested on his left elbow to brush his teeth. As soon as he was finished and straightened up again, he glanced at his face in the mirror one last time. But there, standing directly behind him, stood the faceless image of a man dressed in black. C. J. hollered. "*Whoa!* What in the—" He thought his heart might explode. The blood instantly washed from his face. He whipped himself around but there was no one there. Terrified, he snatched open the shower curtain to hunt for the intruder. Nothing. He stood motionless, too afraid to breathe. He hadn't heard the door open or close. He listened, yet all he could hear was the muffled drone of the clothes dryer. He yanked the bathroom door open and peered out. Although he felt awkward, he breathlessly crept across the hall into the apartment's only bedroom. There, he searched under the bed and over beside the dresser. When he found no one, he jerked open the closet doors. Still, nothing. Slowly, he made his way through the rest of the apartment but found nothing out of order. The doors and windows remained shut and locked, the blinds pulled down.

Standing in front of the couch, made wet by his attempt to clean his own blood from the upholstery, C. J. was just beginning to breathe easier when all of a sudden, the clothes dryer made absolutely certain he knew his uniform was dry.

•

An hour passed. The familiar music of "The Price is Right" was playing on the television set. Fully dressed in the shirt and pants Shane and Deanna had bought for him, C. J. had only just sat down to glance over the morning newspaper when all of a sudden, someone pounded on the front door of the apartment and shot his nerves through the roof. "Police! Open up!"

Still spooked by his vision, C. J. glanced wide-eyed out the blinds. There, standing on the landing, were Officers Vargas and Rayford.

He opened the door. "Okay. So, you're the police and I've opened the door. So ... what's the problem?"

"We've been ordered to take you home," Vargas said. "Let's go."

"Why? It's not like I'm a runaway."

C. J. remembered the pair from the hospital, and as he stood there gazing at them, he realized there was something about them he didn't like. But it had nothing to do with either Vargas's Hispanic heritage nor Rayford's good ole country boy facade. There was something hidden in their eyes.

While Rayford refused to meet C. J.'s gaze, Vargas met it eye-to-eye. "We got our orders. Now you can come with us, or we can cuff you and force you. Either way, you're going. So, what's your choice? Cuffs or no cuffs?"

C. J. leaned his shoulder against the doorjamb, crossed his arms over his ribs, and asked, "And if I choose neither?"

"You ain't listenin' Mr. Taylor," said Rayford. "That ain't the choices."

C. J. instantly shot a glance over to Rayford and laughed to himself when the officer jerked his face away.

Suspicious, C. J. said, "Well, then, let me get this straight. You're here to *kidnap* me to *make* me go home ... to a dungeon, no less."

Vargas snatched C. J.'s arm and yanked him out onto the landing. "I *said,* you're going home! Now, move it!"

"Hey! Take it easy! You'll tear this wound open again. And then I'll have to call the *real* cops."

"Real cops, my foot. We *are* the real cops."

"Yeah? Well, who sent you? Couldn't be my dad ... unless, of course, you went and told him where I was."

Again, Vargas yanked C. J.'s arm. "Get in the car!"

C. J. jerked his arm free. "Unless you've got a warrant for my arrest, I'm not going anywhere!"

"Oh, we can get a warrant. It'll take all of fifteen minutes. Now you've got a choice. You can go of your own free will, or we can wait for the warrant. Which will it be?"

C. J. cracked a sly grin. "We wait. You don't have a reason, so you can't take me anywhere."

But Vargas would not be satisfied. He snatched C. J.'s wrist and caught him in a pair of handcuffs. "Well, I ain't got time. You're going now," he said as he led the young man toward the patrol car.

"Why did I know you were going to say that? You're a part of this, aren't you?"

"Get movin'!"

While the trio was backing out of the parking space, C. J. glanced up through the back door window and noticed the door to Shane's apartment still stood wide open. "Hey, you ought to at least have the decency to turn off the TV and lock the door instead of leaving it open for thieves to walk in. What do you call that? Job security? Nevermind. Don't answer that."

Vargas rolled his dark eyes, slammed on the brakes, and jerked the gearshift into park. And when he glanced over at Rayford, he didn't have to say a word. Rayford jumped out of the car and went waddling up the apartment staircase.

Chapter 8

One would have thought C. J.'s given reputation would have afforded him numerous rides in a police cruiser, but had that been the case, he wouldn't remember.

Standing in the yard, Mrs. Taylor met the cruiser as it pulled into the driveway. Her hands to her hips, and her teeth clenched in gut-wrenching anger, she asked, "Did he give you boys any trouble?"

Vargas had already slid out of the driver's seat and turned to open the back door. "No, ma'am, Mrs. Roxanne," he answered. "Other than a little complaining, he didn't give us any trouble at all."

When Vargas pulled C. J. out of the backseat, Mrs. Taylor was taken aback when she laid eyes on him. "Then, why is he handcuffed?" she asked.

"Insurance," C. J. answered as he cut his eyes over to Vargas, who, to his surprise, came over to set him free.

"Mrs. Roxanne," Rayford began in the most humble of country-boy voices, "we picked your boy up at Westbrook's place. He been there a while."

C. J. had observed Rayford to be the quiet one, but here he was, shooting off at the mouth.

Mrs. Taylor snickered at the dumpling of a man. "*Billy,* do you not remember? *I'm* the one who sent you."

"Oh, yes'um. I 'sho do."

Without a word, C. J. shot a convicting sneer in Vargas's direction while his mother came and took her son's arm and squeezed it hard, said thank you to the officers, and then began leading her boy toward the house. "And you, mister," she began in a very bewitching tone under her breath, "don't you *ever* pull that stunt again! Do you understand what I am saying to you?"

"Yes, ma'am, if you insist."

"You poor thing," she continued. "You've been away for three nights. You must be having horrible nightmares by now. Are you seeing things?"

A drug-induced high, barbiturates in my system, doesn't that make this an interesting turn of events? "I'm sorry. What did you say?"

"Listen, baby, it's been three days since you had your last hot chocolate, and you absolutely cannot afford to miss it. Besides, it's a family tradition."

All of a sudden, C. J. felt certain his mother had slipped a cog and pulled away from her. "No, ma'am, I *don't* understand. You mean to tell me you sent the *cops* after me because of some lousy family tradition? *Obviously* you knew where I was! Why didn't you come and get me yourself? Besides, I don't even *like* hot chocolate!"

Her boy hadn't seemed to notice her sudden profuse sweating and her flushed face. "Baloney!" she cried. "You claim you don't remember anything! So how do you know you don't *like* hot chocolate?"

"Somehow, hot chocolate just doesn't sound appealing to me."

Again, she snatched his arm and hung on tight. "Let's just get inside. I'll make you a sandwich and a nice cup of hot chocolate, or whatever, and then you can relax. Are your ribs still hurting you?"

Knowing deep down that Vargas had to have been her informant, C. J. did not feel surprised when she mentioned the knife wound. But did he dare ask about the mysterious scar? "You know about that too, huh?"

"Why, of course! I *am* your mother!"

Perfect! "Then, why don't you tell me what happened?" He lifted his shirt and showed her the old scar. "And what's up with this other thing? What is it?"

Mrs. Taylor shrugged her shoulders. But then she shifted her eyes toward the floor, as if to find something to say that would satisfy him. "We don't know what happened. We figured it was one of your so-called friends. And as for the other thing, that's simply a birthmark. It's nothing to worry about."

A birthmark, huh? "But you told me you didn't take me to a doctor, yet I've already been stitched up. Does that mean you're a seamstress too?"

"Yes," she admitted. "I'm the one who stitched you up. But don't worry. I can do that because I am a certified RN."

"Oh. That explains how you had access to the Novocain."

Mrs. Taylor stopped dead in her tracks and turned him around to face her. "I'm tired of talking about this. Now, let's change the subject. You look sharp, son. You keep this up, and there's no telling how far you'll get in the department. You might even get to follow in your father's footsteps one day and become chief."

Gazing down into his mother's pale eyes, C. J. held his silence, not knowing how to respond. His only impression of the fire/rescue business had been an instant disaster.

Before they reached the porch, he said, "Okay. I'll change the subject." He hadn't paid much attention to the property when he left with his father early Monday morning, so shielding his eyes from the bright sunlight, he turned himself around and looked it over. It seemed odd to see such a fancy house sitting so far out in the country where but few had reason to travel. And the yard had recently been professionally landscaped. The place would be beautiful when spring arrived. But the rest of the area could not boast such. Over to the right of the house, an unused mobile home sat choked by surrounding vegetation, its rusting tin siding barely visible. To the left of the house, acre upon acre of indigenous loblolly pine trees grew in perfect, man-made rows. Behind the home, an open field lay comatose for want of spring rains and summer sun.

The two-story home itself was non-descript with its gray vinyl siding and black highlights. C. J. felt unimpressed until he turned toward the cow pasture that sat across from the house. Feeling strangely drawn to the watering hole, he slowly made his way across the dirt road while his mother stood back yelling, "C. J., what are you doing? You can't go over there! That crazy farmer will blow your head off for trespassing! Get back here!"

C. J. hadn't meant to ignore her, but he couldn't stop himself. He came to the rusty fence, and when he made note that the cattle were grazing over in the back corner of the pasture, he climbed over it and tip-toed around freshly scattered cow chips to the pond.

"Ooo, you gonna make me mad, mister!" his mother hollered as she slowly and methodically made her way next to where he was standing. "C. J. Taylor, don't you dare ignore me! I *told* you to get back here!"

Standing at the edge of the watering hole, C. J. gazed down into the hazy green water. Other than a school of minnows, he saw nothing out of the ordinary. His suspicions became confused when he turned his gaze to search the ground but could not even find so much as an outline of his earlier footprints.

Mrs. Taylor looked up into his face and saw his troubled look. "What's the matter?"

"Didn't you tell me I was missing a car?"

"Yes. When we found you last weekend, you were home but your Eclipse was not. We have no idea where it ended up."

The question instantly crossed his mind. Should he mention it? He turned his gaze to his left and studied the steep embankment where a vehicle might have gone airborne before landing in the pond. But although he saw nothing out of the ordinary, he pointed toward the water. "Uh, we might ought to think about checking out there a little deeper."

Mrs. Taylor raised her eyebrows. "Why?"

"Because … that's where I was when I woke up."

"*Here?* In this cow pasture?"

He slowly nodded his head. "The pond. I was *in* the pond."

As Mrs. Taylor watched her son, a vicious chill rushed down over her spine. "*In* the pond?" she questioned.

All of a sudden, they heard a gun shot and dropped to the ground.

"The next one will strike! You both be a trespassin'! Git off my land!"

When C. J. and his mother were finally able to catch their breath, they stood up to find a scraggly-looking man of about seventy clad in overalls, a heavy field jacket, and a pair of rubber boots. He was carrying a rifle that he held pointed to his prey. "This here be private property! Git 'yerselfs off it!"

C. J. stood there staring strangely at the man. "We're sorry, sir. And if you'd kindly point that gun the other way, we'll be moving along."

"What you doin' here, anyway?"

"It's just that we think this pond is holding onto something that belongs to us."

The man didn't even flinch. "Too bad, ain't it? It be mine now. You ain't got no right to dump your trash on my land. The way I see it, you Taylors is just slam outta luck. Now, take your momma here and git on out."

C. J. only nodded as he led his mother to the fence and helped her over. But as they were again standing in their yard, he looked toward the pasture and said, "My car … it must be in that water."

Mrs. Taylor's pounding heart hadn't even begun to slow down yet. Her mouth still felt parched. "No, baby … it *can't* be. It just *can't* be. Yes, you were wet, and you were muddy. But it was raining that night, and we live on a dirt road. All you had to do to get that dirty was to walk home. We still don't know what you did with your car."

"You don't believe me, do you?"

His mother again wrapped her arm around his and pulled him toward the porch. "Uh … how about I make sure I talk with your father about it when he comes home tomorrow morning? But for now, you go on up to your room while I fix you a sandwich and a nice cup of hot chocolate."

There she goes again. That room. Hot chocolate. Strike one. C. J. dreaded the thought. "Why are you keeping me in that dungeon? And why do you insist on my drinking hot chocolate?"

"Well, if you don't like your *dungeon,* then *do* something about it! But as for the hot chocolate, that's the way we do things around here. So get over it."

With his lips pursed, he studied the strange woman. His mind raced back to Monday morning when, as he was leaving the house for the job, she'd shoved the mug into his hand and insisted he drink all of its contents. He'd followed her orders well. He'd finished the hot chocolate. And it wasn't long after when his nagging headache had returned. But it was just a few short hours later when he'd learned he'd been drugged. Whether he'd ingested the barbiturates of his own free will or whether he'd been drugged by an outsider remained to be seen.

"Mom, I just finished a big breakfast. I won't be hungry, thank you. But I will go up and do something about that dungeon."

"Go for it, honey. It's *your* dungeon."

She didn't have to say that more than once. "Yes, ma'am."

Inside the house, Mrs. Taylor disappeared behind the kitchen door leaving C. J. standing there alone. Somehow, he'd expected the rest of the house to mimic his dingy bedroom, but he found himself surprised as he took in every inch of the perfectly normal living room; from the leather living room suite and navy-blue tweed recliners to the oak coffee table with its matching end tables. He glanced over to the opposite side of the room and noticed a stone-front fireplace with an ornate oak mantle. And along the wall to the left stood a massive German shrunk complete with framed pictures, knick-knacks, and a plasma screen TV. With its blood red accents to off-white walls, hardwood floors, and recessed lighting, the rich, country-style room looked deliciously inviting and not at all what he had expected.

Curious, he made his way over to the shrunk and studied a grouping of family photographs. But there was something about them that didn't look quite right. He didn't become surprised when he found his own face right in the middle of each one. But if their description of his earlier life had any truth to it, why would Bo's photos include the face paint and spiked hair while his own did not? Could it be that it had all been an elaborate case of mistaken identity? As he stood there gazing at each photo, something caught his eye. There, right beside his own photo, he found what appeared to be a small scratch. And as he investigated further, he found the scratch continued all the way around his own portrait. "Well, what do you know," he whispered to himself. "A cut and paste job." His family must have been so ashamed of his previous identity that they literally cut his old face right out of the family portraits. And not just one or two of them, but all of them.

All of a sudden, Mrs. Taylor startled him. "Hey! Over there!" When he glanced over to her, she was motioning to the staircase beside the kitchen door. She sounded angry. Apparently, she did not feel comfortable with C. J.'s exploring the photographs. "Your room is up that way. Get to the top, turn to your left, and then your door is the last one on the right."

Why does she feel she has to explain to me how to find my room? he wondered, although he knew full well he hadn't paid attention when he'd come down the other day. *Could it be she's finally listening? Or could this be strike two?* "Oh. I ... guess I forgot," he answered, blaming his memory loss. Did he dare mention the discrepancy in the photographs?

"You get yourself up there. I'll bring lunch up as soon as I can get it ready. And then we'll talk."

"Mom, I told you I'm *not* hungry. I *won't* be eating. But thank you anyway."

Perhaps it was the bewitching glint in her eye or perhaps it was the authority with which she pointed toward the stairway that made him say it. "I believe I'm supposed to be on duty today." And he turned and darted for the front door as though he had suddenly become a bullet flying through the air at breakneck speed. But before he could turn the doorknob, she was on him and had squeezed her demonic talons into his arm as though she had become a vicious attack dog. "You *will* get yourself up those stairs and you *will* go to your room."

Without another word, he carefully peeled her fingers from his arm and watched her like a hawk as he turned toward the stairs.

At the top of the stairs, he found the doorway that hid the short flight of steps that led up into the attic. Inside, he felt over the wall until he found the hidden light switch and flipped it up, although the dim wattage of the light bulb made little difference. Knowing his mother was going to demand an apology and deciding it would be best to beat her to the punch, he kicked some of the mess out of his way, sat himself down on the end of the bed, and tried rubbing the burning pain out of his arm. As soon as she reached the top of the staircase carrying a tray with a sandwich, chips, and a cup of hot chocolate, he said, "I'm sorry, okay?"

"Yeah? For what?" she asked while she sat the tray down on top of a dresser and then came over and sat down next to him.

For a moment, C. J. thought hard. He honestly didn't know what to think or what to say. He dropped his head into his hands and answered, "I don't know, Mom! I don't know what's happening to me! What's *wrong* with me?"

The woman reached around behind him and began rubbing his back. "Honey, you're just in a transition. You're reaching manhood and leaving all of this childish stuff behind. That's all it is. It's not a bad thing."

Although she could be right, C. J. did not believe his mother. But what an opportunity. He glanced up at the grotesque symbols of death that permeated every inch of wall space in the entire room. And then he jumped up off the bed and began ripping them off the wall. "Leaving childish stuff, huh? You mean like *this?*"

All of a sudden, it was as if the forty-watt light bulb had morphed into a one-hundred-watt light bulb. He found a window hidden beneath the paper and the room was instantly bathed in glorious sunlight.

"How many garbage bags do you think it'll take?" his mother asked.

Her question surprised him. His intention hadn't been to make her happy. Quite the opposite in fact. His intention had been to make her angry. However, he turned to her and answered, "A bunch. And the black clothes will have to go, too."

"Done."

"And the LEGO bricks?"

"We'll pass them down to Dylan."

"Paint?"

"Color?"

"Uh … maybe blue."

"Maybe a nice royal shade to match your eyes."

C. J. sighed heavily and nodded. *Just what does she want out of me?* "Yes, ma'am. I like blue."

Mrs. Taylor stood up and glanced down at him. "You eat and finish all of that hot chocolate. I'll bring you what few garbage bags I have, and you can continue while I go shopping. Sound good?"

The sudden change in the atmosphere caused C. J. to crack a sweet smile. "Yes, ma'am, it does sound good. Thank you."

•

It had been a busy morning. Shane wished C. J. had been there. He'd been needed. But at lunchtime, when he could get a few free minutes, Shane grabbed C. J.'s paychecks and drove home. But when he came in and found the door locked, the TV off, and C. J. gone, he became real hot under the collar. The kid didn't dare take off without an explanation!

His face violet with anger, Shane jumped back into his Civic and sped off, heading for Opossum Ridge Road. Fully expecting to find someone at home, he came to the door and rang the doorbell.

Up in his attic bedroom, C. J. had looked at cleaning the room as though it would be a treasure hunt. There was no telling what he might find hidden underneath the trash. He began inside the narrow closet where, after pulling out the junk, he found a sixty-one-key midi keyboard lying on the floor, still sealed in its box. And torn pieces of red wrapping paper held on with scotch tape told him it had been a forgotten Christmas present.

Outside the closet, he set bags of gathered trash near the stairwell and then busied himself yanking down the rest of the posters from the ceiling and walls. To his delight, behind the posters, he found another hidden window at the end of the room, just behind the headboard of his bed. In spite of the fact that the walls, ceiling, and even some of the glass panes of the windows had been slopped over with flat black paint, things were beginning to feel better. The room was becoming brighter as he worked, and all of a sudden, he understood the sudden shift in the mood of his mother.

But then, off in the distance, C. J. thought he'd heard the ringing of the doorbell and without giving it a second thought, he dropped the poster he held in his hand, and headed down the stairs. But then he reached for the doorknob and twisted his wrist. The doorknob held fast, causing C. J.'s fragile world to once again come crashing down. The tiny entrance at the bottom of the narrow stairwell had no lighting at all. C. J. could not see the doorknob, but he could feel it. There was no door lock on the inside. Instantly angry, he tried the door again when this time, he was certain he'd heard the doorbell.

Outside on the porch, Shane began knocking when no one had come to answer. "C. J., are you in there? Mrs. Taylor … hello!"

Although he could not hear Shane's voice, C. J. doubled his fists and pounded on the door, hoping to get the caller's attention. "Hey! Get me out of here!" But obviously Shane hadn't heard him, and a few moments later, C. J. could faintly hear a car start. Suddenly, he remembered the first window he had uncovered. It, unlike the window behind the headboard, was on the side of the room. Surely it faced the front side of the house, and in a flash, he rushed up the stairs to try to open it. But it too, like the doorknob, refused to budge. He scratched at the dried paint, but it wasn't coming off either.

His blood pressure skyrocketing, C. J. punched at the wall when the caller peeled his car out of the driveway. Feeling trapped, he returned his attention to the doorknob. Now, it doesn't take a degree in rocket science to figure that a bedroom door ought to lock from *inside* the room and not the *outside.*

It wouldn't be long before Roxanne Taylor had pulled into the driveway; her Ford van loaded with gallons of paint and the like. When she came in and opened C. J.'s door, things changed. She found her son sitting on the top step glaring down at her. "What's the matter now?" she asked when she saw the discontent written all over his handsome face.

"Uh, Mom, do you realize there's not a bathroom up here? There's no kitchen, no refrigerator—no way to answer the door if the doorbell rings."

With a look of confusion, Mrs. Taylor asked, "What are you getting at?"

"Before ... was I really such a tyrant that you couldn't trust me?"

"Son, what is your point?"

"Why are you keeping me locked up in here? Why is the doorknob turned backwards so that the lock is on the outside?"

The look on her face suddenly changed to one of embarrassment. Her China-doll cheeks actually flushed to a pinkish glow. "Oh, no! I'm so sorry! I didn't mean to … sometimes, I lock the door out of pure habit. It was an accident! I sure didn't mean anything by it."

C. J. felt confused. *You've got to be kidding me!* "You mean to tell me that doorknob got turned around the wrong way by *accident?*"

Mrs. Taylor sat down the bags she held and threw her hands to her narrow hips. "Why, *no!* You know full well that doorknob did *not* get turned around by *accident.* It was *fully* intentional. You got a problem with it?"

C. J. held his hands out. "In a word, yes. I guess transitions spread in both directions, don't they? I'm not what I used to be. No face paint, no freaky hair. Even my room is beginning to look.—well, it's beginning to look somewhat better anyway. I mean, Mom, you've *got* to trust me! You've got to have faith in me."

"Oh, I've got faith in you, all right. I've got enough faith to believe you're going to get up off your duff, and come out here to help me unload this stuff."

Totally confused, C. J. couldn't read his mother's mixed signals. What *was* he supposed to think? *I don't get it.* he thought as he stood up, dusted himself off, and followed her outside to the van.

Excited, Mrs. Taylor said, "I got you a couple other

things besides paint; things like a new light fixture so you can have some real light. And I got you some new pants and some shirts, and some—"

Amazed by the sheer volume of bags in the back of the van, C. J. interrupted, "Well, I hope you included a straight-edge razor in with all this stuff."

"No, sir. I most certainly did not!" she cried harshly. "What in the world makes you think I would allow a child to play with a razor?"

"A *child?* You think I'm a *child?* I only asked because the window is painted over with black paint. We'll need something to scrape it off. It doesn't *have* to be a razor but I sure can't scrape it off with my fingernails."

A grin suddenly splashed its way across her pretty face. "I've got just the thing."

Carrying an armload of bags and following her son up into the room, Roxanne again became irate when as she topped the final flight of stairs, she found his lunch still sitting on the dresser untouched. "Carson Zachary Taylor, Jr., I *told* you to finish your lunch!" the woman hollered at the top of her lungs.

For a moment, C. J. was taken aback. He spun himself around. His eyes darted around the room from wall to wall and corner to corner. "Who are you talking to?" he cried. "Who is Carson Zach—" For a split second, he felt his face flush when he realized she was hollering his full name. "Oh. Nevermind."

Undaunted, Roxanne dropped her bags down onto the bed and then came over and snatched up the cup of hot chocolate. "Drink this, and drink it now."

"I don't like hot chocolate."

"I don't care! Drink it all, and drink it now!"

"Mom, I don't like the stuff! I *told* you that already!"

All of a sudden, the irate woman reached up and put a death grip on his jaw. "*All* of it! *Now!*"

C. J.'s hands began to tremble. He didn't dare strike back. She was a woman; she was his mother. "Mom," he attempted to say with his teeth held clenched tightly shut. "I get it. I'll drink it … if you'll let go."

She ignored his request and squeezed her talons tighter.

"Mom … you're hurting me!" he cried while he attempted to pull his head back away from her.

The woman finally released her grip and made absolutely certain he finished every last drop. "Now that I've made myself perfectly clear, shall we begin the painting?"

C. J.'s arm still hadn't fully recovered from his mother's first outburst. And now this. He reached up and tried rubbing the sting from his jaw. "Mom, why the chocolate and not the sandwich?" he dared asking.

Roxanne went over and began scraping paint from the front window with a pancake spatula she'd brought up from the kitchen. "Chocolate makes people happy. And that's what I want for you, to be happy."

If the last few days had taught him anything, it would be that disappointing mother could prove painful, if not fatal. Stunned, terrified, and with a new migraine emerging from the depths of his brainstem, he answered, "Yes, ma'am," with a slight nod. *Strike three, you're out.*

Chapter 9

Sunday, December 11

In a way, C. J. had been correct. Shane's whole life had become routine. Every duty day, he showed up promptly at 5:45 a.m. and immediately headed for the locker room. This particular morning, however, something odd caught his eye and stopped him dead in his tracks. Over in the corner, sitting in the burgundy recliner near the piano sat C. J. dressed in full uniform. He appeared totally engrossed in skimming through pages of notes held together in a two-inch thick three-ring binder. C. J. hadn't yet looked up to notice his friend.

Shane rushed into the locker room, quickly took care of his things, and then came back out with a plastic grocery bag in his hand and stood at the end of the table near where C. J. was sitting. It was when he dropped the bag on top of C. J.'s notebook that the boy looked up. "At the very least, you owe me an explanation," Shane said.

C. J. agreed totally. He nodded and said, "Yes, sir, I—" He hesitated when he caught a glimpse of his father out of the corner of his eye. And after his father disappeared behind his office door, C. J. glanced around the room at the rest of the crew who seemed totally engrossed in whatever little tidbit of nothing they were doing. Finally, he continued under his breath. “Was the TV still on?”

“What has the TV got to do with it?” Shane asked.

“I told them to turn it off. Did they?”

“Who are you talking about?”

“How about the door? Was it locked?”

Shane sat down on the bench near the table and leaned toward C. J. “The door was locked; the TV was off. Now, who in the world are you talking about?”

C. J. lowered his voice to a whisper. “It was Vargas and Rayford.”

“Vargas? Rayford?”

“Oh, come on. You remember. They were the cops who came to question me at the hospital Tuesday morning. They showed up at your apartment and insisted on escorting me home—in handcuffs. And without a warrant at that.”

“Did your dad send them?”

“That’s the kicker. No, he didn’t. It was my mother. She’s in good with those two.”

Shane became confused. “You’re telling me a story, aren’t you?”

It was when C. J. dropped his gaze with an attitude of disappointment that Shane noticed the purple bruise on the side of his jaw.

“Well, then, if you were there, why didn’t you answer the door?”

"I tried to get your attention, but you obviously didn't hear me. The doorknob on the door leading to my room had been turned backwards, and she locked it on her way out. Had you not come to the door, I might not have known."

His brow furrowed, Shane asked, "How'd you get that bruise on your face?"

C. J. leaned back in the chair, picked up the bottle of grape-flavored Propel that was sitting next to him, and took a sip. It quickly became obvious that Shane's observation had made him uncomfortable and he changed the subject. "The dungeon can no longer be called a dungeon. The posters are gone, the walls are painted. And I found a hidden window, among other things." He picked the bag up from off the book and put it down on the floor beside the chair. "I even found time to skim these manuals so that—"

Shane interrupted him when he slapped the top of the manual. "Enough about the book," he said under his breath. "Answer my question. How did you get the bruise?"

C. J. reached up and covered the mark on his face, and then he scanned the others who were scattered about the room. Other than Shane, not a single one of them appeared interested in their conversation. "Oh, um, it pays to look where you're going when there's a door in front of you," he answered to play it safe. But then he leaned forward and whispered, "You don't cross my mother."

"*She* did that?"

"You just don't know how good hot chocolate can taste first thing every morning."

"Your rib cage, your headache, are they better?"

"She's a nurse, and she's real handy with a needle and thread. And hot chocolate? It cures everything. It makes people *happy*."

Sitting over in his corner, Frank had done something that caught Shane's eye. Shane couldn't tell exactly what it was he thought he had seen, but he shot a glance over that way and for a split second, hoping the man had overheard their conversation.

Although he believed the boy, Shane didn't know what to say, or to think, or how to react, so he changed the subject. "So, you're gonna stick it out with us, huh?"

Again C. J. leaned forward and whispered, "They don't leave me much choice."

"Well, I tell you what then. I'll just help you out with some good, old-fashioned on-the-job training."

"Thank you, Mr. Westbrook. I owe you," C. J. said with a grin.

"The name's Shane, and yes, you do. And, by the way, while we're on the subject, in the bag you'll find the uniform you left in the dryer. And you'll also find your last four paychecks." And then, all of a sudden, Shane lowered his voice and got down in C. J.'s ear. "And do yourself a favor," he whispered. "Open yourself a new checking account with the bank. Your dad is on your old account."

Without another word, C. J. nodded his thanks.

•

While he'd been off duty, C. J. had taken the time to

study the first-aid manual his father had given him. But no amount of book knowledge could ever prepare him for the reality of saving lives.

Beyond the interstate overpass, on the south side of town, two vehicles sat tangled together in the grassy median of South Ferdon Boulevard. The late afternoon traffic had come to a standstill for miles in either direction.

Inside the cab of the ladder truck, Zach turned to C. J. and said, "Since this is basically your first, you stay right here and just watch."

C. J. raised his hands in mock surrender. "No problem, Chief." And he watched in fascination as the crew played out the scene as though they were a well-oiled machine. And then, all of a sudden, something over to his right caught his eye. The ditch was deep and thick with overgrown weeds. C. J. strained his eyes until he saw it again. Curious, he jumped down out of the cab and went to investigate. There, made totally obscure by surrounding growth, a third vehicle lay on its roof. Waving her bloodied arm outside the broken door window, the young female driver hung upside down trapped in her seatbelt.

His heart pounding wildly, C. J. rushed over to Taylor and pointed toward the car. "Dad! Dad, there's another one over there!"

Zach was deeply involved with the jaws of life, cutting away a roof to remove a victim. And when he could not hear his son over the roar of the jaws, C. J. grabbed his arm to get his attention and pointed. Taylor glanced over to Shane and nodded in C. J.'s direction. Shane, who was busy taking the pulse of another victim, turned his task over to Jason and followed C. J. "What is it?" he asked once they got out of ear shot of the jaws.

"It's another vehicle! It's turned on its roof in the ditch, and the driver's trying to get out!"

After Shane knocked branches out of the way, he dropped to his knees and peered in the driver's door window. When the young female driver saw him, she cried, "My baby! *Please,* save my baby!"

Wide-eyed, C. J. dropped to his knees next to Shane and looked up through the back door window into the back seat and found an infant's car seat that had been strapped in backwards. Strapped inside was a very tiny newborn whose face had turned to a deadly purple. Instantly, Frank's words came screeching back to him like a freight train. "That kid is *dead* because of him!"

Sweating profusely and shaking like a leaf in a hurricane-force wind, C. J. cried, "I can't do this, Mr. Westbrook! I *can't* do this!"

Busy trying to cut the driver free, Shane hollered, "Yes, you can! Cut the straps and bring him down gently! But hurry up about it!"

"He's blue!"

"Cut the straps!" Shane cried when he shoved a pocketknife his way.

Down on his knees, C. J. grabbed the pocketknife and reached deeper into the car. He didn't dare try to cut the straps of the car seat itself for fear of risking further injury to the baby, so he rolled over onto his back, cut the car's seatbelt to free the car seat, and gently turned it right side up. And then he was able to carefully remove the tiny infant and cradle him in his arms.

"Make sure he's breathing!" Shane cried.

C. J. listened for breath sounds but heard none. "He's not breathing! And his heart's not beating, either! Mr. Westbrook, what do I do?"

When the young mother heard C. J., she cried out, "Please, don't let my baby die!"

Her words cut straight to C. J.'s heart, and all of a sudden, the words of the first-aid manual flashed through his mind. "Infant CPR. Big hand, little heart. Five to one," he whispered to himself. "Five to one." With the baby in his arms, he flipped himself onto his belly and then up onto his elbows, gently pulled the baby's head back, and blew two rescue breaths into him. And then he began chest compressions using his two middle fingers. "One, two, three, four, five, blow. One, two, three—" He refused to give up. He refused to have to account for another dead child. "Come on back, baby!"

Shane and C. J. had become so totally engrossed in the task, they hadn't paid any attention to the tremendous commotion that arose outside the car. "Taylor, that *freak* ain't got *no* business being anywhere near this area!" C. J. thought he recognized Frank's griping voice, but he refused to give up on the baby.

"Come on, little guy. Come back to us." He continued CPR until suddenly, he felt someone grab his ankles and yank him out of the car even before he could kick back. He cradled the infant tightly and held on. And once he cleared the car, in spite of Frank's bellowing, he kept up the CPR until he was rewarded with a tiny squeak and then a wail. C. J. hadn't seen Shane pull the mother out of the wreckage. He hadn't looked up to see the crowd that had gathered around him, nor had he paid attention to the crowd's clapping at the infant's cries. It all seemed totally insignificant to the thrill the very much alive tiny newborn brought to him. Nor could it compare to the young mother's reaction when Frank came and snatched the child from C. J. and took him to his mother. "There you go, ma'am."

With tears pouring down her face, the mother said, "*You're* not the handsome guy who saved my Austin's life! Where is he?"

Red faced, C. J. stood to his feet and brushed himself off. When he came to her gurney, the young mother managed to reach up and kiss him on the cheek. "Austin is only two weeks old," she informed him. "How can I ever thank you?"

With a slight grin, C. J. whispered, "You just did."

On the way back to the station, C. J. turned to Shane and asked, "Do you think that baby will be all right?"

Shane thought for a single moment. "I know this much. If you had chosen to not come back today, two-week old Austin and his mother, Marie, would have been the only casualties."

It sent a chill down C. J.'s spine.

Chapter 10

The busyness of the next couple hours made them zip by. But just as things were beginning to settle down before lunch, two African American women dressed in brightly colored Winnie the Pooh scrubs and heavy overcoats came rushing into the station and were met by Zach. "Can I help you ladies?" he asked.

"Oh, honey, we sho' hope so," the older of the two said. "We got us an e-*mer*-gency! We be lookin' all over the place fo' C. J. Taylor. You know 'im?"

Over in the burgundy recliner near the piano, C. J. had only just sat down and picked up the first-aid manual when he heard his name, and he became totally unnerved when he looked up and found all eyes were turned and focused on him. The older lady took note of the kid in the recliner and rushed over to him. "You ain't *our* C. J."

The boy put his book down, stood to his feet, and stuck out his hand. "Yes, ma'am. My name *is* C. J. Taylor. Can I help you?"

Standing over near the locker room door, Jason hollered, "Hey, lady, you lookin' for the *ugly* C. J. with the painted face?"

The lady turned in Jason's direction. "Yessir! That be the one! Know where we be findin' 'im?"

Before C. J. could get it out, Jason hollered, "Well, ladies, today would be your lucky day! He done gave up the costume mess a week or so back."

The lady turned back to C. J. and asked, "Where in the world you been, boy?"

With a look of confusion written all over his face, C. J. said, "Ma'am, I don't mean any disrespect, but I don't know who you are."

Suddenly, the woman's shiny dark eyes began to glisten with tears. "Miss Sammy tol' us not to come! She tol' us you be mad if we come searchin'! But ya gotta un'nerstan'! We be *needin'* yo' presence! It be lil' miss Mia! Cain't you come on? You ain't gotta have no paint on yo' face. Mia won't be carin' none."

Zach warily approached the ladies. "Ma'am, exactly what is it you need with my boy here?"

"This yo' boy?"

"Yes, ma'am. He's my son. So, what's your business with him?"

The woman looked up at the confusion on C. J.'s face. "He won' let me tell. But it be an e-*mer*-gency! He gotta come with us!"

Zach shook his head. "I'm sorry, ma'am. He won't be leaving. He won't be getting off until six o'clock tomorrow morning."

All of a sudden, she became angry. "You people is in the e-*mer*-gency business! An' we got us an e-*mer*-gency! So yo' bes' let him come on!"

C. J. watched his father for a moment. "Let me go with them, Dad. They seem genuine."

Zach thought, and he thought hard. In the back of his mind, he could imagine his wife's voice. *Absolutely not! Not now! Not ever!* But he felt caught between a rock and a hard place, and finally, he sighed. "All right. Sunday's are usually pretty quiet. I'll let you go ... but just this once."

C. J. turned, grabbed his jacket, and slipped it on as he followed the women toward the door. But his father caught him, pulled him over to the side, and said in his ear, "But if you even begin to think about going back to your old life, you're dead meat, you understand me?"

C. J. jerked his arm away. "When are you going to learn to trust me?"

"I want a full report when you get back."

"Yeah, whatever."

C. J. sat in the back seat of the car as the younger of the two women sped along the road. But when she turned the car onto the interstate, he cried, "Ma'am, I thought you said this was an emergency! Where are you taking me?"

The older woman turned herself around in her seat. "You know where we be goin'! Mia's wantin' you! An' ... she ain't got long."

The younger lady asked, "Mr. Taylor, why'd you go and lie to your daddy like that, sayin' you don't know us an' all?"

The older woman answered, "Now, LaKeisha, girl, yo' done hear'd what Miss Sammy say! She say'd C. J. don't want no body knowin' 'is business."

C. J. smiled. The woman was a class act. "Um … the truth is, ladies, I had a little accident. And I've been suffering with a case of amnesia. So, uh, maybe you should remind me of what my business is, since I don't seem to remember."

"That what happen't to the costume?"

"Is this why I wore it?"

"Some 'o them parents griped 'cause you let yo'self look real bad, but Mia loves ya'. She say you taught her how to face scary stuff. Ain't that why you wear'd the stuff in the first place?"

Embarrassed, C. J. had to admit, "Actually, I don't remember my reason for wearing that kind of get up."

"Ya' say'd it were 'cause yo' believed in facin' stuff yo' was afraid of head on. And yo' was afraid 'o dyin'."

Surprised, C. J. said, "Wait. I dressed like that because I was afraid of *dying?*"

"That's what yo' say'd."

"But … what about the drinking, and the drugs, and the—"

The older woman brushed him off. "Ah, they weren't none 'o that mess. Yo's a good Christian boy! Yo' used to say yo' din't need that mess."

C. J. scratched his head. "Um … what exactly do I do over here?"

"Every month, every single month, them kids seen yo' clown act. Yo' helped teach them not to be a-scared o' nuttin', and yo' brought 'em toys an' stuff."

The younger lady spoke up. "And Mamma Purl, don't forget the flowers for Miss Sammy."

The older lady laughed out loud and clapped her hands. "Yes, Lordy, an' Miss Sammy is sho'nuf missin' yo'! She bad aggravated 'cause yo' left yo' keys. She carryin' 'em around, hopin' yo' come and take 'em back."

C. J. wondered what he'd gotten himself into. In a panic, he cried, "*Whoa!* Wait a minute! *Kids? What* kids? And who in the world is Miss Sammy?"

"The kids is the sick ones … at the children's hospital. And Miss Sammy—"

LaKeisha interrupted. "You ain't won Miss Sammy with them flowers yet, boy, but—"

"But wait till she gets a sight of yo' without the face!" Mamma Purl interjected. "Ooo, honey, yo' gonna knock her socks right off them cute little feets of hers!"

Red-faced, C. J. rolled his eyes. "Oh, brother!" This was looking more like an adventure than an emergency.

The drive into Pensacola took a full hour. And there, as they passed through the doctors' parking lot, in the front of the children's hospital, C. J. took notice of a metallic blue Mitsubishi Eclipse sitting in front of a simple homemade sign. It was a sharp looking car, but why it caught his eye, C. J. could only fathom; it might have been the color, it might have been his mother's use of the word eclipse when they were speaking about his car earlier, or it might have been the combination of the two. Whatever the reason, when LaKeisha pointed out the sign, his own socks were knocked off. Printed in multi-colored crayon on simple cardstock paper, the sign read *Dr. C. J. Taylor.* "Wait! What's all that about?" he asked as they walked past it.

The older lady took C. J. by his arm and pulled him along. "We gotta get inside, honey. Mia be a waitin'. You can play which yo' wheels later."

C. J. kept walking but looked back and asked, "Is that *my* car?"

"Yessir. The las' time yo' was here, yo' spent all yo' money on them kids and din't have 'nuf to put gas in the car to take it to yo' house."

"But—" All of a sudden, the puzzling mystery had taken another turn. "Then ... how did I get home?" *And if* that's *my car, then how* did *I get in that pond?*

"Ain't got a clue."

Inside, in the cancer unit, the two ladies whisked C. J. past the nurse's station and down the hall to a room on the left. While the room had been painted with bright flowers and bunny rabbits, the constant beeping of a heart monitor filled the air. On the bed lay a small African American girl who appeared to be sleeping. LaKeisha sat down on the bed next to her and whispered, "Mia, we found your C. J. If you'll wake up, you can see him." She then reached back, took C. J. by his hand, and pulled him over to the opposite side of the bed.

It quickly became obvious that the boy didn't know what to do, so the older woman instructed him in quiet whispers. "She got leukemia, nuttin' contagious, so go ahead an' sit. She won' mind."

When he sat down on the side of the bed, the older

lady then whispered, "Now, go on an' take 'er hand." C. J. reached down and picked up the little girl's cool, frail hand and held it in his. The woman then whispered, "Mr. Taylor, she be a mighty sick baby."

LaKeisha looked over at C. J. and whispered, "She's just been holding out for you. What she needs is for you to release her. Let her know it's okay to go home to Jesus."

All of a sudden, Frank's words again came crashing back, and C. J. felt a well of emotions building up inside of him. He knew nothing about Jesus, nor did he know how to "release" someone, let alone a small child. But he glanced down at the little girl's pale face and then leaned down and whispered in her ear, "Mia … can you help me out here?" When the little girl responded with a tiny smile, C. J. smiled back. "I had an accident, and I'm not remembering things. Can you help me remember?"

Mia opened her tired eyes and looked up at him. And then she reached up and gently stroked the side of his face. "I always knew you had a pretty face," she said. "Miss Sammy will love you."

C. J. found himself smiling at the thought. He hadn't yet met this Miss Sammy, but he envisioned her as a happy-go-lucky, slightly rotund nurse. "I don't know about that, but I need your help remembering the things I did to help you."

Mia moved her thin, frail arm and pointed to a rather large teddy bear that sat over in her chair. "You gave him to me. You gave everybody one. You said he would protect me from the bad guys."

"Did he do his job?"

The little girl closed her eyes but whispered, "Yes, but I need to go home to heaven now. My Jesus is waiting. If you kiss me good night on my forehead like you used to do, I'll go to sleep like a good girl. Oh. And C. J., can you make sure my protector bear goes to Caleb? He's the new kid on the floor. He needs protection too, like I did."

It almost felt like pure instinct when he leaned down and kissed the little girl on her forehead. And then he hugged her and whispered, "I'll make sure Caleb gets the bear, okay? Now you go on to sleep."

"Hold my hand," she whispered back.

Without another word, he took her hand and held it tight until the sound of the heart monitor changed from a constant beep to a sad, steady hum.

The scene became somber, almost more than C. J. could take. After several minutes of him listening to the ladies' silent weeping, and fighting back his own emotions, LaKeisha whisked C. J. to a doctor's lounge where he could get himself a cold drink. While he studied the selections on the vending machine, he heard what he thought were quiet sobs coming from the side. When he peeked, he found another nurse who had hidden herself in the corner. Embarrassed, she refused to look his way and kept her face toward the wall. C. J. took a couple paper napkins from the center of a table and without a word, handed them to her. She immediately sniffled and straightened herself up. "Thank you," she whispered.

"You're welcome," C. J. whispered back as he

turned away and refocused his attention back to his business at the vending machine. He dug through his pockets and found nothing but lint. And when he pulled out his wallet, he laughed to himself when he realized he was penniless. *Wasn't thirsty anyway.*

After the nurse blew her nose, she wadded the napkins up and mindlessly shoved them into C. J.'s hand. "I know we're supposed to be stronger than this, but… these are children! No amount of time will ever get me used to losing an innocent child!"

C. J. hadn't said a word. He stood there, poised with the used napkins in his hand and a confused look on his face. It grossed him out, but he couldn't help but crack a smile when the nurse suddenly looked up at his hand and snatched the napkins out of it. "Oh, my gosh! I'm *so* sorry!"

Although her face had turned about a dozen shades of red, C. J. noticed she seemed mighty young to be in a nurse's uniform. But she was a pretty girl, her long blonde hair pulled back into a ponytail with gentle wisps of hair fallen down over her forehead. And in her brown eyes, he saw a tenderness he'd never seen in any other. Being a nurse in a pediatric hospital takes a special breed, and somehow, he could see she'd been right for the job.

"Please, forgive me," she said as she threw the napkins into a trash can that was sitting near the door. "Uh, you might want to wash your hands," she said as she pointed to a sink over near the vending machine. "And you might want to use a hand sanitizer too. I've had a little bit of a cold."

C. J. washed his hands exactly the way she said to. Of course, being in the health field himself, he'd learned a lot about good hand washing in the last couple of days. And while he was using the sanitizer, she came and washed her own hands.

While she was drying her hands, that's when she finally looked up and saw his face. She had to catch herself against the sink. "Whoa! Wait a minute! Who in the world—" She suddenly realized she didn't recognize him, so she nervously stuck out her hand and introduced herself. "Uh ... hi. I'm Samantha Gifford. Everyone around here calls me Miss Sammy. I ... don't think I've met you before."

For a moment, C. J. was taken aback. "*You're* Miss Sammy?"

Her eyes wide as saucers, she said, "Yes I am. Why?"

"It's just that you're not at all what I pictured."

"Is that so? Just what did you picture?"

With an embarrassed grin on his face, C. J. said, "Oh, you probably don't want to know."

"Sure I do!"

Oh, dear. How could he get out of this one? "Uh ... well, it's just that ... I thought—"

Thankfully, LaKeisha came in the door, and C. J. felt sure she was going to save the day. She was carrying Mia's bear and handed it to him. "Here you go, Mr. Taylor. If you'll hold on to him, I'll go find out which room is Caleb's."

"Uh, yeah. Thanks," C. J. said as she was heading out the door.

Samantha looked up at him. "Taylor? *You're* C. J. Taylor?" She rushed over to him and punched him hard on his chest.

"*Ouch!* What'd you do that for?" *Women must just plain hate me!*

"Where in the world have you been? And what is up with the *natural* face?"

"What's the matter? You prefer the *old* face?"

"Well, I sure had no idea your *natural* face was so—" All of a sudden, she was forced to catch her breath because she'd never been attracted to him before. She had no idea he could look so unbelievably attractive. "I didn't realize your face was so—oh, for Pete's sake! C. J., you didn't come back this past weekend, and these kids are missing you! They've been asking for you over and over again! They even went so far as to scribble a sign that reads *Dr. C. J. Taylor* and we put it out in front of your car so that you might understand how important you are to them!"

Stunned, the young man turned his gaze down to the floor and rubbed the base of his skull where a dull ache was pounding relentlessly. "You and the other two ladies ... you 're all making me sound like I'm this *wonderful* person, but you're talking about somebody that I don't know. Why can I not remember this?"

"Ah, come on! Now, C. J. Taylor, I *know* you remember! Friday was a week ago. You were ticked off about something. Surely you remember what it was you were so angry about."

Embarrassed, C. J. slowly shook his head. "Do you know what it was?"

"Now how would *I* know? You've sworn us all to absolute secrecy, as if you were ashamed that someone back wherever you came from might find out you were teaching terrified children how to not be afraid of something as drastic and as permanent as dying!" C. J. screwed up his face, straining to remember.

Samantha looked at him with a look of absolute consternation. "What's wrong with you, C. J.? Why the sudden change? How is it you can't seem to remember?"

All of a sudden, C. J. was just beginning to realize how boring his story was becoming. But he felt he had no choice but to try to explain it again. "There was an accident. I got amnesia. The story is getting old, so how much of it do you really want to hear?"

Samantha rolled her eyes. "Oh, forget it, C. J. I've heard all kinds of excuses, and that one's a classic. Besides, it couldn't have been too much of an accident," she said as she reached into her pocket, pulled out a set of car keys, and dropped them into his hand. "You didn't have enough gas in your car to take it home, so I took it and filled it up for you. It hasn't moved since."

For a moment, he stared at her until he found himself a seat at the table and sat down.

As she watched him, the faraway look on his face told her that he was telling the truth. She sat down across from him, placed her hand over his, and asked, "You're not joking, are you? What's going on? What kind of an accident was it?"

C. J. pulled his hand back and shied away from

her. "Um ... I thought ... I mean, I was sure it was a ... oh, the truth is, I just don't know. But it doesn't matter now. I'm fine, and I've got to get out of here." He stood up and turned toward the door. But then a thought occurred to him. "If I swore everyone to secrecy and never let on where I lived or worked, then how did LaKeisha and Purl find me?"

Samantha's face turned red. "It was my fault, okay? You're welcome to be angry with me, not them. But Mia was reaching the end of her battle with the leukemia, and she needed you. All we had was your car, so I took the liberty to go through your glove box and found your registration with your address. From there I went to the internet. I'm not sorry I did it. You did get back here just in time for Mia's sake."

"Well, I hope I did for her what she needed."

"You gave her permission to go home to Jesus, didn't you?"

"I'm not into religion much these days, but yes, that's what LaKeisha told me to tell her."

Samantha furrowed her brow. "Excuse me? Not into religion? C. J. Taylor, you became a Christian three years ago, and you even felt called to become a minister to children! That's where you belong! *This* is where you belong! *This* is where you're heart's been all along. I was there, C. J.! I *know* it was real!" she cried. But when she saw the disdain in his eyes, she leaned back in shock. "You loved leading people to Jesus. You loved being called the preacher boy around here. C. J., what happened to your dream? What happened to you?"

C. J. could only shrug his shoulders and sigh.

"I wish I could answer your questions, but I can't. I don't know what happened to me. I have zero recollection. Whatever I was, I'm not any more. And if what you said was true, that I became a Christian back…whenever, then why do I find religious talk so highly irritating?" He glanced down and saw the tears that were beginning to build in her big brown eyes and dreaded the thought of leaving her like that. "Nevermind. Don't answer that. I've got to get back before my dad manages to give birth to a cow—naturally." Samantha's heart broke. She could not believe her ears. With the tears now trickling down her cheek, she reached over, took the bear C. J. had left sitting on the table, and pulled it to herself. "Are you going to tell him about all this?"

He let out a heavy sigh. "I don't see the point. It's not like he would give a rip about these children. Now, how much do I owe you for gassing up my car?"

"Don't worry about it. You can pay me back later."

C. J. leaned over the table and looked her in the eye. "Look, Miss Sammy, until I can get something in my life figured out, I will not be able to come back to work here again. My nerves are shot, my brain is fried, and I'm flat broke. Please let the ladies know I do appreciate them coming after me, and I do appreciate your taking care of my car. I'll have to get back with you on the money."

Samantha stared back at him, studying his handsome eyes. Oh, she'd heard him all right, but suddenly she found herself searching for a way to keep him coming back. It was strange. She'd never felt that way before. "Only if you bring it to me one dollar a year for the next, say, forty years." He couldn't help but smile. Sure, she was pretty, but he could not shake the feeling that he might be treading into forbidden territory had he been weak enough to allow a relationship to develop. "The bear is supposed to go to a kid named Caleb. I'd appreciate it if you would make sure he gets it," C. J. said with a grin as he quickly disappeared out the door.

•

When he made it back to the station, C. J. came inside the day room and stuck his head in his father's office door. "Dad, I'm back, and yes, it was a real emergency."

But his father was already hot under the collar. "A real emergency, my foot!" he hollered. "You headed back toward Pensacola again, didn't you?"

Somehow, C. J. didn't feel surprised. Disappointed, yes, but surprised—well, it would take a whole lot more to surprise him at this juncture. He pushed the door open with his foot and leaned against the doorjamb with his arms crossed in front of him. "What'd you do? Have your crooked cop spies Vargas and Rayford been following me?"

Sitting in the chair behind his desk, Zach leaned forward. "You were seen turning onto I-10 west. Don't tell me you didn't go there again."

"What's your beef with what I do in Pensacola?"

"I *warned* you not to go there again!"

Outside the office door, neither C. J. nor Zach had seen Shane sitting at the far end of the table trying hard not to be noticed as he was quickly scribbling a note on a napkin and stuffing it inside the manual the boy had been reading earlier in the day.

Up until that moment, C. J. had absolutely no intention of making his way back to the children's hospital—and not because his father had warned him not to go, but because he had no recollection as to why he'd gone there in the first place. But his father's ridiculous ranting and raving could easily persuade him to change his mind. "You know what, Dad? I learned something today. I learned that I was the exact opposite of what all of you fruitcakes have claimed I was." And then he looked up at the ceiling and sighed heavily. "It's sad. After listening to those ladies talk about me, I've come to like the old me a whole lot better than the new me. I was a pretty good guy."

Zachary Taylor was an arrogant man. He sat back in his chair and snickered. "What you was ... what you is ... you *best* tell me what was so urgent!"

"Why is it I get the feeling you don't really give a rip?" C. J. asked as he turned and walked out of the office without waiting for an answer. When he came to the recliner and sat himself down, without a word, Shane turned and handed him the manual. "Thank you," C. J. offered as he opened the book to his marked page, only to find Shane's note. *Since you have your car, follow me home after work in the morning. We have to talk ... and* not *here. It's important.* C. J. looked up toward his father's office, and when he did not see his father standing there, he glanced over at Shane, nodded, and then took the note, wadded it up, and stuffed it in his pants' pocket.

•

In the northwest panhandle of Florida, December nights are usually miserably cold and wet with heavy, dense fog. Just to breathe the air, one might feel as though he would drown.

Miles away from the night lights of Crestview, before dawn on Monday morning, December 12, a lone figure trudged heavily through the unseen part of the Blackwater River National Forest. As he trudged on deep into the night, he stopped momentarily only to shift the squirming, heavy burden he carried slung over his left shoulder.

•

Early Monday morning, December 12

C. J. asked, "What was it that was so important?" as he sat himself down on Shane's couch.

Shane brought a chair in from the dining room, parked it across from the couch, and sat down. His jaw was tight, and C. J. knew something had unnerved him. "While you were away yesterday, there'd been a call. About half of the department was out. No big deal. It happens like that all the time."

"Yeah, I'm learning that. So—"

"So, today, your dad took off out of his office like a bat out of… well, you know. He rushed outside and was yelling at some man in a silver BMW. My curiosity overwhelmed me, so I nonchalantly moved over toward the door, cracked it open, and peeked out."

"And—"

"The car looked expensive. The guy was well dressed … obviously a high roller. And just from what I heard, I took it Zach owes him money … *big* money. The man said something like, 'You'd better pay up by Christmas, or some poor child in your family won't see Christmas.' There was some yelling, and the guy peeled out of the parking lot. I didn't want your dad to know I'd been eavesdropping, so as soon as he started storming back toward the door, I sat myself down and made as if I hadn't heard a thing."

His brow furrowed, C. J. asked, "What was he talking about?"

"He didn't make that clear, but in my mind, all I could picture over and over was your knife incident. After all, you *are* one of Zach's offspring, even if you don't want to admit it. But that wasn't all. There was something else weird about it."

"Oh, great. What else?"

"Now, Deanna would tell you that I'm not intellectual enough to pay attention to appearances. She would tell you that I couldn't see the resemblance in a set of identical twins. And she's probably right. But I gotta tell ya, this guy really stood out. Just like you, the man looked like he'd just stepped out of the pages of *People Magazine.* Where in the world you people come from, I just can't figure."

C. J. found it irritating whenever something about his appearance was mentioned. He'd heard it so many times in the last few days that it was beginning to make his skin crawl. He rolled his eyes, got up from the couch, and walked over toward the door. "What do you mean *you people?* Why do you do that to me? I'm no different than you or anybody else! And I sure didn't come out of some ritzy magazine. Besides, people that look like me come a dime a dozen. It's no big deal. And I can prove it. Just look in a … a *magazine,*" he finished with a snicker.

Shane too got up. "No big deal, my foot! Fact is, people like you are usually the ones who are exploited by Hollywood! People like you are usually not the ones living and working in some redneck city on the other side of the country! My point is, C. J., people like you do *not* come a dime a dozen, especially in *this* part of the country, and that's exactly why this guy stood out. He could have been your brother … or at least, a very close relation."

"Oh, come on, Shane. Surely it's just a coincidence."

"Coincidence, huh? You mean to tell me that it was pure coincidence that you lost your memory and changed from freaky to normal? Was it by coincidence that this replica of you all of a sudden shows up on the scene asking for money? And the knife thing … I know, don't tell me. Just coincidence, right? Not hardly. All these different things are happening at the same time. It's more than coincidence, if you ask me."

"Shane, this is the kind of junk movies are made out of. It's not real life. And even if all this stuff were true, what would it matter now? Without a memory, nothing before this matters, does it?"

"It seems to me that that's the very thing they're

counting on. Your not being able to remember. I think you need to watch your back. I'm telling you, there's something fishy going on here."

C. J. opened the door and stepped out onto the landing. "Speaking of something fishy, if I don't get out of here, Dad will turn me into fish bait. And if I miss our *traditional* hot chocolate breakfast again, Mom will send her cronies after me. And they know where you live," he finished half jokingly.

"Hot chocolate breakfast, huh? Sounds like a dream!"

"I suppose it could be if you liked the stuff. But in our house, it's a '*family tradition*' because '*chocolate makes people happy*'," C. J. mocked, trying to mimic the voice of his mother. "Give me coffee any day."

Shane laughed at him.

"Seriously, she makes us *all* drink it!" He reached up and rubbed his jaw. "It's more important than bacon and—"

Shane stopped him. "You probably don't have a phone in that dungeon of yours, do you?"

C. J. rolled his eyes. "Oh sure! I've got everything a single guy could ever want—all the modern conveniences. I've got it all! Unless, of course that *all* would include things like a television, a bathroom, a refrigerator. There's no running water, no telephone—I'm lucky to have electricity! At least I can *see* what I'm missing." As bad as he made it sound, C. J. found himself snickering at the utter ridiculousness of it all.

"I didn't think so. Wait a second," Shane said as he turned away from the door. And when he came back a few seconds later, he brought out a small cell phone and a wall charger and handed them to C. J. "I left the station during lunchtime today because I had this feeling. You were still gone. If for some reason you feel like you're in trouble, you hit speed dial number three. I have caller ID, so even if for some reason you're not able to talk, I'll still know it was you."

C. J. was taken aback. "Why would you do this for the likes of *me?* What value do I have?"

Shane wanted to say the right thing without making his friend feel pushed. "Um, let's just say it's a God thing, okay? And for now, we'll leave it at that."

"What happens if it turns out I'm the one who's off my rocker?"

"If that's the case, then we'll deal with it. Now, you'd better get on home before the cronies come to take you away."

C. J. left with a smile on his face, honestly thankful for the friend who'd taken his side.

Chapter 11

Friday morning, December 16

It wasn't enough that C. J. could not get the friends he'd met at the children's hospital off his mind. Zach had helped make the decision an easy one.

"Over my dead body!" his father yelled across the breakfast table.

The three younger Taylor children had finished their pancakes and their hot chocolate, and were already on their way to school. It would be their last day before Christmas break. C. J. held back simply to let his parents know of his plans to revisit the children's hospital.

"I *need* to go back, Dad!" C. J. hollered back.

Zach jumped to his feet and shook his finger in his son's face. "*You're* not going anywhere!"

C. J. shot a nervous glance over to his mother. To his surprise, she just sat there without interjecting a single word, staring him down as though she was a vulture waiting for the kill.

"As long as you're living under my roof, you'll do as I say!" Zach continued.

C. J. stood to his feet and leaned over the table.

"I've *got* to go back, Dad! It's important! I'm twenty-one years old, I've got my own car back—I'll even pay for my own gas!"

Zach pushed his plate away and leaned over onto his elbows. "If you even *dare* to attempt to walk through that door without our permission, I'll—"

"*Stop it!* Both of you!" Roxanne finally squealed.

For a breathless moment, C. J. flinched and fought the urge to dive under the table. The woman seemed to have a perfect aim, zeroing her demonic talons from a hundred paces.

"I've had enough!" she continued. "Now you boys listen and you listen good! This is the way it's going to be, period."

Zach furrowed his brow, wondering what his wife was bound to say next. It seemed to him that he'd always let her have the last say, mostly because before the argument was over, she'd figure out some simple solution and end it all immediately.

Clad in the same green bathrobe C. J. always seemed to see her in, Roxanne glanced over at the digital clock on the front of the glass-top stove. "Ordinarily, Son, I would tell you that you'd never be going back to Pensacola, but since you seem so adamant about this, we'll let you go under one condition."

Glaring at her with disdain, C. J. dared not open his mouth. To his surprise, she hadn't yet mentioned his car, that indeed it had not been found in the watering hole.

"If it's the life of drugs, alcohol, and girls that you desire, the way I see it, you have only one choice."

The boy held his silence.

"*If* that's the life you choose, then your only choice is to take me with you."

Zach spat coffee across the table. "*What?* Are you out of your mind?"

"You heard me! You know he isn't going to be doing that stuff with me standing right there. So, either I go along or no one goes."

Even though Zach knew she'd find a solution, her overpowering personality belittled him. But she made perfect sense. And besides, he knew it would never happen. C. J. would balk immediately and prove him right. "What an idea! I dare you to take your mother up on her offer."

To his gut-wrenching surprise, C. J. said, "Challenge accepted. In fact, Dad, why don't you come along, too? Maybe you'll finally understand that I'm not so out of my mind after all."

Zach leaned back and laughed out loud. "On the contrary, it'll only prove I'm right."

Roxanne began picking up dishes from the table and took them to the sink. "No, he's not. In fact, I think it's a great idea. And better yet, since the children get out of school early today, we'll *all* go."

Zach came over and dropped his coffee cup into the sink. "Oh, no! I ain't gonna be seen in public with Bo and that ridiculous get up of his!"

"Dad, they'll love him," C. J. offered.

His father turned and stuck his finger in his face. "Who asked you?"

C. J. held his hands up in mock surrender and backed away.

"Stop worrying. I'll have him shower the instant he gets home."

"Mom, really. They'll love him just like he is."

Roxanne would not be convinced. She turned to C. J. and hollered, "Nobody asked you, Son! Any crowd of people who could love something like that is a crowd of people who ought to be blown away!"

Somehow he believed she would make the perfect assassin to do just such a thing. "Just do me a favor, okay? Wait till you see this crowd before you decide to blow them away."

•

Sitting next to Bo in the backseat of the van, C. J. nonchalantly glanced over at his gruesome brother and then did a double-take. The very sight was enough to send even the most stoic rolling on the floor in laughter. The boy was slouching deep down in the seat and leaning toward the center, the spiked hair taking up most of the head room in the back of the vehicle. "What's the matter? Afraid you'll *break* something?" C. J. asked with a snicker.

Bo simply rolled his eyes.

Sitting in front of C. J., Dylan turned around and said, "Him's hair won' bw'eak, it will 'dus bend."

A couple minutes later, after C. J. regained his composure, he asked, "Bo, why *do* you dress like that?"

"Because *you* taught me too! Remember?"

Somehow, it didn't surprise him, but he most certainly couldn't picture it. "And I did it to face things I was afraid of, didn't I?"

"That's what you *used* to say!"

C. J. turned away, nodded, and thought for a long moment. "You know, I'm not afraid anymore. It's okay to lose the costume now."

"Baloney! You're just giving in! You're turning into a yellow-belly ... like *they* are."

"Hmm ... maybe so. But whatever the reason, I don't need the costume anymore. And I'd almost be willing to bet you don't need it either."

Bo slammed his fist down onto the seat beside him. "Get off my back!"

One full hour and a lot of pavement would pass underneath them before either would be willing to speak again. Finally, Bo said, "You said someone would love me like this. Who?"

It would have been easiest just to brush him off, but C. J. saw that Bo needed some real guidance. "Kids. Kids that are Dylan's age and Julia's age. They'll love you."

"*Kids?* What do you think I am? A clown?"

"Not exactly. There's a lot more to it than that. It's facing your fears ... how to *not* be afraid."

"Afraid of what?"

"Dying. These are sick kids, and they need all the help they can get."

•

LaKeisha was sitting behind the nurses' station desk when she glanced up and saw the approaching family of six. And when her eyes landed on C. J., tears began to fill them. "C. J., Sammy is in her hiding place. We lost another one this morning, and you know she takes these things hard."

C. J. felt his breath catch in his lungs. "Which one?"

"Caleb. He was an abuse case and didn't stand a chance."

C. J., knowing where to find Sammy, rushed down the hall toward the doctor's lounge, leaving his family standing there.

Curious, Zach leaned over the counter and glared down at LaKeisha. "You were one of 'em, weren't you?"

The young nurse dried the tears from her eyes. "If you mean one of the two of us who came to fetch C. J. last Sunday, then yes, sir, you're right. My name is LaKeisha. My mother, Purl, was the other one."

"You said something about a kid named Mia, or something to that affect. I want to meet this kid. I want proof that you actually brought him here."

"Sir, your son is a hero around here. He even helped pay for some of Mia's treatments, which added several precious months to her all too short life. We'd like to let you meet her, however, Mia's extra months came to an end on Sunday. I've just come from her memorial service down in the hospital chapel."

Roxanne's insides began quaking. She wasn't believing what she was hearing. She looked over at the young nurse and asked, "My boy *paid* for medical treatments for a *stranger?*"

"Bone marrow transplants *are* expensive."

Just then, two young boys came strolling along the

hallway, both clad in hospital pajamas and housecoats. One child walked with the aid of crutches while the other sat in a wheelchair and rolled himself along. They chatted quietly among themselves until they caught a glimpse of Bo.

"C. J.! You're back!" the boy in the wheelchair cried.

The other boy said, "We've been missing you! Where'd you go?"

Bo threw his hands up. "I *ain't* C. J.! The name's Bo!"

To Bo's complete surprise, the boy in the wheelchair stuck out his hand and said, "Sorry, Bo. My name is David, but you can call me Davey, okay? My friend here is William. I'm eleven, he's twelve." And then he studied Bo and said, "You look a lot like our friend C. J. He always looked cool. I liked his spiked hair. I'd spike mine, but—"

Sadly, Bo's weak handshake lacked sincerity. He hadn't paid any real attention to the boys until all of a sudden he noticed that Davey had no hair to spike. His head was as bare as a newborn baby's bottom. "The doctor said it'll grow back, but he didn't say when," the boy said while rubbing the top of his head.

Although he didn't know what it was, Bo felt something weird happening inside his chest. He turned his gaze to the boy on the crutches and noticed that his sand-colored hair was terribly thin and nearly gone all together. Bo didn't know what to think. He didn't know what to say and found himself shocked by what slipped out next. "So, what do you guys do for fun around here?"

William had learned early how to find humor in every situation. “Race,” he answered.

Bo glanced down at the boy’s crutches; William was missing his left leg. A race he just couldn’t picture in his mind. “*Race?* How?”

The boys looked at each other and laughed. “Very slowly!” they said together. “Davey always wins,” William added.

“How’s that?” Bo asked out of total ignorance.

The boy laughed loud and hard as he answered, “He’s got wheels!”

Even Bo found himself laughing until William asked, “Why do you look like C. J.?”

“Maybe because he’s my brother,” Bo answered with a matter-of-fact attitude.

Davey, who’d been holding a tablet of drawing paper on his lap, lit up. “Really! Did he come with you? I want to show him something.”

“What?”

The boy opened his tablet and showed Bo a pencil sketch of a futuristic racecar. “This.”

Bo’s attitude instantly changed as he glanced over the awesome picture. “Cool! Did you draw that your-self?”

“Yeah. So, is C. J. here? I’d really like to show him, too.”

“He’s here somewhere, but I don’t know where he went.”

It wouldn’t be long before other ailing children had slipped out of their rooms and headed toward Bo and the others while whispering things like, “C. J.’s back." And before he knew what was happening, the children led him (with little brother, Dylan, clinging tightly to his heels) to a room where there were brightly colored tables and chairs and toy boxes filled to overflowing with toys. Bookshelves were filled with children's books, and a table was littered with wooden puzzles, coloring books, and crayons. All over the walls, autographed childish artwork had been made obscure by a Christmas tree covered with candy-colored lights and homemade angels.

Strangely, Bo felt totally at ease, having drawn their attention by his strange manner of dress. For the first time in his life, he felt welcomed and in his element.

•

Meanwhile, down the hall, Roxanne was leaning over the nurses' counter and directing her full attention to LaKeisha. "Did our son have a *reason* for paying for this child's treatments?"

LaKeisha snickered under her breath. "Ma'am, his reasons were not for what you're insinuating. You see ... Mia was a perfect example of an African American ... like I am. There weren't no racial mixing in her family lines. She was a natural. Besides, C. J. has paid some on accounts of other children as well. Mia wasn't the only sick child who stole his heart."

Zach began to look troubled. "Ma'am, just how long has my boy been coming up here?"

LaKeisha glanced up at him. "Well, sir, I've been employed here for nearly two years, and up until about two weeks ago, C. J. has volunteered his time up here at least once a week every week I've been here."

Roxanne laughed out loud. She'd felt all along that something wasn't quite right with all this stuff. "Miss, there must be some mistake here. You see, unfortunately, our C. J. was a drug abuser and an alcoholic. He spent all of his weekends with his good-for-nothing friends. It's all we can do to stand it! We'd like nothing better than for him to volunteer his time in a place like this, but that's only one of those pipe dreams parents have for their children. It'll *never* happen."

LaKeisha had to think for a moment. Until the other day, she, like everyone else in the children's unit, had never seen C. J. without the costume. If indeed this were a case of mistaken identity, the monkey would lie on Sammy's back. After all, it was she who'd gotten into C. J.'s car and took the registration from it. But LaKeisha knew how to get down to the truth of the matter. "Ma'am, has your boy ever been known to dress like the other kid you have with you? I'm talkin' spiked hair, face paint, the whole nine yards."

Roxanne shot a stunned glance over to her husband. "Are you listening to this?"

The arrogant look on Zach's face told her exactly how he felt. He didn't believe it either.

LaKeisha continued. "Our C. J. Taylor is not a drug addict or an alcoholic. He dresses in that Gothic mess, just like your other son. Now, I admit, no one here has ever seen him without the ridiculous costume, and I'll admit I was a bit leery when he wasn't able to remember, but I'm positive we got us the right one. Besides, I think Miss Sammy's grown sweet on him … now that she's seen his real face. Never knew the boy was a looker."

"You're not hearing me, ma'am! There's no way!" Roxanne cried. "Our C. J. would never do this sort of thing!"

LaKeisha jumped to her feet, leaned over the counter, and whispered in her loudest whisper. "Then answer my question. Did he or did he not do the costume thing?"

C. J.'s choice of appearances had become such a source of contention that Roxanne thought she might never get over her anger about it. "Yes, he did," she admitted.

"Then, there is *no* mistake."

"Look, miss, you don't understand."

"Oh, on the contrary. I understand perfectly. You don't know anything about your own kid. C. J. Taylor might have made bad choices about his appearance, but he's a good Christian boy … every chance he got, he went to Sunday school and church where people don't judge him. Volunteers right here at the children's hospital. He ain't into drugs or alcohol. If there's a case of mistaken identity here, it's yours."

•

Inside the doctor's lounge, beyond the gentle hum of the vending machines, C. J. could hear Sammy's muffled weeping. Instinctively, he took a couple napkins from the dispenser on the table and held them out around the corner of the machine. He kept his head back, hoping she wouldn't recognize him.

"Thank you . . . C. J.," Sammy said in between sobs.

A half smile graced his face, and he stuck his head around the corner of the machine. There she was, the beautiful maiden, crouched down in the corner with the teddy bear clutched tightly to her chest. Thick streaks of black mascara ran down her cheeks. Was she ever a sight?

"Am I that easy to read?" C. J. asked.

Another wave of sobs came barreling out of her. "Ye . . . s!" she cried.

C. J. reached down, took her by the hand, and gently pulled her to her feet. "I'm sorry. I'm really sorry."

Sammy melted into his chest. "He was just a baby, C. J.! He didn't deserve this!"

Something about the news of little Caleb's death struck a chord deep within C. J.'s heart. Sammy was right, of course. No child deserved to be so hated by its mother. But what was it? Could it be he had once known someone in Caleb's situation? Or could it be that he'd felt it himself? He couldn't be sure of the answer, but either way, it brought an unexpected tear to his eye.

Sammy looked up when she felt something fall onto the top of her head, and when she saw his tears, she used the napkins to gently dry them off of his face. But all of a sudden, something struck her, and she pushed herself away from him with a very confused look on her face.

"Oh no. What'd I do this time?" C. J. asked.

With a furrowed brow, Sammy studied him intently. "Who are you?"

"What do you mean?"

"I mean, C. J. Taylor *never* held me when I cried! And C. J. Taylor *never* seemed moved by these things! He *sure* never cried about them! So, who are *you?*"

Sighing, C. J. backed away and sat down at the table.

"Answer me!"

"I *can't,* okay? I don't *know* the answer! They tell me my name is C. J."

Sammy really wanted to believe him. She felt something for him. But was it love or had she simply become infatuated with his off-the-wall charm and out-of-this-world good looks?

"You told me the other day that you weren't coming back. What made you change your mind?"

C. J. became very uneasy and fidgeted with a salt shaker. "Uh ... I brought somebody I want you to meet."

Sammy laughed out loud. "You drove all the way over here to Pensacola just so I can meet some friend of yours? Are you crazy?"

This wasn't exactly the reaction he'd hoped to receive. "Uh ... yeah ... maybe I am. This wasn't exactly what I had planned, but this is how it turned out. They simply want proof."

"*Proof?* Of what?"

Out of the blue, their attention was stolen by a gentle knock on the doorjamb. When they turned and looked, there stood Julia, waving her hand. C. J. motioned to her, and she came and climbed up into his lap.

Sammy studied the similarities in their looks. She was a pretty little girl with her blue eyes and dark chocolate hair. Any parent would be proud; yet, Sammy's heart wanted to die. He'd never one time let on that he was even married, let alone the father of a child. She instantly felt embarrassed. But she brushed a lock of hair from the little girl's forehead and asked, "What's your name, sweetheart?"

"Julia Nicole Taylor."

"Well, Julia Nicole Taylor, you have a very… um, a very nice daddy, here."

Julia giggled, but C. J. on the other hand, turned bright red. That Sammy would think he could have fathered the child totally floored him. But he laughed it off and introduced the little girl. "Miss Sammy, I'd like for you to meet Julia… my little *sister, not* my daughter."

Like C. J., Sammy's face also turned bright red. "Oh, my goodness! I'm *so* sorry, C. J.!"

After they all laughed the embarrassment away, C. J. said, "At first, I hadn't intended to come back because it was too much all at once. But… I couldn't stop thinking about it, so I finally decided that I needed to come back and at the very least, apologize for leaving so abruptly on Sunday. Will you forgive me?"

Sammy's heart leapt for joy. "Apology accepted! Are you planning to stay?" In her heart, what she really wanted was to take him back to church and show off his new look, yet, after last Sunday's meeting, she didn't dare push it. Besides, she already knew her motivation was wrong.

Again, C. J.'s face turned red. How could he tell her his parents wouldn't let him without making it sound childish? "Since Sunday, this stuff has plagued my mind until I decided to come back and to try to relearn the things I used to do here. Problem is I'm still living at home. And as long as I'm still under their roof, I have to abide by their rules. So ... I asked permission."

"That's a good change, C. J."

"I don't know. Is it? You see, in a way, it backfired. They refused to allow me to leave ... unless they came with me. *All* of them."

"*All?*"

"My parents, my brothers, and my little sister here." Julia laid her head against C. J.'s chest. "They only want proof."

Sammy glanced down at Julia and smiled. "I'd love to meet them ... *all* of them."

C. J. sighed. "Okay. But you might want to wash your face first," he said with a grin.

Sammy gasped, grabbed a napkin, and rushed over to study her reflection in the glass front of the microwave oven. "Oh, no!" she cried while wiping her cheeks with the dry napkin. "That's what I get for investing in cheap mascara!"

•

Down in the northern Gulf Coast region of the country, the warm atmosphere of summer will sometimes drag on through the month of December. The air might remain volatile and prone to afternoon storms with dangerous lightning, deafening thunder, and torrential rain. The storms are sometimes accompanied by straight-line winds, tornadoes, and hail stones that range in size from marbles to baseballs.

On the road again, while the sun shone bright outside, the four Taylor siblings remained strangely silent on the inside of the van while a vicious storm was beginning to brew up in the front seat. Like a flash of lightning, a swinging fist cut the air. Like thunder, their voices grew louder and louder. The van lurched this way and that as Zach jerked to avoid the flying fist. "You *lied* to me!" Roxanne screamed, her pretty face violet with rage. "You *told* me he was—"

All of a sudden, the storm ended as abruptly as it began when Julia began to cry. "No, Mommy! Don't be mad again!" the little girl cried as she snatched her seatbelt off and climbed into the back seat in between her older brothers. "Make them stop, C. J.! Make them stop!" Julia had always been a rather shy child, keeping mostly to herself. And in a home filled with abusive tension, C. J. had been her only refuge.

As he wrapped the middle seatbelt around his baby sister and latched it for her, C. J. noticed a glint in his mother's eye.

"And *you,* mister," Roxanne hollered as she glared back at her eldest, "if you even remotely think I'm going to allow you to go back there, you're out of your mind! There will be no alcohol, no drugs, and *no* girlfriends! *Nothing!* We're *not* going that route! It's *not* going to happen! You get it? *I'll* be the one to pick out the girlfriend! Understand?"

"Mom, could you not see that there were no drugs or alcohol involved? It's all about the children—the sick and the dying ones! It has nothing to do with drugs, or with alcohol, or even girls for that matter!" C. J. answered. "Have your eyes been blinded to the obvious?"

Bo punched his brother on his right shoulder. "What do you think you're doing?" he cried under his breath. "Don't you dare make her madder! She'll punish all four of us!"

C. J. leaned against the back of the seat and shot a sympathetic glance to each of the children. *I'm sure she'll try to dig her talons into me, but she'd better not touch you.*

"Things around our house are changing," Roxanne announced. "Just look at yourself in the mirror." And then she pointed to Bo and said, "And you, buster, you, me, a pair of scissors, and a washcloth have a date. If you won't wash that mess out, I'm going to do it for you. And I can promise you will not like it when I get finished."

"But, *Mom!*" the boy hollered. And then he turned to C. J., shoving him against the window. "This is all *your* fault, you know! They fought about you when you were cool! Now they gotta fight because you wimped out and went and changed! Man, if only you'd left everything alone—"

The hair on the back of C. J.'s neck stood on end. He brought his fist up ready to swing, but then looked into each of their faces and saw the tears and the anger. And worse than that, he saw the terror. Bo had been perfectly correct. It had been his fault. If only he could remember. He slowly brought his fist down and turned to Bo. "How old are you?"

"Who cares?"

"He's fifteen," Julia interjected.

"Be quiet, Julia!" Bo hollered. "Nobody asked you!"

"So!"

And then Dylan, who was sitting in the middle seat just in front of Bo, shocked them all when he turned and cried, "When are we 'donna 'dit our *old* C. J. back?"

Cuddling up against her oldest brother's right arm, Julia glanced up at Dylan and cried, "I love our *old* C. J. but I love our *new* C. J. too!"

"Where *is* our old C. J.?" Dylan asked.

Finally, Roxanne had enough. Until now, she hadn't considered how the three younger children would react to C. J.'s sudden and unexplained transformation. Keeping her ears perked and her face forward, she yelled, "He's the *same* C. J., now will you kids *please* get on another subject and leave him alone?"

Julia had paid attention to her mother's demand, but in her childish innocence, she asked, "But, where is he?"

Cutting his eyes forward, C. J. waited for his mother's reply. But when she did not come back with a response, he had to think. What could he tell the child that she would understand? "Uh … in the accident … the *old* C. J.—" he'd begun when he saw his mother as she turned her head slightly toward the back, and he knew she was listening. His father, on the other hand, seemed to be paying no attention at all. Did C. J. dare speak what had crossed his mind? Would it sound even slightly like an accusation? He figured only time would tell. "I think the old C. J. died in that accident ... and ... I came back to take his place."

That's funny. He'd only made up the story, trying to pacify the child. But all of a sudden, something about that puzzling concept seemed to make perfect sense.

But Julia continued. "Did the old C. J. go to heaven when he had his 'oopsadent?"

Heaven. In his mind, C. J. could not fathom how any human being could grow to become a staunch supporter of such a place as heaven nor of a concept such as Christianity. Neither concept fit with the five senses. They were not something that could be seen or heard, touched or tasted. Neither would have a scent. Yet, all of a sudden, it seemed oddly comforting just hoping there was such a place. Anything but this. "Um, I don't know, baby girl, but if what those people back at that hospital said about me is true ... then yes, I'm sure the *old* C. J. went on to heaven when he had his ... his 'oopsadent."

C. J. couldn't help but smile at Julia's childish vocabulary. But after a moment, as he slid his left hand into his pocket and viciously crumbled the piece of paper that contained Sammy's phone number, he turned his uncomfortable gaze away from his mother and out the window, watching the water as they passed over Escambia Bay. After the embarrassing scene his parents had made back at the hospital, he fully understood why he'd not allowed his friends from the hospital in on his personal affairs. He'd never again be able to show his face.

He hadn't seen his mother's face turn violet. Neither had he seen the color wash from his father's.

Chapter 12

Monday, December 19

The weekend passed all too slowly. Saturday had been busy at the station, but C. J. spent all of Sunday locked up in his attic bedroom. And he would have spent Monday there as well, had Shane not called on the cell phone before breakfast was ready.

"Man, they're keeping me locked up in this miserable attic," C. J. whispered into the cell. "They don't allow me the freedom to just get up and go anywhere I please."

"Then I'll call your dad and ask his permission. And I won't let on that you and I have talked about it, okay?"

"Listen, you've gotta want me to come with you pretty bad in order to take that kind of punishment. You know he can be a pain."

"Let's just say I've got an ulterior motive. It'll be worth it. Now, hang up and hide that phone."

"Ulterior motive, huh?"

"Hang up!"

"Whatever you say, boss. See ya," C. J. whispered

as he flipped the phone shut and slid it down into his pocket.

It was only a moment later when he heard the main house phone ringing, and he quietly slipped down the stairs and pressed his ear against the door to try to hear the conversation, but the only audible sounds he could hear was muffled hollering. He chalked Shane's request up to a waste of time.

About an hour later, after C. J. had been allowed downstairs to eat and after breakfast was finished, Zach waited to put down his morning paper until after the three younger children and the missus were out of ear shot. The man then turned to his eldest, and said, "Mr. Westbrook called this morning. You know anything about that?"

Of course he knew about it, but he didn't dare let on. He took his father's question as an insult. "How would I know anything about a phone call? You keep me locked up like I'm a prisoner. There's no phone, no TV. There's nothing up there."

"He wants you to go somewhere with him … something about picking out a Christmas gift for his fiancé."

"Yeah? Like, you're going to let me go?"

"Actually, son, your mother and I have discussed it and have decided to allow it. Mr. Westbrook is harmless."

For a moment, C. J. felt confused. "If Mr. Westbrook is so harmless, then why did you send your cop buddies to track me down when he was only trying to help me out?"

Just then, Roxanne came in through the kitchen door. "Carson Junior, if you backtalk your father again, I'm going to lock you up in that attic for the rest of your life!"

C. J. turned and stared strangely at the woman. Comebacks danced through his head as though they were ponies on a carousel. *Going to? The rest of my life? What life? You're killing me here!* He snickered to himself when he took his empty hot chocolate mug to the sink and headed for the kitchen door. *Hey! What a concept! Knock me in the head, claim I was brain damaged, and starve me to death. What would it take? A couple weeks?* He stopped at the door and for a brief moment, studied his parents. *Come to think of it, I could save myself a whole lot of trouble if I just got her mad enough to*—Much as he would have liked to have hollered everything that had just crossed his mind, he shook his head and instantly dismissed the thought. He just couldn't see the point of voicing the blatantly obvious, knowing full well she could, and probably would carry out her threat, had he given her half a chance. "Yes, ma'am," he finally answered in a whisper. *Whatever!*

"Boy, what exactly is it you want out of life?" asked his father.

C. J. snickered to himself, knowing the man couldn't care less. "Why? What's it matter?"

His father startled him when he brought his fist down hard onto the kitchen table. "If it *didn't* matter, I wouldn't waste my time asking now would I?"

For a moment, C. J. felt forced to think. Anger

and frustration now permeated his days. Fear and disappointment filled his nights. And still there was the ever-present, nagging headache. They were supposed to be his parents, and yet they seemed totally unconcerned. "I just want to know the truth about what happened to me and I want to know why!

"I don't have a clue as to why all of a sudden Mr. Westbrook would be asking *me,* of all the people in the world, to go somewhere with him. But don't you worry. I won't be going. I won't be going anywhere other than upstairs to my cell. Don't forget to lock the door behind me. In fact, don't bother. I'll save you the trouble." He pushed through the door and double timed it up the stairs, leaving his parents standing in the kitchen gawking at each other.

Up in his room, C. J. curiously inspected the window that looked out to the front side of the house. It wasn't enough that the window had recently been nailed shut. He didn't recall finding those nails on the morning he'd torn the posters down and uncovered it. But at the top, he found a thin wire and a tiny white box, something else he hadn't noticed after he'd scraped all the black paint off. The window had been connected to the brand new home alarm system. But it didn't matter now. Even if it hadn't been nailed shut, the alarm would prevent him from opening it, not to mention a jump from a third floor window might seem tempting but would more than likely prove rather painful.

A few moments later, when he heard the creaking of his door, he turned and watched as both of his parents came quietly up the stairs. When they reached the top, he turned away and stared out of the window toward the cow pasture.

Zach came over first and sat down on the side of the bed. "I take it you really wouldn't mind going with Mr. Westbrook."

"I don't even know where he's wanting to take me. So what's it matter whether or not I want to go?"

"I already told you that you *could* go."

"What's it going to cost me? Some outrageous curfew ... ten minutes for something that takes fifteen?"

"Don't be ridiculous."

C. J. spun himself around. "*Me ... ridiculous?* My life has been ripped away from me so I could be turned into some movie star-looking freak, only to be kept in prison! I *don't* get it! Why?"

Roxanne threw her hands up in the air. "We did that for your own good! If you'd kept up the charade, you'd never make it in life!"

"You call *this* life? When are you going to figure out that you can *trust* me?"

"Trust is a mutual thing, Son," his father answered. "You have to trust that we know what we're doing too."

C. J. came close to his father's face and looked deeply into his dark brown eyes. "Dad, I'm sure you think you're doing right. But it's *not* working. All I'm asking is that you unlock the door. Let me see the outside of this place. Let me watch TV with the rest of you. Let me ... I just want some freedom!"

"Then get yourself dressed. I'll call Shane back and let him know to come pick you up."

"Why can't I just drive to his apartment? I've got a car, and I pay for my own gas."

"Because you don't know how to get there!" Roxanne answered.

Confused, C. J. shot his mother a strange glance. *How could she forget already?* "Mom, I spent three days over there. Why would I not remember how to get there?"

Zach sighed heavily and pushed himself up off the bed. "All right. We'll just see how far trust can go. Let this be a test. It's 8:00 a.m. You go ahead, and you drive to Shane's apartment. You go with him wherever he wants to go. But be home no later than five o'clock this evening."

Shocked out of his mind, C. J. thought he'd better get out while the going was good. But he had one last question. "And how many of your cronies are you going to sick on me?"

His father grinned. "All of 'em." C. J. laughed out loud. Was the man serious? C. J. didn't know the answer, but in the back of his mind, he fully expected Vargas and Rayford to be lurking around a corner somewhere. At the moment, he didn't care. At least he'd get a glimpse of the freedom he longed for, but not if he didn't rush out of there before his mother could change his father's mind.

When C. J. reached the bottom of the lower staircase, Bo was just starting to head upstairs. C. J. stopped his brother and looked him over. Their mother had kept her date with the boy, just like she'd promised. His hair had been washed out, cut short, and styled neatly. His face was clean. But what C. J. noticed wasn't Bo's cleaned-up look; it was the disappointment that had filled the pale-skinned face where the black paint had once taken up residence. "Are you okay?"

"What do you care?" Bo's anger had grown sickening. He pushed C. J. back into the wall. "All this changing junk is *your* fault!"

At the top of the stairs, Zach and Roxanne had come from C. J.'s bedroom door and started down the main staircase, arguing. "What are you going to do?" Roxanne asked as she followed her husband down the stairs.

"I'm going to get a screwdriver! I'm going to turn that doorknob around the right way, and that's the way it's going to stay! And *this* time, you'd better leave it alone!"

Astonished, C. J.'s eyes grew to the size of saucers, and a half smile crossed his lips. "Isn't it funny how they argue about us that way?" he asked Bo.

"*Us?* They're not arguing about *us.* They're arguing about *you!* The rest of us don't amount to a hill of beans!"

"I've told you, Roxanne, you *can't* cage him up! If this is going to work, we've got to keep him happy! And right now, he's not!"

"Oh, *you're* a fine one to talk—Mr. All American Fake of the Year!"

The pair passed right on by Bo and C. J. as if they weren't there.

"See what I mean?" Bo asked his brother. "It's all about *you.* It's *always* about you."

"This is *your* adventure!" Zach hollered back to his wife.

"All right! So I've been a *little* overprotective," Roxanne admitted, following right behind him.

"A *little?*" Zach cried. His voice was beginning to fade as the pair disappeared into the kitchen.

C. J. knew Bo was right. They were arguing about him again. But although he hated to admit it, he agreed with his father. His mother had been overprotective. And then all of a sudden, an idea crossed his mind. "Hey, Mom, would you mind if Bo goes with me?" he hollered, hoping she would hear him through the kitchen door.

His mother stuck her head in. "Not a chance!"

But his father poked his own head in and hollered louder, "*Yes!* If Bo wants to go, take him with you. Just be back when I told you to!"

"Yes, sir!" C. J. answered. And then he turned to Bo. "Would you like to come with me?"

"With *you?* Like Mom said, not a chance!" And again, Bo shoved his brother backwards. "*You're* the reason for all this mess! It's all *your* fault!" He shoved C. J. again. "Get out of my face!"

C. J. couldn't hide his disappointment. "At least tell me what I did wrong!"

"Man, ever since Mom bought that lousy ticket, everything has been turned upside down. *Nothing* is normal anymore!"

A look of complete confusion crossed C. J.'s face. "*What* ticket?"

For a moment, Bo dropped his head and shifted

his eyes to make certain his parents were out of sight. He'd been instructed to keep his silence about it, especially around his brother. But he believed C. J. had a right to know. After all, it concerned him. He sighed heavily, came close to C. J.'s ear, and whispered, "I'm not allowed to tell you. *You* aren't supposed to know. But a few months ago, Mom bought the only winning lottery ticket. That's why all the new junk around here … the flowers and the plasma TV, the new furniture, and the alarm system."

C. J. about choked on his own spit. "And all this time, you've been blaming me."

"Man, you gave in to them! You *gave* in! It was only after that when you conveniently *lost* your identity … the costume. And then you went and ripped your identity out of your room. And because *you* did, they *forced* me to do the same thing!" Bo shoved his brother one last time and hollered, "Now, if you don't get out of my way, I'm going to—"

C. J. grabbed his arm and stopped him. "If I've heard you right, then changing you into a monster was my fault, too! So go ahead! Blame me for your turning back into a human. Costumes are great but *not* for everyday life. It's time to *grow up.* Besides, what part of you were you trying to hide behind that ridiculous makeup anyway? You have a sickeningly perfect face." It was true. C. J. had observed that his brother, like himself, had somehow survived puberty without having to face the acne challenge, or the buck teeth.

"Yeah? Well, so do you, so get out of my way before I have to disfigure it," Bo threatened as he yanked his arm free and rushed up the stairs.

C. J. threw up his hands in mock surrender. "Whatever!"

•

When he climbed into the driver's seat, C. J. looked over to the floorboard of the passenger side. He'd forgotten that his attic prison and his car had belonged to the same previous owner, his previous self. The trash on the other side of the car had been piled shin deep. Oh, sure, he'd seen the mess the other day when he brought the car home, but he hadn't yet been allowed outside long enough to get it cleaned out. Aggravated, he found a plastic bag amongst the mess and began snatching up the trash and throwing it into the bag. But when he reached the bottom, something he gathered up into his fingers drew his attention. It was a fabric neck strap with a plastic credit-card style picture ID attached to the end of it. Something told him not to touch the badge, so he tossed it up onto the dashboard and finished picking up the mess. As he was heading for the outside garbage can with the full bag of trash, again something crossed his mind, so he tossed it into the backseat of the car, started the engine, and crept out of the driveway.

When he reached the apartment, Shane hadn't even gotten the door shut before C. J. asked, "Is your fiancé working today?"

"Yeah. Why?"

"Can I borrow a couple freezer bags?"

Shane went into the kitchen and brought back two large zipper bags. "What do you need these for?"

Outside, in the car, C. J. picked up the badge he'd tossed up onto the dashboard, being careful not to touch the plastic. But before he slid it down into the bag, he studied the picture of the face that was on the front. When he showed it to Shane, he asked, "This *isn't* me, is it?"

Shane glanced at it and nodded his head. It was C. J. all right … in full costume.

But C. J. shook his head. "I don't think so."

"C. J., this is your ID badge, the one taken when you used to wear the stuff."

"Maybe it's just my imagination, but look at my eyes. Can you see a difference in the color?"

With a look of consternation written all over his face, Shane glared down at the ID badge and then up into his friend's eyes. The picture was too obscure. "Cee'j, you know I'm on your side, and I don't mind at all taking you to see Deanna. But it's impossible to make out the eye color on this badge."

"Like I said, maybe it's just my imagination, but for my own peace of mind, I've gotta check it out."

Using a napkin, C. J. carefully picked through the garbage bag he'd saved, removed three used drinking straws from their empty counterparts, and slid them down into the other zipper bag. He didn't have to explain his actions to his friend.

At the police station, C. J. handed the bags to Deanna. "I know it's a lot to ask, but I need to know if there are any fingerprints on the ID; if there's any DNA on the straws, do they come from the same source; and if so, are they mine. And probably most important, keep the information away from both Vargas and Rayford. Somehow, I don't trust them."

The beautiful blonde carefully took the bags from C. J.'s hand. "Shane's told me as much as he can. Don't worry. It won't be a problem, Mr. Taylor. But in order to keep the info from Vargas and Rayford, I'm going to have to send this stuff off to a lab outside of our office here. It'll take a few days before we get the results back."

With his lips pursed, C. J. said, "Not a problem. I can tolerate whatever I have to until I find out the truth. If this comes back as a match to me, then I'll never again question who I am."

For Deanna, it was just routine … the DNA swab, the fingerprint chart. But for C. J., it made him feel more like a criminal than a victim. But in a matter of a few minutes, Shane laid a lip lock on his girl, C. J. waved goodbye, and the boys were off on their quest for the perfect Christmas gift.

Chapter 13

The Critters and Claws Pet Store had been opening early just before Thanksgiving for those hoping to adopt a pet for the holidays. Its manager, Mary Sanderford, was a barrel of laughs. The overweight single woman strolled through life blowing bubbles with a wad of bubble gum. One of her favorite pastimes had been to tease her male customers by batting her false eyelashes at them through her thick-lens glasses. She didn't have a care in the world, other than the few employees who remained steadfastly loyal to their fun-loving employer. One such employee, a timid young girl by the name of Keeli McKenzie, had become Mary's number one concern. She took to the beautiful brunette like a mother to a daughter.

The instant Shane and C. J. came inside the door, Mary glanced up, gasped, and nearly choked on her bubble gum. After a coughing spell, she dried tears from her chubby cheeks, cleared her throat, and asked in a raspy voice, "May I help you boys?"

While Shane asked Mary some questions about puppies, C. J. caught a glimpse of the woman as she nonchalantly turned toward him and batted her eyelashes. With boiling laughter nearly spilling out of him, he sucked in a deep gulp of air and held it tight as he backed away and began wandering curiously through the store. And when he momentarily glanced back, he noticed the woman behind the counter was gawking wide-eyed in his direction. He'd expected to see Vargas and Rayford, but for his father to stoop to this level was just too much. It cracked him up! It was a pure struggle, but he held on to his calm, cool facade and turned away as fast as he could move his head, pretending he didn't notice.

A moment later, C. J. heard a door open from the back of the shop, and a fair-complected, petite girl came in and was walking toward him. The girl was beautiful in her hunter green smock and blue jeans. But with her eyes focused downward, her soft face appeared sad and slightly reddened, almost as though she'd just lost her last friend.

The girl hadn't paid much attention to the dozen or so customers who were scattered throughout the small pet store, although she could sense their presence. She came over toward where C. J. was standing and was busying herself with a few scattered boxes of birdseed when she asked, "Can I help you?" She hadn't looked up to see his convicting blue eyes or his soft dark hair. Nor had she seen the silly smirk on his face.

C. J. nearly lost his breath. His heart began pounding, and his mouth went dry. He jerked his shy eyes away from the beautiful brunette, and backed into the shelves, knocked over the birdseed, and fell onto his backside to the floor. He made an embarrassingly loud racket.

The girl gasped and threw her hand up to cover her mouth. "*Oh my gosh!* I'm so—" All of a sudden, when she came to help him up, she noticed his eyes, tripped over her own clumsy feet, and fell right on top of him.

Shane and Mary, and several of the other customers came rushing over.

Their faces had turned blood red. Neither could say a word. But he'd caught her. She hadn't hit the floor. And where her long, dark hair cascaded over his arm, it felt like electricity. He glanced down into her shiny brown eyes for only a moment and smiled shyly. "Are you okay?"

Absolutely smitten, she looked up into his sparkling blue eyes and felt the electricity. "I didn't mean to ... I mean, I didn't mean to ... oh, I don't know what I didn't mean to do. But I am okay. Are you?"

C. J. quietly nodded.

Laughing, Mary came and gently picked the girl up from behind. "Keeli Jenae McKenzie, now, *that's* what I call falling for someone!" And after Shane came and helped C. J. to his feet, Mary looked the boy over from head to toe. "My friend here is unattached. Interested?" And then she batted her eyelashes at him again.

When the crowd began laughing, the girl cried, "Miss Sanderford! I *can't* believe you just ... I didn't do it on purpose! I just tripped over ... I tripped ... it was an *accident!*"

"Uh huh. *Sure* it was!" Mary laughed.

With her beautiful face glowing dark red, the girl cried, "*Mary!*" and she pushed through the crowd, rushing toward the door to the back room as fast as her feet could carry her.

Laughing to himself, Shane turned to C. J. and saw him rubbing his left elbow. "Hurt yourself?"

C. J. shook his head, but he wouldn't take his convicting blue eyes off the chubby, lash-fluttering manager. The smile that had been on his face was long gone. "Why'd you embarrass her like that? It wasn't her fault. I fell first, and she tripped over me. You owe her an apology."

It was probably the first time in Mary's life that her own face had turned beet red, and she was left speechless.

Finally, the crowd dispersed. And while Shane went on about his business with the red-faced manager, C. J. continued strolling aimlessly through the aisles, hoping to get a glimpse of the timid girl once again.

Back in a nook of the store where more than a dozen aquariums bubble round the clock, C. J. stood, gawking at the colorful fish and other curious critters. The walls and ceiling of the nook had been painted to mimic a night sky. Strategically placed black lights made the stars and some of the fish appear to glow in the dark.

Behind the nook, a door marked *employees only* stood cracked open. The angry girl had come, picked up her jacket and purse, shut out the lights, and started out. But when she cracked open the door and glanced out, standing in the darkened nook was the wonderfully handsome and strangely familiar young man with whom she'd just made a complete fool of herself. Her face burned red, and she gasped, nearly slamming the door shut. But something inside of her made her hold the door open. *Who is he? Why does he look so familiar?* she wondered, thankful he could not see her.

C. J. took his time. He curiously glanced into each aquarium until he came to the one that held a single brown tarantula. He reached up to rub a chill out of his arms and slowly backed away.

As the girl watched, she couldn't help the smile that spread across her lips. *There's no in between. They're either loved or they're hated,* she thought. *He hates them. And that's okay with me because so do I.*

Suddenly, C. J. felt something wet on the back of his left elbow and pulled his arm up to find a couple droplets of blood had soaked into his sleeve. The girl also noticed the blood and swallowed her pride, dropped her things onto the floor, and quietly slipped out of the room. "You're bleeding," she choked as she came up beside him. "You must have hit your elbow when we—"

With a grin on his face, C. J. took a deep breath. "It's probably just a scratch. It's really all right."

"Um, my name is Keeli McKenzie, and if you wait right here, I'll go get something to clean it up with."

It certainly didn't feel natural to C. J. to allow a perfect stranger to make a fuss over him. But she was so beautiful, gentle, and kind that he found himself saying, "Um, my name is C. J. Taylor, and—I'll be glad to wait."

In the few moments the girl was away, Shane and Mary came to the back. And when Mary disappeared behind the employee door, Shane joined C. J. at the tarantula aquarium. "Hey Taylor, think I ought to get Deanna one of these instead of a puppy? I mean, they're already house-trained and everything. And I'm sure he can't eat as much."

C. J. screwed up his face. "Uh, in a word, *no.* Only met Deanna once, but I'd almost be willing to bet she's not too particularly fond of those eight-legged creatures. Even if you were to stick one of those in a box with some nice wrapping paper and a pretty bow, I seriously doubt you'd have a very happy Christmas. But you get her whatever you think she'd like. Just don't expect me and that thing to be riding in the same car at the same time."

Shane laughed. "I take it you're not particularly fond of them either are you?"

With a smirk, C. J. answered, "Not particularly."

All of a sudden, the look on Shane's face changed to one of deep concern. "Hmm ... that's strange."

"What?"

Just then, the ladies interrupted their conversation when they returned from the back room. Mary came over and made herself busy showing Shane the numerous fish and other critters while Keeli bandaged the scratch on C. J.'s elbow. As soon as she was finished, Mary came to them both and apologized. And after the apology was accepted, she said, "Okay. Now that that's out of the way, follow me. We've got some really great puppies over here."

In the glass-enclosed room where the puppy cages were kept away from curious fingers, Mary led the trio to the cage in the far corner where a cute ball of fur lay sleeping. She opened the cage, picked up the puppy, and held it close to her. "She's eight weeks old and has been separated from her momma now for the last three days. That's hard on a baby dog."

While Keeli and Shane were making a fuss over the little dog, C. J. stood there staring, straining his mind to remember. The puppy was a tri-color Shetland Sheepdog—an expensive breed of show dog. Her thick coat was solid black with a pure white mane that came over across the top of her neck. On her face were brown patches while her underside and paws were totally white. She was a beautiful puppy, although she seemed awkwardly docile. But to C. J., there was something familiar about her. As he stood there staring, another vision came to him. He could see himself standing in a field of freshly cut grass. He saw trees, and the faint glimmer of a rain-washed sidewalk glistening in the sunlight. In his right hand, he held a yellow ball, and at his feet sat a dog, not at all unlike the puppy Mary held in her arms.

Suddenly, C. J. was snapped back to reality when Shane touched his arm. "Earth calling C. J. Come in, C. J. Hey, you're losing your head again, aren't you?"

C. J. found himself staring at the puppy, but Mary thought he was staring at her. "He's still angry with me, I think," she said when she noticed the scowl on his handsome face.

C. J. smiled. "Oh, uh, no, ma'am. I'm sorry. I'm not angry at all. I was just thinking about the pup." He then came over, took the dog from Mary's arms, and held her, petting her head and neck. "I, uh, I used to have a dog like this."

Surprised, Shane held his silence while he watched C. J. with the puppy. *Interesting. The Taylors have never allowed their children to have pets of any kind.*

By the look on Shane's face, C. J. knew he'd just said something weird, so he handed the puppy over to his friend. "Mr. Westbrook, she's perfect. Deanna will love her."

Shane handed the puppy right back. "Then you hold her until I finish paying for her."

C. J. just smiled, gladly took the puppy, and while he and Keeli made small talk and made a huge fuss over the cute ball of fur, Shane and Mary gathered things Deanna would need and finished the transaction.

On their way back to the apartment, while C. J. coddled the puppy on his lap, he remained strangely quiet until Shane reached over and picked a shiny penny from a cup holder in the console of his car and laid it on his friend's left knee.

"What's this for?" C. J. asked when he picked up the penny.

"Haven't you ever heard the phrase, a penny for your thoughts?"

"Yeah."

"I was just paying in advance. And I was thinking. Back there, you said you'd had a dog like that before. Are you certain?"

For a long, awkwardly silent moment, C. J. stared out of the window. "It was a female," he finally answered. "And I believe her name was … Molly … no, it was La—oh, I don't remember what her name was. But she was black and white with some brown places on her face, just like this one."

All of a sudden, Shane felt his insides quivering. "C. J., the Taylors have *never* had a dog. And the deal with the spiders, C. J. was the only human I know of who was incredibly brave enough to pick up one of those big brown wolf spiders and carry it outside to let it run free."

C. J. turned and looked at him with a matter-of-fact expression on his face. "If you're asking me if I'm surprised, the answer is no." And then he tossed the coin back into the cup holder. "But the stuff I gave to Deanna, if those tests confirm our suspicions, what will it matter? Without a memory, I'll never completely know the truth."

Shane glanced over his way for an instant. "You know, you look sharp, C. J. You're a decent, well-dressed, clean-cut individual—nothing at all like the old C. J. Taylor."

C. J. cringed. Although he appreciated the gesture, words of affirmation seemed to make him feel horribly weird. Not to mention he'd not been gifted with an abundance of words himself and did not know how to respond. "What are you getting at?" he asked.

"What I'm getting at is that you don't look like the kind of guy someone would just throw out and forget. You know what I mean? If indeed it is true, that you've been taken against your will, then someone somewhere will be looking for you."

"What will it matter if I don't remember?"

"It'll matter to them, whomever they may be."

"Okay. But then all this begs another question. Where is the real Carson Junior?"

Shane's heart leapt into his throat. "Now you're giving me the creeps."

"You and me both."

"Either way, I would advise you to make sure you stay in the Taylors' good graces, just in case. Treat them like they *are* your parents and honor them like the Bible tells you too."

C. J. laughed. "The *Bible*... says to *honor* them? Like *that's* going to happen," he said with heavy sarcasm.

"Yeah, it sounds crazy. But I'm serious. It could mean the difference between life and death."

"Yeah. Mine."

"That's right. And you can't afford to die yet. You ain't ready."

"Do you know anyone who *is* ready to die?"

Shane thought for a moment. "I sure do. Me. Deanna. I know many people who are literally ready. But you're not one of them... not yet."

"Well, I appreciate that."

"Maybe.

"Now let's change the subject," Shane said as he maneuvered the car through heavy Christmas traffic. "The girl was gorgeous, wasn't she?"

"What girl?" C. J. asked with his eyes focused on the highway and a sly grin plastered on his face.

"Uh huh. Like you *didn't* notice."

C. J. reached into his shirt pocket, pulled out a slip of paper, and waved it in front of Shane's face. "I may look weird, but I'm still all male. Of course I noticed!" he admitted. "What do you think I am? A robot?"

Stopped at the red light where Airport Road intersects Highway 85 on the north side of Crestview, Shane gawked at the paper. "Her *phone number? Already?*"

"Sure! Why not? How long did you wait before you tried to get Deanna's number?"

Shane laughed. "Just to get up the nerve, it was like ... *years!*"

•

The in-dash clock read 4:37 as C. J. brought his car to a stop at the western corner of the cow pasture. There, he slid out of the driver's seat and stood staring out over the fence and across the upper side of the embankment toward the pond. He stood there staring for what seemed like forever but could find nothing out of the ordinary. While the fence had recently been repaired, there were no tire tracks on the embankment. He strained to see down into the pond, but the water was still too cloudy to reveal shadows.

When he finally turned and started for his car, he stopped short of the driver's door just as a silver BMW came peeling out of his driveway from across the pasture. And when he made eye contact with the driver, the man gunned it, spinning the tires and throwing red clay up into the air.

"*Whoa!*" For a moment, with his brow furrowed

in absolute confusion, C. J. strained his mind to recall the driver's face. *Shane was right. That guy* does *look like me.* And then in a sudden panic, he rushed toward the house and came barreling inside the door by the time the clock on the wall read 4:50.

"And with ten minutes to spare!" his mother cried when she saw him coming inside the door. "Dinner's going to be ready at five. How was the shopping trip? What did Mr. Westbrook get for his fiancé?"

C. J. had already forgotten about the puppy. He hadn't noticed the delicious aroma of southern fried chicken or the sweet essence of hot apple pie. Shaking in his shoes, he looked around, half expecting to find blood and bodies. Yet, everyone and everything seemed to be perfectly fine. He took a deep breath and calmed himself down. "What I want to know is who was the guy in the beemer?"

C. J. was oblivious as his mother glared toward his father and then quietly ducked into the kitchen. He didn't see her hold her breath as she stood with her ear glued to the door.

In the living room, Zach was sitting in his chair reading the newspaper. "What beemer?" he asked without looking up from an article.

"Oh, come on, Dad. I'm talking about the car that just peeled out of our driveway a couple minutes ago. What was he? An insurance salesman or something?"

Zach furrowed his brow. "It just happens he was a friend of mine. And if my business with him had been any business of yours, I would have told you what the business was. But it wasn't, so I didn't, now you can drop it."

"But Dad, that friend of yours looked like he could be my twin! And when he passed me, he made it abundantly clear that he wasn't too thrilled about seeing me. Doesn't that bother you?"

His father crumbled the newspaper in his fists, threw it to the floor, and jumped up out of his chair. "How am I supposed to know what his problem was?" he yelled. "Maybe he just didn't like the way you look!"

C. J. sucked in a deep gulp of air and held it. Every muscle in his body tensed. The hair on the back of his neck stood up. The stranger's familiar face and the angry scowl that was written all over it sent chills down his spine. But suddenly, he remembered Shane's words—that something he said about honoring the parents—and C. J. realized he had nothing to lose. He dropped his gaze to the floor. "Maybe you're right, Dad." He sighed heavily. "It seems there's a lot of that going around here lately… you know, people who don't like the way I look. But why would that make somebody angry?"

"I suggest you drop it. My business with that man had nothing to do with you. Now get yourself cleaned up for dinner before you get on your mother's bad side."

"All right, already! I'm going. Don't get so excited!" He turned and bounded up the stairway with his wide-eyed father staring after him.

Chapter 14

Tuesday, December 20 - Early morning

Living alone in a small apartment on the west side of town, Jason Cruz, the station clown, lived a glorious single life. Nobody nagged him about dirty dishes or laundry, as was evident by the condition of his apartment. A healthy crop of dark green and black mold stood like alfalfa sprouts in dirty dishes that lay strewn beside the sink, beside the refrigerator, beside the stove, on the table—anything with a flat surface. There were dirty dishes stacked on the floor buried underneath a load of mold-encrusted pizza boxes, empty cans, maple syrup bottles, pancake mix boxes, and any other sort of garbage. The rest of the apartment wouldn't be too difficult to imagine for the observer. Laundry was no big concern either: shoes, socks, pieces of uniforms, and wet towels lay in piles across the floor, the furniture, and the shower. The apartment reeked of BO, dirty socks, and mildew.

Tiptoeing through the deep clutter, wearing only a white muscle shirt and red silk boxers, Jason picked up the pair of pants from the arm of the couch. "Ah, yes. These must be the clean ones. The ones I wore yesterday ... and ... the day before that ... and ... maybe the day before that ... oh, who knows? Who cares, for that matter?" he asked himself while shrugging his shoulders. He used the proven method of testing for cleanliness by pulling the pants up to his nose and sniffing. "Good grief, I gotta get me a wife!" he cried, carelessly tossing the smelly pair of pants over his head and continued his search. "I know there's another pair around here somewhere."

His uniform shirt was not in any better condition; but again, he shrugged his shoulders and held his breath as he slipped it over his head.

When he started back toward the dining room table, he tripped over something on the floor. He barely caught himself, looked back, and saw that he'd tripped over one of his work shoes. "There you are, you little vagrant," he said when he picked it up. "Now, to find your partner."

Back at the table, he plugged in his electric waffle iron, the one his mother had given him when he moved away from home. Waffles had always been his favorite breakfast, and she wanted to be sure he had something to remind him of home.

He attempted to set the iron down amongst the wads of stacked junk mail cluttering the table so he could mix some pancake batter, but the clutter caused the waffle iron to sit so precariously that he decided to clear an area for it first. He set the open, hot iron down in a chair to clear a corner of the table. He pushed on the clutter until some of the junk started tumbling off the other side. "There, that's enough." And then he set his hand down on the now uncluttered area only to find sticky, spilled maple syrup. "Oh, yuck!" he cried in disgust. "I *really* gotta get me a wife!" He tiptoed back over to the sink to get a dishcloth but his mission was interrupted by the phone.

"Hello?" he answered in his most sultry voice, hoping the caller was Alicia, the girl he'd met the night before. But Jason hadn't paid attention to the unavailable message flashing on his caller ID. Staring off across the room and focusing on nothing in particular, he stood still and listened very carefully for several moments before he finally mumbled, "I understand," and hung up.

After a moment of deep thought, he finally shook his head, breathed a heavy sigh, and went back to his task. "Now, what was I doing?" he asked himself while looking over toward the table. "Oh, yeah!"

He grabbed the wet, soured dishcloth, wrung the slimy water out of it, and then danced back over to the side of the table when something on the floor caught his eye. He turned back and yelled, "Hey! I need you, too!" as he bent over to pick up a black sock, his back toward the chair containing the now very hot waffle iron.

The strange phone call still on his mind, he sighed, and dropped himself into the chair.

•

At the station, the call came in. Zach turned to Shane and said, "Westbrook, you got C. J. on this one. Cruz is a no-show."

Since C. J.'s transformation, Shane had been

paired with Jason. Although he had never believed in C. J.'s "curse", he said nothing.

He and C. J. brought the ambulance to a halt in front of the apartment building and got out to gather their equipment. Neighbors, on their way to work or school, stopped to check out the commotion.

"Which apartment is it?" C. J. asked.

"Downstairs. Right."

C. J. found the door unlocked and entered with Shane following him. "Hello? Is anybody here?"

Over to the left side of the room, they heard Jason's moaning. Turning, they saw him lying on the cluttered couch, face down, wearing only the uniform shirt and bright red silk boxers, with the very deeply toasted imprint of a waffle on the back flashing like a radio tower beacon. In his right hand, he was clutching a cordless telephone.

"*Cruz?* Is that *you?*" Shane cried with a snicker. He came around the glanced down into Jason's face. "*No wonder* you didn't make it in today! Chief called you a no-show, and you know what that means, don't you?"

Jason rolled his eyes and hid his face in the cushion. "He ain't happy."

With a weird smirk on his face, and his hand over his nose, C. J. glanced down at Jason's injury. "Ooo … that's gotta hurt."

Cruz moaned when he turned and glanced up at his colleagues. "Is it bad?" he whimpered. Shane knelt down and tied a tourniquet onto his arm to begin an IV.

"Well, *Fireman* Cruz," Shane started, trying his

best to control his shuddering insides, "we're just *measly* paramedics, but neither one of us believes silk was meant to take that kind of heat."

C. J. had tried his best to keep a straight face, but once they had their colleague loaded into the ambulance, he hopped up into the back, turned toward the cab window, and cried, "Hey, Mr. Westbrook, grab that video camera you've got hidden under the seat!"

"*Taylor,* don't you dare!" Jason cried. "*Westbrook,* don't even think about it!"

So much for another boring day.

•

All was quiet back at the station. Too quiet for C. J.'s taste. As the day dragged by, he found himself staring over at the old piano. Out of pure curiosity, he tenderly laid the fingers of his left hand on the keys. He gently pushed down on the keys, acting almost fearful that someone might hear him.

"C. J., don't be afraid of the thing!" Shane sat down at the table and pulled a game of checkers over in front of him. "It's not going to bite."

C. J. pulled his hand away in an instant. "I don't know anything about a piano."

Somehow, his partner didn't believe him. "Yeah? Well, something tells me you've got more talent hidden in your little finger than most of us could ever dream of. Far as I know, nobody here has ever tried to play that thing. In fact, I tell you what. Tomorrow, we'll be off, and it's Wednesday. I have to go to prayer meeting at six o'clock tomorrow night, and then I have choir practice afterwards. I dare you to come with me."

C. J. laughed scornfully. "Yeah, right! Like *I'm* going to show up at a church somewhere, let alone sing. Give me a break!"

For a long, awkward moment, Shane stared at his friend and breathed a silent prayer, wondering how to answer him. Finally, he shook his head. "Nope. No breaks. It's better to walk into a church on your own two feet than to be carried in by six pallbearers."

C. J.'s face turned dark red. "Is that what this is all about? After all this time, you choose to become my *friend* so you could convert me to some fruitcake, front-door-hopping religion! Why? Are you after the money too? Isn't that what you all do? Go door-to-door begging for money? Well, I'm *not* interested! It *ain't* happenin'!" He went back over to the recliner and dropped down into it, snatched up a magazine, and quickly flipped through the pages as if he were speed reading.

Shane threw his hands up and rolled his eyes. *Oh, great. Here we go again!* he thought, remembering other times he and C. J. had clashed. He came over, snatched the magazine out of C. J.'s hands, and got down in his face. "Taylor, I think that by now, you should *know* me better than that. And we Baptists, *we're* not the ones peddling bicycles from door-to-door or begging people to buy our pamphlets. You've got us mixed up with somebody else."

Fact was, C. J. did know better than that. He could not deny that Shane's friendship had been genuine.

So genuine, in fact, that he found it difficult to continue to stand his ground in his own beliefs or the lack thereof. He pulled the lever to let out the footrest and threw his arms over the arms of the chair. And he sighed. *As if* she *would allow me out of the dungeon long enough to go to* church*!* "Yeah, so I do know better than that. And I'm sorry I yelled. But do you really think they'll—"

"They let you go to the mall with me, didn't they?" Shane interrupted. "Just tell me you'll think about it, okay?"

For a moment, all C. J. could think about was the insurmountable strength his petite little mother had in those long, bony fingers of hers. He could almost sense her coming after him again. "Okay. I'll *think* about it."

Shane nodded. "Good enough. Now get yourself over here so we can get this checkers marathon started."

"You do realize it's *my* turn to win."

Shane laughed. "Yeah? As long as I *let* you win, right?"

Chapter 15

Wednesday evening, December 21

Knowing C. J.'s qualms about church life, Shane had not offered to pick him up. He knew that if C. J. had meant what he said, he'd find a way to get the permission he needed to show up on his own. And Shane felt it best to leave it at that.

The church's denomination was Baptist, Southern Baptist to be specific. And it was situated out in the country, north of town. All through prayer meeting, although Shane had kept his head bowed, he kept one eye cracked open and on the door, hoping C. J. would quietly sneak in. But when there was no sign of him, Shane was not surprised. A little disappointed maybe, but not surprised at all.

However, just outside the sanctuary doors out in the foyer, C. J. stood peeking in through the crack between the double doors. Although deep within the caverns of the long hallways that stretched out behind him, he was able to hear children laughing and playing coming from one direction and screeching strains from guitars and drums coming from another, he hadn't met another soul. He'd come in late. The congregation had already dispersed to their respective classes. In his solitude, C. J. stood there quietly watching, dreading the possibility of contact with another of those money-hungry *Christian* fanatics. Why he felt like he should have come was a question he could not yet answer. As it was, it had taken a proverbial act of congress for his father to talk his mother into it. “We have to allow him to be as normal as possible,” Zach had whispered, sure that C. J. was not able to overhear him. But C. J. had overheard. It had not been the first time that statement was made.

Suddenly, he was startled when he heard whispers coming from behind him.

“Hey, who are you?”

When C. J. turned around, he found a pair of young girls, about nine years of age, standing there whispering to him. “What’s your name?” the blonde child asked.

His first thought was that it was a shame that this group of fanatics had had the nerve to sucker even the children. And he couldn’t believe that when he tried to answer them, his voice cracked. After a long, awkward moment, he cleared his throat and tried again. “I’m nobody special. Why do you ask?”

The girls giggled quietly and then the sandy-haired one said, “Because you look like somebody else.”

With a half snicker, C. J. said, “Oh. I look like *somebody* rather than *nobody*. Okay. So, who do I look like?”

The girl giggled. “You look just like Cory Richardson. He’s a really famous music star. Is that who you are?”

A sweet smile slowly crept across C. J.'s handsome face because they seemed genuinely smitten. "Nah. I hate to disappoint you girls, but I don't know anybody named Cory Richardson. My name is C. J. Taylor, and I'm not a famous anything. I'm sorry."

"That's okay, Mr. Taylor," the little blonde whispered back to him. "You're still just as cute as our Cory is."

While the girls headed off down the long hallway, C. J. dropped his head and laughed to himself. *Well, at least they didn't come asking for money.*

After the prayer meeting was over, the church's dozen-member choir had gathered in the choir loft and was glancing over some new music when the director was given word that their pianist had gotten a flat tire on her way to church and would be late.

Sitting up on the top row, in the tenor section, Shane, like the others, was busy glancing over the new music when cries from the soprano section drifted up toward him. "Check out the young, handsome, new choir member!" cried one of the younger and bolder sopranos.

"Now, Allison, don't you go and embarrass that poor youngin'!" cried another. "Just because he ain't been here before doesn't mean you can—"

Shane usually managed to ignore the ladies and cut off their usual comments from his mind. But this time, his curiosity got the better of him. He looked up from the music and glanced down the center aisle between the pews. There, slowly walking toward the choir loft, was C. J. Shane closed his eyes hard and opened them again, sure it was only a vision. But when he opened his eyes, C. J. was still there.

Shane felt it was his duty to come and welcome his friend, but just as he reached him, the music director came over, looked down at C. J., and asked, "Pardon me, young man, but we have an emergency need of a pianist. You wouldn't by any chance—"

C. J. turned his red-faced gaze downward. *You have got to be kidding me!* he thought. "Um … I'm sorry. I … know nothing about the—"

The director didn't let him finish. "Well, maybe you can at least help us out by playing a few keys here and there. Come and let me show you."

When C. J. looked up and caught a glimpse of Shane's grinning face, his friend held his hands up and refused to bail him out. Right or wrong, C. J. would have to handle this himself. "Well … I can try."

A very shocked and very wide-eyed Shane Westbrook slowly made his way back up to his seat in the choir loft while the music director gave C. J. a crash course in piano.

Sitting on the piano bench, C. J. stared down at the music. And when the director pointed to a single note and called it middle C, all of a sudden, it came flooding back. The half notes and quarter notes, rests, sharps, and flats. The treble clef, the bass clef, time signatures, and measures. The chord fingering over the ebony and ivory of the baby grand felt perfectly natural, and the music that flowed from the inside caused chills to wash over Shane's arms and neck.

Before practice could begin, a searing realization

suddenly shot through Shane's mind as if it were a missile. He rushed down from the choir loft and took C. J. by the arm. "Concert's over. You need to get out of here," he said under his breath.

Confused, C. J. turned to him. "Why? What did I do wrong?"

Shane came close to his ear. "I was right when I said you have more talent in your little finger than most of us could only dream of having. But the *real* C. J. Taylor didn't have a musical bone in his body. He had no sense of timing, and he couldn't carry a tune in a bucket, let alone, play one on the piano. But if word gets out that you do—"

C. J. interrupted him with a heavy sigh. "Message received loud and clear."

"You go home and don't say a word about this. I'll see you at the station Friday morning. Just keep that cell phone close."

To the dismay of the choir leader, C. J. got up, but as he was leaving the sanctuary, he overheard Shane. "Hey, fearless leader, sorry for ruining your new piano player, but it used to be that guy couldn't carry a tune in a bucket!" Shane hadn't thought to introduce his friend to the rest of the choir. And at the moment, he felt sure his forgetfulness had been divinely inspired. "The crash course you gave him was a pure miracle! Think you could do the same for me?"

It was only a short time later when the church parking lot quickly emptied. Shane alone had stayed behind to make sure the doors were locked. And when he came out to his car, he found C. J.'s car parked right alongside his own. His imagination running wild, he could picture only one reason why his friend would have left it sitting there. His heart began pounding wildly until he found C. J. sitting in the driver's seat with the cell phone in one hand and a small piece of paper in the other. Shane climbed into the passenger seat up front and stopped C. J.'s hand from pushing the buttons on the phone when he saw he was dialing Keeli's number. "Don't. Not her."

"Why? What have you been doing? Praying that your *God* would keep me from getting through? I've been trying for the last forty-five minutes, and all I've gotten is a busy signal."

"No, I *didn't* pray for that, but had I realized you were going to use my phone for that reason, I might have. And even though I didn't pray that prayer, it wouldn't surprise me to find that the busy signal is divinely inspired."

"Then tell him to back off!"

The hair on the back of Shane's neck stood on end, and he reached over and knocked C. J. on his head. "Get your head out of the clouds! Use your brain, *not* your hormones! Think about somebody other than yourself. Picture it. The DNA tests come back and prove you don't belong here. The police come, arrest all the bad guys, and take you home."

"Sounds like a plan to me."

Shane reached over and snatched the cell phone out of C. J.'s hand. "At the risk of sounding like your father, *now* is not the time to go stupid! The results ought to be back any day now, and until you get them, don't you dare go down there and lead that girl on! Don't you dare start something you might not be able to finish."

"Is that what you think I'm doing? Leading her on? What makes you think I'm not simply going to buy one of those puppies? I might have two brothers and one sister who would probably love to get one for Christmas. Like it or don't, life goes on."

Frustrated, Shane opened the door and poured himself out of the little car. "Go on home, and *don't* do anything stupid!" He tossed the cell back onto C. J.'s lap and slammed the door shut. And then he stood there, waiting for the boy to drive off.

•

It was a little after nine when C. J. arrived back home. His curfew for the evening had been ten. Other than the kitchen, and the sparkling glow from the lights of the Christmas tree, he found the house unusually dark and quiet. His father and siblings had already hit the sack. But in the kitchen, he found his mother drying and putting away the supper dishes. Like any mother, she wouldn't rest until her boy was safe at home.

Finding her alone, C. J. took advantage of the golden opportunity. An unexpected peck on the cheek drew a pleasant smile to Roxanne's normally serious demeanor. Holding a kitchen towel in one hand and touching her cheek with the other, she turned to her eldest. "What was that for?"

C. J. had taken Shane's advice seriously. He leaned back against the kitchen counter. "Just a little bit of the Christmas spirit, I suppose. And also to say thank you for letting me go tonight."

His mother finished drying the last plate and quietly stacked it on top of the counter with the others. "You mean to tell me you actually *enjoyed* a church service?" She believed her son's thoughts on church were very similar to her own: vague at best. Church was not a subject regularly discussed.

"I admit," he began when he dropped his eyes and stared down at his shoes, "the best part was the music."

"Why did I know you were going to say that? Hmph ... you boys and your music."

Had he said the wrong thing so quickly? He gently picked up the stack of clean plates and quietly sat them in their place in the cabinet while his mother began drying the glasses. "It's okay, Mom. It was simple Christmas music. You would have liked it."

His mother's expression changed to a scowl. "No, I would not have liked it. Music is just noise pollution, and I'm not into that scene. So, if you're trying to butter me up to ask for your CDs back or for a new stereo, forget it."

Undaunted, C. J. began putting away the dry glasses. "Nah. I was just going to try my luck for a piano." And then a silly grin crossed his lips.

Roxanne rolled her tired, pale-blue eyes, but she didn't dare let on that her heart was pounding inside her chest. It was absolutely not going to happen. She couldn't allow it. "A piano, huh? I know you're not serious. With your inbred lack of musical talent, don't make me laugh! Now, get yourself upstairs because it's getting late."

"Then I guess I'll stick with the keyboard," C. J. said.

Puzzled, the woman asked, "And what keyboard would that be?"

"You know. The one you gave me for Christmas last year."

"Oh. That keyboard." Again, the wheels in her head began turning.

C. J. tried to think nothing of it as he turned, but then he stopped short of the door. "Oh, yes. One last question. May I go Christmas shopping tomorrow?"

"Christmas shopping? For whom?"

With his lips curled into a silly grin, C. J. answered, "Oh, I wouldn't know. Maybe for my brothers or my sister. Maybe for Dad, or maybe for my favorite mom in the whole world—"

"Okay! Okay," Roxanne said with a perturbed sigh. "Maybe for your brothers and your sister. But as for me, I've thrown out and given away more knick knacks than you can shake a stick at."

"That sounds like a yes to me."

With a half smile, Roxanne said, "I'll talk it over with your father, and we'll let you know in the morning."

"Oh, come on, Mom. We both know who's the boss in this family."

"Get yourself to bed!" she cried with a snicker.

C. J. bolted for the door. "Yes, ma'am! Night!"

For the first time since her son's strange and questionable return, Roxanne felt as though things were finally going to work out. Keeping her home life as normal as possible had become a tremendous struggle, a struggle she had felt she was about to lose until this encounter. C. J. finally seemed to be blossoming. Maybe there was something to this church thing after all. Making sure he felt content had been her goal.

With a smile, she gently touched her cheek where he'd kissed her.

Chapter 16

Thursday morning, December 22

The following morning, promptly at eight o'clock, C. J. left on his own Christmas shopping trek, with ample blessing from both parents. Getting into his mother's good graces, he was being generously rewarded, just like Westbrook had advised him. It would be an hour later that he pulled into the parking lot of the mall and parked near the main entrance.

Like C. J., Keeli too had the day off. But for her own safety, she felt it best to meet him at the store and stick close to common ground. Although he looked vaguely familiar to her, she was not accustomed to giving her home address to just anyone.

Nervous, Keeli came out of the employee lounge just when the clock on the wall read 8:58. And to her most pleasant surprise, she found C. J. patiently waiting outside the barricade for the store to open.

When Miss Sanderford noticed C. J. standing outside, she grinned at him and began fluttering her eyelashes, just as she had on Monday.

C. J. wanted to crack up. He turned himself around to try to avoid embarrassing her by his laughter. But when he looked up, to his great astonishment, there was Vargas, standing about ten paces behind him, holding a cell phone to his ear. C. J. dropped his gaze and wagged his head until a thought came to him. "Hey, Vargas," he called.

Vargas pretended he hadn't noticed C. J. He looked up at the boy, mumbled something inaudible into the cell phone, and then flipped it shut. "What do you want?" he asked in a most derogatory tone of voice.

Vargas's attitude didn't phase C. J. one bit. A huge grin crossed his lips and he motioned toward Mary. "Has that thing got a camera on it?"

"So what if it does?"

"Check it out! Take a picture!"

Vargas glanced over at Mary, and when he noticed the false eyelashes flapping like a leaf in the wind, C. J. laughed. "I think she's speaking your language!"

Over at the store entrance, after the metal gate was moved out of the way and the store was officially open, Keeli came out and met C. J. "Hi," she said softly.

Totally enamored by her radiant beauty, C. J. nearly choked on his own spit when he asked, "Where should we start?"

With a sweet smile that could stop the world from turning, Keeli gently took his arm and led him past Vargas. And when C. J. lifted his eyes and glanced up at Vargas again, he asked, "Is it worth what she's paying you?"

Vargas only moaned.

Concerned, Keeli turned around and watched the man. "Who was that?" she asked.

C. J. smiled. "Ah, just my bodyguard."

Confused, Keeli looked up at him. "If he's a bodyguard, he's not doing a very good job, is he?"

C. J. laughed. "That's the joke of it."

"Okay. Well, shall we start at the beginning?"

"The beginning of what? The mall?"

"No, silly. At the beginning of your shopping list."

"Duh!" C. J. pulled a folded piece of paper from his pocket and handed it to her.

•

The noon hour was fast approaching, and Christmas was bearing down like a storm. The crowd at the mall rushed around like gale-force winds. No store would be left un-shopped. No sale item would be left unpicked. But unlike the other shoppers, who rushed about carrying shopping bags loaded with brightly colored packages, C. J. hadn't yet spent a penny. Instead, he and Keeli had spent the entire morning sipping fresh-squeezed lemonade from the Chick-Fil-A restaurant and making innocent small talk while sitting in the crowded food court.

It had been a glorious three hours, but still, C. J. could not comprehend what he was feeling inside. Keeli's innocence and beauty had given him a genuine view of himself and left him with a sense of how to be a gentleman. She hadn't pried into his personal life, and he felt secure keeping his problems to himself.

Was it love?

Likewise, Keeli had been given a sense of herself and what it meant to be a lady. Looking up into his sapphire eyes, her heart went pitter-patter. Her mouth went dry, and her palms became sweaty. He was perfectly handsome and so strong too.

Was it love? Or was it infatuation? Could this feeling last for a lifetime? Somehow, she felt she should cherish the moment for tomorrow may never come.

Suddenly, an eerie silence fell over the crowded food court. When C. J. and Keeli turned to look, they found the rest of the crowd watching a hoard of uniformed police officers, TV news reporters, and TV cameras as they came flooding into the food court.

There was something about it that gave C. J. an uneasy feeling, although he refused to make it known to Keeli. Instinctively, he stood to his feet and took her hand. "Let's get out of here."

As she stood up, Keeli looked over the crowd of people. "Who are they coming after?"

"I don't know, but this can't be good. Let's get out of their way."

Mingling with a crowd of shoppers, they strolled along toward a toy store. But back in the area of the food court, there arose a loud commotion. Like everyone else in the mall, C. J. and Keeli stopped and turned to watch the commotion until all of a sudden, someone grabbed them from behind and forced them into the back of a sporting goods store.

It was when C. J. instinctively grabbed Keeli to protect her that Shane's warning hit him like a ton of bricks. His being with her might actually endanger her very life, blessing or no blessing. Suddenly, he felt sick to his stomach that he'd put her in that situation.

Frightened out of their minds, neither Keeli nor C. J. had been able to utter a sound until they turned around and found a very red-faced and angry Shane standing behind them. Clad in a baseball cap, he grabbed C. J. by his arm. "Let's go."

Once C. J. caught his breath, he yanked his arm free. "*Why?*"

Shane found a rack of baseball caps and sunglasses in the back of the store, took one of each, and handed them to C. J. "I knew you were going to ignore my warning. Now, put these on, and let's get out of here."

C. J. threw the cap and sunglasses back at him. "What's the big deal?"

"Keeli! *She's* the big deal!"

"I'm *not* leaving this place without her!"

"That mob out there, the cops, the reporters—they're after you! I don't know what you've done to get so many people mad, but I'm sure once Miss Keeli finds out you're a fugitive, she'll be glad to let you go. Won't you, honey?"

Stunned, Keeli couldn't say a word. She wanted to choke.

Shane turned and looked into the pretty girl's sad eyes. "Listen, honey, you gonna have to trust me on this one. He's not right for you."

"I don't believe you!" Keeli cried.

"Indulge me this once."

"Not a chance!"

Just then, the manager of the store came to them,

threw his hands to his hips, and asked, "Is there a problem here?"

C. J. turned to the man. "No, sir. We're just—"

But Shane threw his hand up and stopped him. "Yes, sir, you could help us find a safe way out of this place."

The manager gave him a stern look. "The only safe and legal way in or out is through our front entrance. I suggest you use it, but not before you pay for the cap and sunglasses."

Shane snatched the price tags off and handed them to the manager along with a twenty-dollar bill. And after the man had rung up the purchases, he handed the change back and then pointed to the front entrance. "That is the only way out. Go before I call security."

Shane pulled at C. J.'s arm. "Let's go."

C. J. jerked away.

With his jaw tightly clenched, Shane got in his face. "If you don't walk away now, I'll wash my hands of all of it. You have a choice to make, and you'd better do it quickly. Vargas is out there watching."

"I *know* he's out there!"

"*What?*"

"It's not like I don't know what he's doing! And he knows I'm on to him. He's got my parents on the other end of that phone he's got planted in his face."

Just then, when the commotion out in the mall grew deafening, Shane gasped, pulled the baseball cap down over C. J.'s head, and said, "Let's go."

C. J. rolled his eyes, turned to Keeli, and looked

down into her teary eyes. "Listen, I'm really sorry. He's right. I don't have any business being here. I'm sorry."

"Something told me this was going to happen. But, please don't lose my number."

He didn't know what to say. He kissed her on her forehead, and then he and Shane split before the mob could reach them.

•

Outside in the parking lot, away from the maddening crowd, C. J. snatched the cap off his head and threw it down onto the pavement. "Are you *satisfied?*"

"Why didn't you listen to me? You have *no* business being here!" Shane then glared at the blue sky. "Lord, he's becoming a very heavy burden!" Looking over at C. J. again, he said, "Cops? Reporters? Who in the world *are* you? And *why* are they after you?"

Puzzled, C. J. shot his friend a confused look. "I thought you believed me."

"I *did!* I mean I do! Oh, I don't know what to believe any more," Shane cried as he came over and snatched the baseball cap up off the ground. "For your sake and for hers, I'm praying this thing pans out good. Now go home."

C. J. headed for his car. "You fanatics and your holier-than-thou *Christian* ethics. Don't bother *praying* for me! If that God of yours was so great, I wouldn't be in this boat in the first place."

"Is that so? Does that mean you think you're such a hot shot that God should do the bowing down? And why would that be? Because you have a disgustingly handsome face, which, by the way, he *gave* to you!"

"Give me a break!"

Mr. Westbrook had been known for his long-suffering patience. But his patience was being stretched to the limit. He felt like Job of the Old Testament. "I told you I don't give a rip about the opinions of others, and that would include yours. But until those test results come back, I have taken you on as a divinely inspired assignment."

"Is that so?" C. J. mocked. "Does *that* mean if those results prove I really am C. J. Taylor, you'll finally *quit* praying for me?"

"Look, Bud, it don't matter how many times you insult me. I'll never stop asking God to help you out. Now, you're either going to go home on your own or I'm going to take you. Which is it going to be?"

C. J. spun around and opened his car door. "I'm not going back to that dungeon until I have to." He got in his car and squealed out of the parking lot.

Standing next to his own vehicle just a couple rows over, Shane took a deep breath and counted to ten. And in his heart, he prayed, "I'm sorry, Lord. It's just that he's getting under my skin. He's a prisoner with just enough freedom to hang himself, and I don't know how to help him. How can I keep this robin from—"

All of a sudden, Shane's prayer was cut short when he heard another vehicle peeling out of the parking lot in the same direction C. J. had gone. And when he turned and saw that it was Vargas's black SUV, he quickly picked up his cell phone and dialed C. J.

"Don't tell me you called to apologize," came C. J.'s voice from the other end.

"No, sir, I didn't because I'm right, and you know I'm right. I called to tell you that Vargas is hot on your trail. He's driving a black SUV, so watch out for him."

Shane could hear C. J.'s heavy sigh through the phone. "I suppose you still expect me to go straight home, don't you?"

"You know what? You go wherever you want to go. Have a nice day." Shane hung up the phone.

C. J. snapped his phone shut and tossed it onto the floorboard. And then he glanced up into the rearview mirror, and what did he see but a black SUV closing in fast. He knew Shane had been right, although he'd been too full of pride to admit it. Home might have been the only place left open to him, but he wouldn't go without a fight. Working with the department for the last eighteen days had taught him a thing or two about Crestview's city streets. He glanced down at his gas gauge, noticed the tank was still half full, and then a grin crossed his lips. He slowed down and waited for Vargas to catch up and then led him on a wild goose chase up and down the back streets of the city.

After driving for over an hour, C. J. finally looked up and noticed the man was no longer behind him. Heading west on Airport Road, he stopped where Highway 85 intersected. When he glanced across the highway at a gas station, he found the SUV with

Vargas standing next to the pump filling the tank. With a smirk, C. J. turned right onto the highway and gunned the engine, leaving Vargas and his P. I. duty in the dust.

With the house coming into view, C. J. looked ahead just in time to catch a glimpse of Shane's car as he backed out of the driveway. All the way home, he had felt lousy. Guilt had been plaguing his mind, but seeing Shane's car at the house became the straw that broke the camel's back. He slammed on his brakes, grinded to a halt, and pulled the car over to the left, off the road just in front of the cow pasture. He shut the engine off, reached for the cell phone, and quickly punched in Keeli's number. It was probably the dumbest move of his life, leaving the most beautiful girl he'd ever seen stranded and at the mercy of the mob. He owed her an apology and would not be satisfied until he could speak to her. It had taken a lot of nerve to ask her out in the first place, and he doubted she would ever be able to forgive him. He was not surprised when there was no answer. He pushed the end button and sat there in total silence, staring out toward the pond in the middle of the pasture.

And then there was Westbrook, the only true friend he had, and yet he'd driven him away by his foolishness.

It would be getting dark soon. Trapped in a lifeless prison without a friend in the world, out of the blue, the pond seemed to be whispering his name. All of a sudden, a burning sensation came over his face and neck. It was an overwhelming and unexplainable feeling of fear. He sucked in a deep gulp of air and held it, forcing his chest to expand until an idea came to him. From the pond he came, and to the pond he would return.

Leaving the keys in the ignition, he tucked the cell phone and his wallet into a jacket pocket and headed for the water's edge. As the blue sky was quickly fading to oranges and purples, he stared out over the greenish water. The surface was as smooth as glass. Again, he heard the silent whisper. Again, fear overwhelmed him. Determined to stop the insanity, he kicked his shoes and socks off, dropped his jacket to the ground, and held his breath tight as he waded out into the brutally cold water. His muscles began to stiffen immediately. But he forced his body deeper and deeper. His lungs burned for oxygen. His pounding heart throbbed in his ears. He waited, even hoped it would all just stop and he would finally be at rest—until all of a sudden, his hand brushed up against a huge metal object near the bottom. Confused, he opened his eyes and found a Ford van lying on its roof. The vehicle was an ambulance with Alabama tags. The back doors had crumbled and were wedged open by the murky bottom. The gurney had been thrown clear and was lying twisted under a layer of silt just a few yards away. By the angle, C. J. knew immediately that it had run off the embankment and flipped upside down before it landed in the water.

Jolted to reality, he swam around and peered through the windshield; to his utter shock, he found two bodies strapped into the frontseat. Like a rocket, he shot to the surface only to be snatched by somebody's hands. He fought until he was finally able to turn himself and find his father in the water with him.

"What are you doing?" Zach hollered at the top of his lungs.

C. J. managed to push himself free and began swimming toward the edge. "I could ask you the same question! What are *you* doing? Trying to drown me?"

After they finally reached the shore, Zach hollered, "We break down and give you permission to go Christmas shopping, and what do we get? I trust you have a reasonable explanation for this stupidness!"

C. J. refused to answer.

"We're living in the woods, there's not too many people around this part. But you're still trespassing. That's against the law. And second, we may be in the state of Florida, but it's still cold enough this time of year that swimming in this water in the month of December is nothing short of suicide!"

C. J.'s silence was only feeding the man's anger.

"Is that it? Have you decided *suicide* is your answer?"

There was no confusion. Yes, that was his goal, but that wasn't how it turned out. He wanted to blurt out his discovery, but something stopped him. "Like you really care."

Zach picked up his son's shoes and jacket and shoved them into his chest. Did he care? The question had crossed his mind ... once. "Get in the house."

•

The tension inside the house had grown thick enough to cut with a knife. Inside the door, C. J. glanced up and caught a glimpse of the children sitting side-by-side on the couch in absolute silence. And by the terrified looks on their faces, C. J. could see they'd had a bad day.

Roxanne met him just inside the door, demanding, "Hand over the car keys!"

Refusing to speak, C. J. motioned toward the door with his thumb.

"Bo, come over here!" his mother hollered.

"Ma'am?" Bo answered in a frightened voice.

"Get out there and get the keys out of your brother's car."

C. J. noticed the boy appeared strangely downtrodden and seemed to purposely keep his eyes off his brother.

"Uh … shouldn't it be moved into the driveway first?" Bo asked with deep caution.

Zach interjected, "*I'll* move the car. Bo, take your brother and sister into the dining room and eat your dinner!"

"Yes, sir," he said under his breath as he quickly moved to usher Dylan and Julia out of the line of fire.

Again, Roxanne turned her attention to her eldest. "Mister, you'd better explain to me why your face is being plastered all over the television screen, and you'd better explain who the girl is because I already told you there would be no girls unless *I* approved!"

C. J. glared at her with disdain in his eyes. *Lady, you might plan to tear through me with those claws of yours again, but this time, I'm not going down without a fight!* "If you don't already know, then obviously your miserable cop friend makes a lousy private detective. You ought to advise him to keep his day job."

Roxanne shook her finger at him. "*I* am your mother! I have a right to know where you are at *all* times! I will *not* apologize for hiring Vargas, so don't bother complaining because I'm *not* listening!"

"Don't you think this prison thing would be a whole lot easier if you would just tie me up, gag me, and throw me in the basement?"

Mistake number one.

After he picked himself up off the floor, C. J. grabbed his left temple. "I didn't *do* anything wrong! Apparently those people thought I was somebody else! That's not *my* fault!"

"And just *who* do those people think you are?" his mother squealed.

"You say you're my mother! You tell me!"

Mistake number two.

This time, Zach snatched his wife's wrist before she could make contact. "Not again," he warned. And then he turned to C. J. and said, "Get on upstairs and get changed. Dinner's ready."

"No, thank you. I won't be interested in dinner," C. J. whispered as he made his way past his parents and toward the stairs.

He had just reached the top of the first flight before he overheard his mother. "He's *my* son, it's *my* money, and I'll *do* with it whatever I please!" Overwhelmingly curious, C. J. hid himself behind a wall and listened to his father's low voice.

"Your stranglehold is driving this kid to suicide. Blow your money on that."

"*No,* that's *not* what I want! *I* am his mother! Those Richardson people had *no right* to teach *my* son how to play that piano or how to gallivant across some stage where hoards of girls can chase him down! They had *no right* to exploit his talent or his handsome looks! Who do they think they are?"

"Well, why didn't you just buy back the *other* one?"

"How *dare* you!"

The other one? Richardson people? Cory Richardson? C. J. wondered. One-by-one the pieces of the puzzle were beginning to fall into place. But his father went on in a most derogatory tone of voice. "Oh yes. How dare I forget. There is no place for the *perfect*... unless of course, you kill the *defective.*"

C. J. knew the woman swung a mean fist, but he didn't know she would have the nerve to swing it at her husband. It sounded, however, as though Zach had caught her hand again.

"Look at what untold thousands your one-nighter with that Cantrella dude has cost you. The perfect for the defective. Had you aborted like the man told you to do in the first place, there would have been neither, would there? There would have been no extravagant medical bills. The rest of the world would have never known, and we wouldn't be in this predicament, would we? The problem—you didn't listen. You insisted on doing it your own way. Now there are more people out there who know the truth than we can try to fool in a lifetime."

C. J. couldn't move. He couldn't breath. Wet and cold, his body shivered hard. *Defective one? Me?* He gently rubbed the six-inch scar that wrapped around his left side. It was just a narrow, white line, with the classic railroad track signature of a skilled surgeon's hand. Could it mean he had been the defective one they were talking about? Or maybe Bo? Julia? *Dylan?* He didn't dare ask.

Undaunted, his mother whispered, "Then he, like the other, will simply have to die. A stronger dose of Triptazine ought to do the trick. They'll call it a self-inflicted OD and should come as no surprise." She breathed those deadly words with a bone-chilling, matter-of-fact arrogance. "Now, you get up those stairs, turn that doorknob back the way I had it, and then get out of those wet clothes while I get Vargas on the phone."

From the top of the main staircase, C. J. had been able to clearly understand every breathless word. And although he felt sure they had been talking about himself, the other children were no less victims. But how could he protect them while trying to save himself?

All of a sudden, he gasped and darted for his door when he heard his father's heavy footsteps reach the bottom of the stairs.

Chapter 17

Thursday night, late December 22

Wrapped in a heavy blanket and sitting in a ball on the floor beside the bed, C. J. shivered hard as he nervously punched Shane's phone number into the cell phone he held tightly clutched in his cold hands. Over and over again, he dialed Shane's number. Over and over again, he dialed Keeli's number. But he could get neither of his friends to answer. And dialing 911 was not an option, not as long as Officer Vargas was still on the prowl.

His room was dark. The house was dark. Frustrated and scared out of his mind, sleep would not come easily. He sat watching the changing of the bright orange numbers on his digital alarm clock, fully expecting the final blow at any second. He expected to hear the familiar squeaking of the floor beneath heavy feet and the creaking of the door hinges like he'd heard when his father had busied himself switching the doorknob around again. Yet, there was nothing. He searched the closet for the keyboard and found it had mysteriously disappeared. As the minutes turned into hours, his eyes grew heavy, his mind weary. And in the silence, his mind slowly faded to the ambulance and the bodies in the pond ... and to water swirling over his face ... and to the feminine hand that had held him under.

•

Friday morning, before dawn, December 23

Bo too found sleep difficult to come by. He too had overheard his parents' conversation. Like his brother, he waited for the frightening sounds of the night. The evening's newscast played over and over in his mind like a broken record. His mind refused to rest. The label the media had given to his mysterious brother played on and on until a revelation finally hit him as though it was a slap in the face—the proverbial ton of bricks. He bolted out of bed, grabbed the flashlight he kept hidden under the bed, and began fishing for an elusive object through his dark closet.

When he reached his bedroom doorway with the flashlight and the object in his hand, the antique clock on the fireplace mantle down in the living room chimed. In his mind, he counted the chimes: one, two, three, four. It was four o'clock in the morning. He didn't have much time.

After he made a quick stop in the kitchen, he crept back up the stairs but stopped dead in his tracks when he heard a faint whimper. Maybe it was his imagination, or perhaps it was the strange, human-like screech of the panthers that had made the surrounding woods their home.

When the noise stopped, Bo quickly headed for C. J.'s door. Just as he reached for the lock, there it was again: a soft whimper … a garbled cry in the night. It was coming from C. J.'s room. In sheer panic, Bo silently pleaded, *No, God! Give him a chance!* as he quickly unlocked the door and rushed up the inside stairs to his brother's bedside. Bo found his brother lying flat on his back, staring straight up at the ceiling with eyes of terror. C. J.'s face was ashen, and he held his arms straight out as if trying to grasp hold of something or someone.

Bo shook him. "C. J.! Wake up!" he cried in his softest voice. Convinced his parents had done something drastic in the middle of the night, he didn't dare rush down to their first floor bedroom and wake them.

It looked as though C. J. was saying audible words, but there was no sound nor any air moving between his lips. He was not breathing. "God, please! Not yet!" It was a sight he would never forget. He dropped to the side of the bed and shook his brother again. "C. J.! Please! Wake up! You've got to breathe!" When he didn't wake up, Bo jumped up, grabbed him by his arms, and yanked him up to sitting position. "We can't let them win, God!" he cried in a quiet panic.

All of a sudden, C. J. threw his head back and gasped for air. "No! I'm not ready to die!" he cried. For several moments, he struggled to catch his breath.

Shaking in his socks, Bo stood still, trying to catch his own breath. "Psst … wake up. C. J., it's me, Bo."

The room was dark. His left eye swollen almost completely shut, C. J. could not see his brother clearly, but he could hear an unusual concern in his voice. He could sense it in his somber mood. "*Bo?*"

Bo shushed him and sat down on the side of the bed. "Are you okay?"

The last C. J. remembered, he'd been sitting on the floor. He hadn't remembered climbing up onto the bed nor did he remember dozing off. "What happened?"

"You weren't breathing!" Bo whispered loudly. His heart pounded hard inside his chest. "I thought they'd already … listen, we've gotta talk. Are you with me yet?"

The nightmare had been vivid. A bathtub full of water, and a woman kneeling beside it. She was weeping as she reached in, put her hand over his face, and held him under the water. Beside the woman, there stood a dark-haired boy, crying, hollering, and pounding on the woman with his fists. He was trying to stop her.

C. J. tried rubbing the sleep out of his eyes. "What are you doing here? Did they send you to finish the job?"

"No, they didn't send me, and if they find out I'm here, they'll hang me. Listen, C. J., God sent me to you, even though it may cost me my life. Something crazy has been going on here, and you've gotta hear me out."

C. J. rolled his tired eyes. "Don't tell me you're one of them too," he complained with heavy sarcasm.

Bo's voice began to waver with panic. "Yes, I'm a Christian … and so was the *real* C. J."

"Well, *this* real C. J. isn't one, and if religion is all this talk is going to be about, then I would greatly appreciate it if you would just go on back to bed. I'm not interested."

Bo threw a pleading glance up at the ceiling. "Come on, bro! Hear me out!"

Could he trust the kid? C. J. wondered. He sighed, brought his knees up, and rested his elbows on them. "All right. I'm listening."

"Last night your face, and the face of that girl, was plastered all over the television news. The cops are after you. And so are a lot of other people. And then I heard Mom and Dad arguing about it after they sent you up here. C. J., they're planning to have you killed ... just like they did—"

C. J. interrupted him. "Are you convinced I'm not your brother? Do you believe me?"

Bo pulled a CD case and a sandwich bag containing a small, white pill out from under his pajama top. With a shaky hand, he handed C. J. the sandwich bag. "Up until last night, when I realized you were trying to commit suicide, I'd been blaming you for all the junk going on around here. But God himself told me I was wrong."

"Yeah? And I suppose your God told you to apologize too, didn't he?"

"Yeah. So, I'm sorry, okay?"

"Why would God care about whether or not you apologize ... especially to me? *He* doesn't care about me."

"That's not true. He doesn't like what's happening any more than you or I do."

Although his heart yearned to know the truth, C. J. felt bitter against God. "Then *why* did he let it happen in the first place?"

"Like you, Mom and Dad do not belong to him. They're *not* Christians, and I'm sure they're *not* asking his permission. Now, look at the pill. Mom has been crushing one of these into your hot chocolate every morning, and she doesn't know that I've been watching. I don't know what it is because there's no label on the bottle. But I'm sure you've got friends who can do a chemical analysis to tell you what it is."

"Why are you telling me this now?"

"The news … the argument … I believe my brother has been murdered and that you've been brought here, against your will, to take his place as a cover-up. And then I found this." He handed his brother the CD.

The cover of the CD boasted nothing spectacular. The picture was obscure at best; maybe an abstract of a distant mountain range. C. J. couldn't tell. "I thought Mom confiscated all of our CDs."

"Yeah, well, she missed one. Open it up," Bo commanded.

C. J. flipped the case open and glanced over the inside. "Why would you keep this particular one hidden? It doesn't look any different from any other."

Bo reached over and pulled the word booklet from the case. "This is Christian music."

"*Christian* music? But I thought—"

Bo shook his head. "You thought wrong," he interrupted. "The music, the posters, the costume … it was all just a front because if Mom ever found out it was Christian stuff we preferred, she'd have a cow. Christian music is where it's at."

"What makes you think I don't agree with her?

Aren't you Christians nothing but narrow-minded fruitcakes?"

With a half smile crossing his lips, Bo flipped the word booklet open to the inside back cover and handed it back to his brother. "You know, you don't surprise me at all. Even if you could recall your past, I'd expect you'd say the same thing." He shined the flashlight down onto the cover. "Check this out."

When C. J. looked down at the booklet, his eyes nearly exploded out of his head. He had to force his lungs to take the next breath. Inside the back cover of the booklet was a picture of four young men. One of the faces was that of a fair-complected natural blond. A couple of the others had sand-colored hair. But the last face, the second from the right, was a blue-eyed brunette ... C. J.'s double.

"The name of the group is Spirit of Peace," Bo said. And then he reached over and tapped the face in the picture. "This guy is Cory Richardson, the keyboard artist and the adopted brother of the blond guy."

That name again. Cory. "But ... it can't be me! I'm not—"

"Because you're not into Christian music. News flash! Cory was the only *non*-believer of the group. However, he's just plain good. That's why they let him tickle the ivories."

C. J. looked up and held the booklet out. "Bo, you're out of your mind. These people are the real busy kind, you know, out on the concert circuit, signing autographs, and stuff like that."

Bo leaned forward. "That's the kicker. That's what

the newscast was all about last night. Twenty-one days ago, just after Thanksgiving, Cory Richardson was attacked while in the backyard of his parents' home in Ozark, Alabama, a place not so far from here. He'd been stabbed. An ambulance picked him up to take him to the hospital, but it never got that far. Neither Cory nor the ambulance has been seen since. And that's why, when you were seen at the mall yesterday, people went nuts."

C. J.'s insides began rattling. He felt as though his brain was on fire when visions of the ambulance and its dead occupants flashed across his mind like a television screen. "Do you believe them?"

"Listen, I heard them last night. They're planning to kill you, and once they find out I told you all this stuff, they'll come after me next. I don't care if I die. I know I'll be going to heaven. But if they kill you, all your nightmare will do is get worse.

"Cory, I'm afraid… not because I might be killed for finding out the truth and telling you, but because of how your family will be hurt, if after all this, you end up dead like my real brother. Your family is desperate to find you. The whole Christian music world is desperate to find you. They're all scared out of their minds and are praying for you like crazy. I know it sounds like I've lost my mind, but it's the truth. Please, Cory, give God a chance. Let's fight this battle together on level ground. All you have to do is ask Jesus to forgive your sins and take over your heart, your life, your everything. Even though you're not at fault in this mess, it's still more than likely you'll have something you need forgiven of… like unbelief."

Bo had said one thing right. They hadn't seen eye-to-eye on anything. But here he was, a young man who suddenly seemed to be carrying the weight of the world on his shoulders.

"If I tell you I'll think about it, will that make you feel better?"

"No! You don't have time to just think about it! You've gotta act now! Either you believe or you don't. What's it going to be?"

Cory found it almost comical. "All right, already! Good grief, you're worse than Westbrook! And speaking of Westbrook, why was he here yesterday?"

"You're avoiding the issue here!"

"But it's still a critical question! Why?"

"Because Mom is planning a surprise birthday party for you tonight at the station, and she wanted him to do something for it."

"And do you know what that something might be?"

"I don't know, um, something like take you away from the station for a while so she can set it up, or maybe it was to pick up a cake from the bakery. It sounded innocent enough. But please don't let on that I told you. Mom may be little, but she packs a mean punch."

Cory reached up and rubbed his aching shiner. He'd learned firsthand about the woman's vicious claws and punches. "Is she the one leaving those bruises on your face?" he asked, remembering the purple marks on Bo's face.

The silence became strained when his brother refused to answer the question.

Cory read between the lines. "Enough said. Are you going to be at the party?"

"She never lets us out of her sight."

Cory nodded. "Good. Because I've got a feeling this birthday party is going to be one no one will ever forget."

Bo slowly stood to his feet. "Cory, I'm scared," he admitted humbly. "How you ended up here I don't know, but I do know that God sent you to get us out. Julia, Dylan, and I have no one else we can turn to. We're trapped unless you can help us."

Cory sighed. The boy's concerns were definitely genuine. "All right. For now, don't change anything, including my name. I'll stay C. J. until I know you, Dylan, and Julia are safe."

"I don't understand why she's doing this to you. I don't know where my real brother is. But ... whatever happens, please—don't leave us here." Bo hesitated as he glanced over his shoulder. "I've got to get out of here before Dad comes up and finds me," he whispered before he rushed down the stairs and quietly shut and locked the door behind him.

Cory sighed heavily. Sitting alone in the quiet darkness, he allowed his eyes to drift over to the alarm clock. It read 4:10 a.m. He still had twenty minutes before he needed to be ready to hit the shower. But just then, Bo's words rushed back into his head like a freight train. "Give God a chance, and let's fight this battle on level ground."

Chapter 18

Twenty minutes later—with a pound of bacon sizzling in a large cast-iron skillet on one stove burner, a pot of grits boiling on another, and a tea kettle beginning to show steam on a third—a very unnerved Roxanne found herself standing at the kitchen counter, staring down into the mug C. J. would be using for his ritualistic morning hot chocolate. Sure, her stone-cold exterior had been a strong armor, stoic and tough. But inside, she had become weak as a kitten. She hadn't slept a wink, and with her mind a jumble of panicky thoughts and her heart pounding ninety to nothing, she pulled the small pill bottle down from a cabinet, pulverized two of the tiny pills to powder, and sprinkled the powder into C. J.'s mug.

Drawn by the delicious aroma of the bacon, the two younger children came trickling into the kitchen and sat down at the table, patiently awaiting breakfast. And when Bo came through the door, his mother sent him to unlock C. J.'s door and call him to the table.

She hadn't seen Bo as he watched her through a crack in the door. She didn't realize he knew about the medication, let alone the sudden increase. She might never have believed he was capable of paying attention to the little things. She hadn't seen him during the night when, before his talk with his brother, he took one of the pills from the bottle and hid it.

Bo didn't balk when he was asked to wake his brother. He gladly complied and rushed up the stairs. One might have thought he was simply excited because Christmas was coming just around the corner. Or one might have noticed he was on a mission.

Bo knocked on the door before he opened it and found Cory sitting at the top of his stairs, waiting to be let out. Cory looked as though he could have used one of those nights that lasted about three or four days long. He was obviously struggling with a lack of sleep. His pajamas were twisted and his hair tousled. As he came down and brushed by, Bo whispered, "What are you planning to do?"

Bo could see the wheels in the stranger's head were turning. He could also see the shiner his mother had left him. Bo knew that pain all too well.

"For now, we play the game," Cory whispered. "I need a shower."

"Hey, don't drink the chocolate," Bo warned. "She's doubled up. It could be her weapon to finish the job."

Cory acknowledged the warning with a nod and would have answered something intelligent, but Roxanne broke their quiet conversation when she hollered from the kitchen door. "Bo! C. J.! Get yourselves down here this instant!"

"Yes, ma'am!" Bo answered. And then he turned to Cory. "Come on. Get your shower later. We don't want to make it worse."

•

Down in the kitchen, Cory pretended to be groggy and disoriented. "Mom, where is Lacey?" he asked, referring to one of his many strange dreams.

"Son, I *warned* you about those girls!" his mother hollered with a heart full of caution.

"I'm talking about our dog! You know, the little black-and-white sheltie. Don't you remember? We used to call her Lacey T. Knothead. What happened to her?"

Julia laughed out loud. "We don't got a dog, you silly goose!"

"What's a knothead?" asked Dylan while scratching his head.

Roxanne only wagged her head as she set an empty plate down in front of each of her children. And when she came to Cory, she said, "Son, to the shower as soon as you're finished eating. It'll help wake you up."

Cory nodded. "Yes, ma'am."

A few moments later, with all the innocence of a heavenly angel, Julia came to her eldest brother, climbed up into his lap, and laid her head against his chest. "I love you, C. J.," she whispered while she tenderly rubbed his arm.

Cory had grown to love the pretty little girl. He wrapped his arms around her and whispered, "I love you more." He gently squeezed a giggle out of her. But when his mother came toward the table with the pot of hot grits in one hand and a large spoon in the other, he perceived a jealous glint in her eyes. And when she splattered a spoonful of grits onto his plate, he looked down at his little sister and said, “Baby girl, I think Mom’s ready for you to sit in your own seat.”

Without a complaint, Julia got up and climbed into her own seat. Roxanne, however, surprised the stew out of them all when the glint in her eyes became a flood of tears. She finished serving the grits, put the pot back onto the stove, and then quickly turned herself away and dried the tears from her cheeks before she served the bacon and eggs. “C. J. Taylor, why do you have to be so—”

When she hesitated, Cory became puzzled. “So what?”

“Why did you have to pick today to become so tenderhearted?”

Cory leaned back in his seat and glared at the woman. He didn’t know her. He didn’t understand her. And he certainly didn’t trust her. “I don’t know, Mom. I’m sorry I didn’t realize loving my siblings was such a crime.”

“Oh, it *isn’t* a crime, for Pete’s sake! Just finish eating while I make your hot chocolates.”

It had been the same ritual every morning, like clockwork. Four uniquely different mugs, four different spoons. Each child had his or her favorite. Each claimed his or her spoon. Cory’s mug had been the cobalt blue one, his spoon the one with intricate scrollwork on the handle.

Shaking down to his socks, and wondering how he could make it work, Cory picked at his breakfast while watching the woman out of the corner of his eye. Four envelopes of hot chocolate mix, water from the whistling teakettle on the stove, and three marshmallows each. She did absolutely nothing out of the ordinary. It was her daily routine, and it remained unchangeable. Cory felt he had no choice but to at least taste the stuff. Thankfully, the extra pill made the bitterness unbearable, and the very first sip ended up sprayed across the tablecloth.

He didn't allow the woman time to retaliate. He dropped his head into his hands and rubbed his aching temples. "I'm sorry, Mom. It just won't go down. I don't know what's in it. But isn't there another way? Hot chocolate isn't supposed to taste like this … or is it?"

Roxanne dismissed the three younger children to their rooms. And then without a word, she went to the cabinet, pulled down the hidden pill bottle, and sat down across from him.

For an awkward moment, they sat in silence, staring at each other until she cautiously said, "Okay. You win. You're a persistent little devil, aren't you? I guess you come by it honestly." And she sighed heavily. "Yes, I admit you're on medication, but it's to ease the trauma of the nightmares. And yes, I've tried to hide it in the hot chocolate. But I'm not sorry I tried to make taking medication easier on your overgrown male ego. Your problem is mental, not physical: high anxiety, nightmares, mood swings, and panic attacks. You feel like you belong somewhere else, but we all know better. If you want a normal life outside of a mental hospital, you will have to take this medication every day for the rest of your life," she finished, proud of herself for having come up with such a wonderfully perfect, albeit wildly believable, defense.

Boy! She didn't miss a beat! Stunned by the woman's story, Cory took the bottle from her hand and made note of Bo's words: there was no label on the outside. He opened it up and stared down inside. The tiny white pills were no larger than a saccharine tablet.

"What's it called?"

All of a sudden, Zach came flying through the door in a rage and snatched Cory up by the hair of his head.

Cory winced hard and reached up to try to relieve the pressure from the man's grip. "What did I do this time?"

"You have fifteen minutes to get yourself upstairs and get ready for work!"

"Uh, Dad? Hey, Dad … you can let go of the hair. I'll be ready, I promise."

Zach let go of his hair and shoved him forward. "Hurry up."

Roxanne jumped to her feet. "Not before he takes his medication!"

With a sweep of his arm and fire in his eyes, Zach knocked the hot chocolate and the pill bottle across the room. The hot chocolate splattered everywhere and ran in long, brown chords down the front of the white refrigerator. The pills lay in small white mounds of chocolate-soaked powder. "It's a joke! The stuff doesn't work!"

"You don't know what you're talking about!" Roxanne hollered.

Thankful that the bitter hot chocolate situation seemed to resolve itself, Cory interrupted. "Uh … I'll just go up and get into my uniform now." And in an instant, he rushed out the door but stopped himself short of the stairs. For fear his benefactors might hear his very breath, he held his lungs tight as he stood with his ear perched against the kitchen door, soaking up every last word.

Roxanne's voice hit a high decibel level. "What *is* your problem?"

"This!" Zach slammed something plastic down hard onto the table. "I found it lying on his bed."

Cory was certain he heard something crack.

"Where would he get this CD?" Zach asked.

"You're asking *me? You're* the one who let him go to that miserable mall yesterday! I *told* you he shouldn't go!"

"Don't get onto *my* case! *You're* the one showing him the pill bottle!"

Cory hiked it on up the stairs and locked himself in the bathroom. He knew he had to be brave for the sake of the other children, but truth be known, he didn't have a brave bone in his body. He was terrified. From the deepest pit of his stomach, he longed to know there was somebody on his side: a warrior willing to see him through. But so what if he'd found his true identity. There was still no one to help. Shane had tried to warn him, but now he was gone. Keeli was not answering. The aloneness was quickly turning to helplessness and despair. Not only was he responsible for freeing himself, now he felt responsible for the safety of the other Taylor children as well. But if he couldn't help himself… ?

Chapter 19

The trip to the station was tense. Cory held on white-knuckle tight as Zach peeled the pick-up out of the driveway and fishtailed it down the dirt road, throwing dust high up into the air. When they reached pavement, Taylor pulled the CD from the inside pocket of his jacket and slammed it against Cory's chest.

"Ouch!" Cory cried when he rubbed his chest. But something told him that creating a bruise was not Zach's full intention. "Gee, Dad, if killing me was your plan, you're going to have to try a little harder."

"Where'd you get it?"

It was the Spirit of Peace CD Bo had given him. And what he thought he'd heard from the kitchen was correct. The outer case had cracked when Zach slammed it down onto the table.

Although his heart pounded and his mouth felt dry, knowing the lives of the children would depend on his answer, Cory chose to play innocent. When he noticed the CD player on the dashboard of the truck, he asked, "Are they any good? Can we listen to it?"

Zach's laughter reeked of sarcasm as he shattered

the CD with his fist. "What's the matter with you?" he hollered. "Do you think this is some sort of a joke?"

Cory's shoulders tensed up hard. The hair on the back of his neck stood up. He knew that if he implicated Bo, it would more than likely cost the boy his life. "Oh, come on, Dad. You saw the condition of that room. I know Mom stripped us of all musical paraphernalia, but you can't tell me you're angry because she missed one," he lied. "Give me a break!" And then he grinned. "But that's not what's got you so uptight, is it? It's your wife, isn't it?"

Taylor momentarily cut his eyes toward the boy. "My *wife* happens to be the woman who gave birth to you! Do you think your resemblance to your mother is only coincidence?"

Cory smiled. He wasn't about to be fooled again. "Oh, no. She's not my mother."

"Oh, but she is. And the man in the beemer ... he would be your father. In the real world, they call it adultery. You are the product of an affair; a one-night stand. Your very existence is a joke."

Although he felt confused, Cory continued. "I know that's a lie," he accused. "You see, you're trying much too hard to keep me from putting the puzzle together." He picked up the broken CD case and shook it. "But it hasn't worked. Now she's ticked off and you're uptight." He carefully removed the word booklet from the broken case, flipped it open to the back page, and laid it down on the seat. "The puzzle ... it's who I used to be," he said while tapping on his face in the picture. "It's where you took me from and how you got me here. It's how you made the real C. J. disappear, and how you can try to fool so many people into believing your lie. It might have worked, but the problem is that too many people already know me. And now I fully understand her ripping music out of our lives."

After he rolled down the door window, Zach snatched the word booklet out of Cory's hand, picked up the CD case, and flung both of them out. And then the guy relaxed himself back in the seat and said with an arrogance that could cut through lead, "This plan *is* going to work, and I'll tell you why. Because there are three young kids in that house whose very lives are based solely on whether or not you accept your place in your new home. What are they worth to you? If you choose to reject the offer, which one would you choose to have sacrificed first? A single misplaced word will cost another life. I believe we understand each other."

Disheartened, Cory asked, "Why is it you couldn't be satisfied with just destroying my life and C. J.'s life? Why do you have to destroy theirs too?"

"I *said* I believe we understand each other!"

Not only did it make Cory feel sick, it cemented Bo's request. "I hope you don't expect any respect from me. You sure give new meaning to stooping low."

As they barreled along down Highway 85 at seventy-five MPH, Zach didn't see the highway patrolman sitting in a hidden nook on Blueberry Curve. And as he listened to Zach's lame excuse to the unfamiliar officer, Cory fought the urge to make a break for it and run. The terror had been etched as deeply in his memory as it had been in their young, innocent faces.

Zach mumbled something incomprehensible as he handed over his driver's license and vehicle registration. "I know, I know, you're going to ask where the fire is, aren't you?"

As the young patrolman was glancing down over Zach's license, he cut his eyes up and said, "I'll get to it when I'm good and ready." And then he noticed the fire department insignia on Zach's sleeve and laughed to himself. "Chief Taylor, now you know as well as I do that without the lights and sirens, you ain't gonna get there any faster than the average Joe … legally speaking, that is."

Taylor's face was quickly turning red. "Well, maybe if you'd cut the small talk and get on with it, I could!"

When the highway patrolman flashed the torn word booklet from the CD, all of a sudden, the deep red color washed from Taylor's face and he broke out in a cold sweat.

"Chief, you got a problem with *Christian* music?" the patrolman asked.

"Uh … no, the style … it had nothing to do with—"

The officer interrupted him with a warning. "As a law-abiding citizen, you probably know there's a five-hundred dollar fine for littering in the state of Florida."

"So I know! And I'm sorry, okay? I'll take it back!" cried a highly agitated Taylor. He tried to yank the booklet from the officer's grasp, but the officer called his bluff, snatched the booklet away, and slid it underneath his ticket pad. And then he began scribbling. "Come on, man!" Taylor whined. "I'll throw it in the trash myself if you'll just let me have it back!"

"Not to mention," the officer continued as if he never heard Taylor's plea, "there are about a million pieces of CD scattered all over the highway. Given the *legal* fifty-five MPH speed limit on this stretch of highway, and weather conditions, one of these pieces could penetrate a tire and cause a blowout and ultimately a lawsuit. That, coupled with a speeding ticket . . . you're looking at a hefty—"

Taylor mopped heavy beads of sweat from his brow and began quickly rolling his fingers on the steering wheel. "All right, all right already! I'll go back, pick it all up, and I'll throw it in a real trash can! Now, can I please have the trash back so I can get out of here?"

All of a sudden, the man glanced up from his ticket pad and noticed Cory sitting on the other side of the cab. "Wait," he said. "Haven't I seen you somewhere?"

Cory shot a glance up at Taylor's pale face and momentarily shied away.

The officer returned his attention to his scribbling on the pad. "What's the matter with the kid? He deaf?"

Taylor pounded the steering wheel. "Would you *please* hurry up?"

The officer cut his eyes up again. "Impatience is what got you here in the first place, mister. One more blow up like that, and that fire will just have to put itself out."

Cory again turned and made eye contact with Taylor. "Take it easy ... *Dad,*" he said sarcastically. "Or you'll spend *this* fire sitting in a jail cell."

Taylor shook his finger in Cory's face. "You've already been warned! Don't you dare try me!"

The officer again glanced up from his ticket pad and looked at Cory's face. "I know I've seen you somewhere before."

Once again, Cory was in a fix. He had to carefully choose his words, knowing several lives depended on it. And then it hit him. "Well, I guess it all depends on *where* you look," he answered while shooting a strange, wide-eyed glance down toward the officer's ticket pad. "They call me C. J."

With a furrowed brow, the officer snickered. "*Taylor? C. J.* Taylor?"

"Some would say," Cory answered while letting his eyes drift back and forth from the officer to the booklet underneath the ticket pad.

"Well, if that's so, where's the face and the hair? You don't look anything like the C. J. Taylor I remember. And should I be surprised that you don't seem to recognize me either?"

"I'm sorry," Cory answered, finally turning his eyes away. "I don't remember a lot of things these days."

"Thompson! Mack Thompson! How could you forget? You and I were enemies all through high school. I can't believe you wouldn't remember the fights. You were such a dork."

Cory snickered out loud when visions of C. J.'s costume popped into his mind. "Yes, sir, he ... I mean ... dork was my middle name."

When the officer laughed too, Zach nearly hyperventilated. "The kid had an accident and suffers with amnesia! Now, can we get this over with?"

"I tell you what," the officer continued. "Since your boy and I are old acquaintances, I'll send you off with just a warning, but only this once. Don't go speeding through my territory again without the lights and sirens. And by all means, don't be stupid enough to throw garbage out of the vehicle. That's not cool for someone in your position."

"Yes, sir. Now, will you please hand me that trash so I can get on to the station?"

The patrolman pulled the booklet out and again flashed it. "You already threw it out once. Now it's mine. I'll take care of it myself. You get yourself moving. You've got a fire to squirt, but you'd better make sure you get there within the parameters of the law."

Sweating bullets, Zach gunned the engine and tore out, leaving the officer in his dust while Cory looked back, hoping the old friend would open the booklet.

•

The officer grew suspicious when he glanced up in time to see Zach physically redirect Cory's attention to the front of the truck. Curious, the officer quickly flipped through the pages of the booklet, wondering what about it could have made both Taylors act so weird. What was in the book that C. J. so desperately wanted him to see?

Cory's hope was immediately answered when the officer came to the torn picture, smoothed out the rough edges, and instantly recognized the face. Suddenly, the muddy water began to clear, and he picked up his radio's mic and thumbed the call button.

Chapter 20

At the station, the Christmas rush was on. Throughout the night, there had been one tragedy after another. Faulty Christmas lights, poor fireplace ventilation. You name it, the firefighters encountered it.

It was still early that Friday morning. Many of the A-shift crew had not yet trickled in to relieve the obviously exhausted C-shift crew. The C-shifter's faces were smudged with soot. Their uniforms were covered in dirt and reeked with smoke and sweat. It seemed perfectly typical. However, as he headed for his usual corner, Cory couldn't help but notice that the atmosphere of the station had taken on an eerie silence. While a couple of the men made wise use of the showers, those left held themselves back from Cory, whispering and staring at him with contempt.

Feeling confused and momentarily too chicken to ask, Cory shied away from their stares and impatiently tapped away the minutes on the arm of the recliner, waiting for Westbrook to show up. Shane was not known for being late and would tell him everything. But six o'clock came and six o'clock went. The whole of C-shift was gone now, on their way home, leaving the whispering and staring to A-shift. But Shane still had not yet clocked in.

Angry and unnerved by the stares, Cory jumped to his feet and rushed to Taylor's office door. What had once been a distinguished glass office door was instantly reduced to a flimsy aluminum frame and a massive pile of glass shards.

"Where is Westbrook?" Cory hollered.

Behind the desk, Taylor's empty chair sat spinning. Taylor was nowhere in sight. When Cory came around the desk and looked underneath it, Zach slowly crept out from under it and whined, "That was *stupid!* You scared the life out of me!"

Outside the shattered door, the whole of A-shift had gathered and stood gawking at Cory's mess. But their gawking didn't phase Cory one bit. He snatched Taylor up by his shirt collar and yelled, "*Answer* me! Where's Westbrook?"

Zach managed to break free of Cory's grip, shove him into the corner, and drop himself down into his chair. "Maybe Westbrook just got tired of looking at your ugly mug and finally put in for the transfer he requested years ago. You're stuck on inspection detail with Frank and Jason."

Outside, Frank's harsh voice startled the whole of the A-shift crew. "*What?* That ain't happenin'! I ain't no *babysitter* … especially to *that* freak!" But what they hadn't seen was when Frank turned and shot an inquiring glance to Jason. Nor had they seen Jason's secretive thumbs-up response.

In the office, Cory's face turned dark red. The veins

in his neck began bulging. He got down in Zach's face and in a ferocious whisper, cried, "This is your plan, isn't it... picking them off one at a time?"

"That's up to you, isn't it?" Taylor whispered back. "How many people are you willing to risk?" The man leaned back in his chair, snatched a pen from his desk, and began twirling it in his fingers, a sickening grin spreading across his face. "There are people dependent on you, so I suggest you heed the warning. Now, get out there, and find a broom. Oh. And FYI... your little temper tantrum is gonna cost ya."

•

Out in the day room, this being his first day back after the waffle iron incident, Jason Cruz held two brooms in his hand. "C'mon, C'eej. I'll help you clean it up."

When Jason handed Cory the second broom, Cory said, "Thanks, but I can handle it."

"I know you can," Jason said as he began to sweep the glass into a pile. "But together, we'll get it done in half the time."

Cory knew deep down that Shane's strange disappearance was more than just a transfer request, and he didn't dare risk getting another soul involved. He glanced up at Cruz with vicious anger in his eyes. "I *told you* I can handle it!"

Cruz got the message and tossed his broom back into the broom closet. "Have it your way! See if I give a rip!"

It wasn't long before Cory had the glass cleaned up and had again taken his seat in the recliner when

Cruz chanced coming to him a second time. "I've got a question for you."

"Yeah? Well, answer me one first. Did Westbrook really transfer out of here?"

Jason pulled a folding metal chair over and sat down. "Gee, C'eej. Don't you remember? I missed a day."

"Guess it's a good thing that burn wasn't serious. You might have been waffled for life."

For a moment, Jason found himself glaring at the kid. "Funny, Taylor."

"Get out of my face before I—"

"Before *what?*" Jason hollered as he jumped up and knocked the chair over with a deafening clang. "Think you're big enough? Come on! Let's go outside!"

C. J. dropped his gaze. "No," he humbly admitted. "That's not what I meant."

Jason picked up the chair and dropped down into it again. "Then listen to me. The guys are saying some stuff. What happened between you and Westbrook? Did you guys get into it about something? Is that why the black eye? And was that really your face we saw on the news last night?"

Cory dropped his head into his hands and rubbed his aching temples. "Cruz, the best thing you can do is back off."

"Answer me! Was it you or not?"

When Cory looked up, he noticed all eyes were trained on him, including Taylor's soul-piercing glare. He had to choose his words very carefully. He felt he had no choice but to get mean. He snatched Jason by his shirt collar. "Back off!"

After Zach disappeared back into his office, Cory whispered in Jason's face. "This is your final warning. If you don't back off, you'll vanish the same way Westbrook did. Now, get out of my face."

When Jason managed to jerk away, he accidentally knocked over the table of books and magazines as well as the metal chair he'd been sitting in. "You're out of your mind! You're *totally* out of your mind! You need to get in touch with reality. That's what you need."

Finally sitting there in total solitude, Cory could only wish Jason was telling the truth. He thought, *Out of my mind, indeed. If only.* Losing himself in deep thought, he reached down to pick up the fallen books when something caught his attention. A Bible, its inscription indicating it was a donation to the department by the Gideons, had landed on its spine and flopped open to chapter ten of the book of Romans.

With a nervous hand and a scowl on his handsome face, Cory drew a deep, tense breath and instinctively picked up the Bible when the words of verse thirteen caught his eye. *For whosoever shall call upon the name of the Lord shall be saved.* There was something about that word, the word *whosoever*, that made his heart begin to pound. He flipped back several pages until he came to a stop at the very first verse of chapter eleven in the book of Hebrews. "*Now faith is the substance of things hoped for, the evidence of things not seen. For by it—*" When the words left a burning sensation deep within the pit of his stomach, he reared back and threw the open Bible across the room where it slammed hard against the wall, barely missing Jason's head.

Jason jumped up. "*All* I did was offer to help you clean up your mess! And *this* is the thanks I get! You gotta go and throw God's Word at me! If it's a fight you want, I dare you to step outside! I'll pound that sickeningly handsome head of yours right down into the ground!"

Of course, the rest of the men sided with Jason with their whooping and hollering.

Even as the Bible left his hand, Cory wished he could have taken it back. It was quickly becoming obvious that God might just be the only friend he had in the world, and yet he'd just thrown him out. Cory could not understand how a loving God could allow him to hurt so desperately. "Go ahead, Cruz! Make my day!"

But when Jason drew his fist back, the station alarm sounded, stopping him in his tracks. "We'll finish this when we get back!"

Cory could only hope. He longed to go and pick up the Bible. He longed to have God as a friend and not a foe. He felt desperate and clueless.

Chapter 21

Far away from the busyness of the city, deep in the heart of the Blackwater River Forest, the small wood-framed house sat hidden from the wandering eye. Surrounded by pines and scrub oaks, only the thick black billows of smoke gave away its location. By the time the fire department pulled its trucks down the narrow dirt driveway, the house had already become fully engulfed. Whatever or whoever was left inside had already been incinerated. Zach wasted no time in declaring it a total loss.

What was left of the house was a scene right out of a horror movie. The surrounding trees stood singed by the heat, leaving a black hole in the forest. The roof had caved in; the walls had collapsed into heaps of black dust. Ashes swirled upwards in a whispering breeze. Puddles of blackened water glistened like shining pits of tar where a single white body bag was being carried away. All that stood was the charred remains of what had once been a doorway to a small bedroom closet in the back.

Dressed in full bunker gear, Cory, Jason, and Frank stood back, waiting for the tanker crew to finish dousing the flames. As soon as the embers were doused, it would be their job to investigate the cause.

The hours passed. The fire was out. A trickle of smoke here and there danced in the breeze. The hoses were being stored once again into their places on the truck. Jason donned his digital camera and began snapping photos while Zach approached Frank. "It's your turn. Just make sure C. J. does his job."

Frank's brow furrowed in vicious anger. "What *is* your problem, Boss? Do I look like a *babysitter* to you?"

Taylor didn't flinch. Nor did he raise his voice. "I don't recall hearing myself asking your permission. I simply gave you an order … that's *if* you plan to keep your job. Now get on with it."

Frank must have caught a glimpse of something odd in Taylor's eye. Or he might have heard evil in his voice. Whatever it was, he backed down. "Yeah, whatever."

Cory stood back and waited. Soon he, Frank, and Jason were the only three left on the eerie scene. When he came to Frank, he said, "If you'll just tell me what to do, I'll make sure you keep your miserable job."

"Yeah? Well, I'd sure call babysitting a *miserable* job!" Frank hollered with a scowl on his face. But out of the blue, his expression changed when he momentarily cut his dark eyes toward the woods. "So, brat, do us a favor. Go lock yourself in the truck, and stay out of the way!"

It seemed like a rather ridiculous request, locking himself inside the truck, like he was going to let Frank in when it was all over. But he was the boss—temporary as it may be. So, spinning on his heel, Cory turned. "Whatever," he said, mocking the man as he made his way toward the truck.

With the doors locked, he pulled the cell phone from his pocket and dialed Westbrook's number. When again there was no answer, he dialed Keeli's number and got the same message.

Disappointed, Cory shoved the phone back down into the deepest part of his pocket, slid down into the seat, and watched Frank as he rummaged through the ashes with a long, rusty nail. Over to Frank's right, Jason carefully moved up and down between smoldering ashes, snapping random photos of what seemed like nothing. What Cory hadn't seen was when the pair occasionally cut their eyes toward the woods.

The day had been a long one. Shadows were growing long as the evening sun was beginning to set in the western sky. All of a sudden, a piece of paper inside the cab drew Cory's attention. When he saw that it contained the name and address of the homeowner, it drew his breath away. Against Frank's orders, he climbed down out of the truck and carefully made his way through the rubble. "Do I read this paper right?" he asked Frank as he was moving to another location.

Frank flew off the handle when he saw Cory standing there. "*What* did I tell you to do? You'd better get yourself *back* inside that truck or else I'll—"

"*What* are you going to do, Frank?" Cory interrupted. "Tell my *daddy?*"

When the man had no answer, Cory continued.

"Now, answer me! Was the dead man we found here the cop called Rayford?"

"So what if it was? What's it to ya?"

Jason came over when he heard the two arguing. "Taylor, you'd better do what Frank said unless you plan to finish our scuffle right here!"

"How hard can it be to say yes or no? It's a simple question! Does this place belong to the cop called Rayford?"

"So it does! Why?"

"Either of you know a cop called Vargas?"

Frank again flew off the handle and snatched Cory by the arm. "I *told* you to lock yourself in the truck! Now *go!*" he hollered with a shove.

Jason managed to pull Frank off and looked over at Cory. "What's Vargas got to do with this?"

Straightening his shirtsleeve, Cory focused his attention on the closet door. He didn't answer Jason's question. He didn't see Frank's awkward glance toward Jason. Nor did he see him as he motioned toward the woods with his eyes and mouthed words that only a trained eye would understand.

"You plan to tell your friend his partner's dead?" Cory asked.

Frank curled his nose up, turned away, and began inspecting another section of the house. "First, Vargas ain't no friend. And second, I inspect fires, not carry bad news. That's your daddy's job, not mine. You couldn't pay me enough."

For a moment, Jason watched Cory. When Cory's attention seemed drawn to the door that was left standing, Jason asked, "What is your problem, Taylor? Why the weird questions?"

For a moment, Cory shuddered. "I don't know. Hopefully it's nothing. But—"

As he carefully made his way toward the door, something told him to pull out the cell phone and dial Shane's number one more time.

From the other side of the house, Frank hollered something incomprehensible, but Jason picked up his camera and followed Cory anyway. "Taylor, you're weird, and I'm gonna prove it to the world."

Cory seemed to take no notice of the camera's flashes as he listened to the air with an intensity Jason had yet to witness. And then without warning, he hollered something the others could not understand and violently kicked debris away from the doorway.

The camera flashed.

"What in the world is he—" Frank began to complain until Jason put down the camera and hushed him across the distance with a simple hand gesture.

From the other side of the door, they could hear the faint, muffled twittering of what sounded like a ringing cell phone.

"Cruz, are you deaf? Didn't you hear that ringing phone a few minutes ago?"

Jason acted surprised. "But I thought it was coming from a house next door."

Cory cut his wide eyes to Jason. "Are you blind too? Look around this place! There *aren't* any houses next door!"

He returned his attention to the charred door and

carefully pulled it open. And when he looked inside, his breath caught in his throat. The cell phone he held in his hand crashed to the floor, and he collapsed to his knees with a thud.

The closet was very small, not fit for sardines. And it was very black inside; the purest sunlight could not penetrate its darkness. From his vantage point, Frank could distinguish nothing more than a pair of human feet. But it was enough. He lumbered over the debris and punched Cory hard on his shoulder, throwing his hands up in the air. "I *told* you, you were a *curse!* I *told* you to *stay* in the—" He turned and headed for the truck, muttering something about death all the way.

When Jason donned a flashlight and shined it in, he too fell to his knees. Stunned out of his mind, he became exasperated. "But … how?" His eyes nearly bugged out of his head. His hands shook when he turned Cory's face to him. "The people on the news last night. They were right, weren't they?" Cory felt sick. He could feel the color as it washed from his face. He knelt there in shock; unable to speak … unable to breathe … unable to see through the clouds forming over his sapphire eyes.

From the side of the truck, Frank hollered, "Cruz! How many?"

Jason nearly choked on his own spit. Again, he shined the flashlight into the closet. "Uh." He coughed. "Uh … three."

Cory cut his eyes up to Jason. "Cruz … tell me this is just another nightmare. Tell me … this *isn't* real. And don't you dare lie to me."

A moment later, Frank returned carrying two blankets and three white body bags. He hadn't heard the conversation. And he still hadn't seen inside the closet. When he threw the blankets and body bags down onto Cory's lap, he pointed with his arm and said in his booming voice, "Your daddy told me to make sure you do what you're told, so make your worthless self useful! Get over there and spread these things out on the ground."

One glance at the body bags was all it took. Cory jumped to his feet, threw the bags and blankets back in Frank's face, and then turned tail and ran like the wind.

He didn't get far. In a moment, Jason tackled him to the ground and jumped on his back. "Oh no you don't, buster! You ain't goin' anywhere!"

Spitting dirt, Cory hollered, "Get off!"

Jason managed to flip Cory onto his back and held his arms down under his knees while Frank duct-taped his ankles together. "We're not going anywhere! And if you know what's good for you, you'll keep your mouth shut!" Jason said in a harsh whisper.

"Why didn't I pay closer attention? You creeps are—"

Before Cory could say another word, Jason had unwrapped a piece of candy, shoved it into Cory's mouth, and then slapped his hand down over it. "Hope you like real chewy toffee. Frank, bring that tape up here."

In a split second, Frank came and stuck a piece of duct tape over Cory's mouth. "Enjoy the candy, brat."

Cory had felt powerless against Frank alone. A six-foot-four, three hundred-pound mass of pure muscle, his mere size had been intimidating. But with the two of them together, he didn't have a prayer. He fought as hard as he could, kicking and squirming. Before he knew it, his arms had been crossed in front of his stomach and his upper torso had been completely wrapped in duct-tape. It made breathing rather difficult. His only choice was to give in, to stop fighting them. He felt the battle was over, and he'd lost.

After Frank and Jason had muscled their helpless catch into the cab of their fire truck and locked him in, they went on about the business of removing the bodies from the closet, leaving Cory alone to watch through the windshield.

There was no mistaking the victims' identities. Although covered in a heavy blanket of soot, Shane's body was easy to recognize. And Cory had learned enough about the real C. J. Taylor that recognizing his body had proven unmistakable. But when Cory recognized Keeli's lifeless form and her long, dark hair, his emotions finally overwhelmed him and he collapsed over onto the seat.

Chapter 22

Back in town, news of the quadruple murder-by-fire had not yet reached the police department. Sitting in front of a computer screen, Deanna typed feverishly while Police Chief Gil Donavon and Highway Patrolman Mack Thompson huddled around her. In his hand, Chief Donavon held the results of Cory's DNA and fingerprint analysis.

Likewise, Patrolman Thompson held the CD booklet.

As she typed, Deanna said, "Shane's been suspicious ever since this kid first turned up here. And then C. J., or should I say Cory, himself came in requesting this analysis be done. I just don't understand why this computer didn't—wait a minute!" Deanna interrupted herself when suddenly, her cursor brushed across the icon in the bottom corner of the screen and a message flashed up. "Check out this date of record modification!" It read December second.

"We've got to find them," the chief said in a flurry of motion.

"Fire department," Patrolman Thompson offered. "I caught them speeding this morning. That's how I came upon this—"

Thompson was interrupted when all of a sudden, a fair-faced, blond heartthrob who could not have been any older than eighteen years of age appeared at the desk. He stood there alone, obviously in some distress. "Hi. My name is—"

Deanna stood to her feet, shook his outstretched hand, and hushed him. "Honey, you need no introduction. You're Brandon Richardson, aren't you?"

For a long, silent moment, he studied their faces: that stern law enforcement glance, that convicting glare. But his heart leapt into his throat. "Judging by the looks on your faces, I take it I'm in the right place."

Deanna chewed on her bottom lip and slowly nodded her head. "Yes, sir, you are. Have a seat. We need to talk."

•

It seemed like only a moment had passed when Cory felt himself being lifted up. When he opened his eyes, he looked down only to find his body caked with red clay. The candy had long since dissolved, and Frank and Jason were pulling him from the truck with Jason at his feet. When he looked up, he recognized the ceiling of the engine bay. Powerless, he laid his head back against Frank's shoulder and forced himself to take slow, deep breaths. He felt groggy and helpless. His head was splitting, and the overhead lights weren't doing him any favors.

When they came inside the day room, a tremendous gut-rolling laughter broke out from the rest of the crew. Zach stood in his office doorway, leaned against the doorjamb, and after he found himself snickering, said, "Well, that answers my question."

Frank glanced over at Taylor with a look of deep disdain in his eyes. "Boss man, the way I see it, you got two choices. He can either join our janitorial company, or I hear they's lookin' for cashiers down at the grocery store." He spoke with a lazy lisp in a mocking tone of voice. "Either way, he's o-fic-i-a-lly off my crew," he said, dividing the word into five syllables. "Now, your kid here, he needs his-self a shower. Guess that's a bit obvious. So, we gonna take him in and make sure he gets that shower. Then he's all yours."

With a grin on his face, Zach threw his hands up into the air. "Have at it!"

•

In the shower room, Frank and Jason carefully laid their catch onto the cold tile floor of a single shower stall. While Jason busied himself slowly ripping the tape from Cory's ankles, Frank knelt down beside him, pulled a switchblade from his pocket, and snapped it open. While Cory kept a wary eye on the shiny blade of the knife, Frank leaned over, held his hand over the top of the tape that covered his mouth, and whispered in his ear, "Number one, it's absolutely imperative you keep your mouth shut."

Stunned, Cory flinched as Frank ripped the piece of tape from his mouth. "Why are you doing this to me?" he asked in a hoarse whisper.

Frank again slapped his hand down over the boy's mouth. "I *just* told you to keep it shut!"

Cory nodded.

"Number two, innocents are being slaughtered because of you," Frank continued under his breath, "and there's no guarantee you yourself will survive." He picked up the knife and began cutting through the tape that was wrapped around Cory's body.

"Number three, the way I see it, you haven't got many friends left. So, about all that really matters to you right now would be the lives of the three younger Taylors. Am I not right?"

Cory hadn't yet been with it enough to give the situation much thought. Something in the candy knocked him for a loop. But as his mind slowly began to clear, he realized that if there was anyone left worth fighting for, it would be the children. Suddenly, he remembered Bo's mentioning the surprise party, and that they would be arriving soon. He tried to jerk himself away. "If you touch one single hair—"

Again, Frank covered Cory's mouth. "Sounds like a request. Ain't that what you hearin', Cruz?" He picked up his lazy accent again.

Jason came over and glanced down into Cory's tired eyes. "Yep. That's what I'm hearin'."

"Now, do what I say or the tape stays."

After Cory sighed, he again nodded.

"Westbrook, the girl, they were your friends," Frank said under his breath as he began peeling off the tape one strip at a time. "They're dead. And you best begin prayin' because, like I already said, there ain't no guarantee you gonna keep on survivin'. And it's for sure them kids could use the prayer."

As soon as his right arm was freed, Cory bolted like lightning after Frank's jugular. "If you go anywhere near those children, I'll—"

Frank fell backwards onto the floor trying to catch his breath when Jason dodged for Cory's arm and pulled him off. "Mr. Richardson, we need your help!" Jason barked in Cory's ear.

"*Help?* What are you? *Crazy?* Wait. What did you just call me?"

With his hand wrapped loosely around Cory's jaw, Jason looked him dead in the eye. "Yes, Cory, we know who you are," he said in a low whisper. "And you should be able to remember soon. The candy I stuffed in your mouth was laced with the antidote to the Triptazine, the drug she's been doping you with."

Stunned out of his mind, Cory pulled away, pushed himself toward the back of the shower stall, and tried to rub the tension out of the back of his neck. "You *knew?* All this time, you knew?"

Jason continued. "Ain't none of us illiterate. We all read the newspapers. We're here to help free you. But the Taylor kids are also in danger." He finished pulling the tape off and then stood to his feet. "One last message. That forgiveness thing, it ain't no joke. God don't mess around. Either you got it or you don't. And if you don't, it's for sure your nightmare is only just beginning." His whispers had grown louder and louder until he had removed all of the tape and rolled it into a ball. He glanced down and tapped the face of his watch. "You got fifteen minutes, and you best use 'em wisely."

Oh no! The party! "But, the children. They'll be—"

"Yes. They'll be arriving soon. Fifteen minutes. Use them."

After Frank finally recovered and made it to his feet, he hollered in his usual booming voice. "Cheer up, kid! I'll make sure you get that application from the grocery, even if I gotta go get it myself!" And then he spun the cold water faucet on full blast and laughed hard and loud as he turned and followed Jason out of the room.

Chapter 23

The sunlight had gone for the day when the inspection team returned to the station. The bodies had already been transported to the county morgue. The inspection report had already been completed … minus one slightly minute detail: the identities of the three surprise victims.

In Zach's office, standing with their arms crossed, Frank and Jason waited while Zach fiddled with the report. He looked up at Frank with expectation in his eyes. "If you've got something to say about that worthless kid of mine, just save it. I'm not interested."

"Yeah? Well, if I were you, I'd quit worryin' 'bout that kid and begin worryin' 'bout yourself."

Taylor slammed the report down onto the desk and jumped to his feet. "*Me?* What's your beef with *me?*"

Frank snatched the report from the desk and shoved it into Taylor's hands. "Read it!"

Taylor glared at the man with contempt and then shifted his eyes to the paper. "*Bodies?*" he hollered after several silent but very tense moments. "You found bodies?"

Frank returned Zach's convicting glare. "You and your crew missed 'em, and we sure would like to know how you did that."

Suddenly, the color washed from Zach's face. "Who were they?"

"Now, boss, you know we don't know that!" Frank lied. "They was all burned up clear beyond reca'nition! You want that info, call the morgue yourself!"

With Jason on his heels, Frank turned and pulled the brand new glass door open. But before he walked through it, he turned back and said, "I hear they's lookin' for cashiers down at the grocers. I'll be pickin' ya up a couple applications."

Jason snickered to himself as he nudged Frank out the door.

•

Meanwhile, back in the shower stall, the blast of cold water sent Cory into a frenzy. It wasn't until he managed to roll himself out of the stall and onto the floor that he realized just how weak he'd become. While the headache was finally beginning to subside, the heartache was not. Stunned out of his mind, he changed the water over to warm, kicked his shoes off, and sat down on the floor of the stall under the spray, fully clothed. He felt dazed. Did he dare trust the pair of renegades who called themselves firemen? Did he have a choice? He'd already given up twice, but somehow a miserable blast of cold water managed to shock him back to a very unwelcome reality.

Deeply entrenched in a longing he'd never known,

he doused his head with shampoo and let the warm water wash the soap and the chill down the drain. Convinced he was losing his mind, his heart of stone suddenly and completely crumbled to powder. And in a moment of blind desperation, he turned his face up into the warm spray of water and cried, "I can't do this, God! I can't do this! I'm scared out of my mind and I don't understand why you would let Shane, Keeli, and the real C. J. burn to death when *I'm* the one who doesn't deserve to live!" He buried his face in his hands and allowed a flood of unexpected tears to pour from his eyes and mingle with the water as it swirled down around the drain. "I'm no good, Lord, and I've hated you without a reason. But … I can finally see that it's *my* fault! *Me! I'm* the one to blame! Not you! And now people are dying because I'm a miserable sinner. God, please, I'm begging you, forgive me, help me free the children, and get me out of this place so I can come up there with you and so I can be with my friends again. Please, God. I believe Jesus died for me, too. I believe. I beg you, Lord, change my name to Whosoever and take over. It's all yours. It's *all* yours. Everything I have, everything I am—I just want to go home."

Cory became amazed when all of a sudden, the empty place deep inside his chest had suddenly been filled. He turned his reddened eyes upwards and breathed a heavy sigh when an unmistakable feeling of peace came splashing down and showered him with a sensation of warmth so rich, it was as though his heavenly Father himself had come to wrap him in a heavy fleece blanket on a cold winter's night.

Everything Shane, Bo, and yes, even Frank had told him about the Lord suddenly became perfectly clear, and for all the abundance of words he could have hollered at that moment, all he could manage was a soft whisper. "Wow."

It was a moment he could bask in forever—until a loud knock on the door startled him.

"C. J., Dad said to hurry up!" Even through the door and over the running water, Cory could sense anguish in Bo's voice.

The party! Lord God, I can't let any more ... we *can't let any more innocents die! I* have *to save the children! But I know, God, that I can't do anything to help them unless you lead the way. Please, Lord—please get us out of this place.* Cory silently pleaded as he snatched a bath towel and came barreling, soaking wet, out of the shower room and into a crowd singing "Happy Birthday." Although the song sounded half-hearted and off-key, it was being sung to him. The rest of the crew must have seen it as a small price to pay for a free dinner. On the table sat a huge sheet cake with twenty-two brightly burning candles. Over to the side, there were tubs of ice cream and boxes of delivery pizza stacked ten deep.

Cory wrapped the towel around his shoulders and stood stunned. He looked down at himself and snickered. Water—dripping from the ends of his hair, from his elbows, from his shirttails, and from the bottoms of his pant legs—created puddles down around his bare feet. His toes curled under against the coldness of the concrete floor.

Although he did his best to appear surprised, the tables were turned when, from behind the crew, out stepped Samantha, LaKeisha, and Purl—the three nurses from the children's hospital. A million thoughts ran through his mind, and he could feel an internal dagger stabbing at his heart when he saw the beautiful blonde Samantha.

Purl bounded over to him and gently punched him on the shoulder. "Boy, what you been doin' bathin' in 'yo clothes?"

When Cory looked down at himself, his face turned pure red, and his lips curled into a tight grin. When Julia and Dylan came squealing to his side and wrapped their arms tightly around his water-logged waist, his heart melted. The little girl turned her face up and looked into his tear-filled eyes. "Happy birthday, my very favorite, and my very wettest C. J. in the whole world! I love you!"

"Me, too!" Dylan added.

Cory knelt down, wrapped his wet arms around their necks, and hugged them both back. "I love you both more than you'll ever know." Even Cory was surprised at the honesty he felt.

When Roxanne saw that her son was soaked to the skin, she ran to him, flailing her arms and trying to pull the children off of him. "*Cor* ... uh ... I mean—"

It was a simple mistake, but a mistake of monumental proportions. When she stumbled over her words, the room suddenly took on an eerie silence.

"Carson Junior, what are you doing standing there soaking wet?" Roxanne tried to continue as if no one had noticed. "Get in there and get changed into something dry!" she cried loudly, hoping to recover from her blunder. "What's the matter with you?"

With the children holding on tightly to his waist, Cory dried his eyes with and end of the towel, and then looked up and made eye contact with Bo. He could see anguish written all over the boy's face, and the new bruise next to his left eye sent another dagger. Their lives had been threatened, and their fear was ripping him apart.

"Uh, Mom," Cory began, trying to play on her goof, "you've been calling me *C. J.* for years. Why change my name now?" he asked with a hint of sarcasm in his voice. "I mean, it's not like I wouldn't like a name change. I mean, everything else about me has changed. Why not my name, too? Why go by plain ol' letters anyway? Carson ... Carson ... what was my middle name?"

"Zachary," answered Julia, "the same as Daddy's."

"Oh yeah. That's it. Carson Zachary Taylor, Junior. I don't see anything wrong with Carson," Cory rattled on. "I'm officially changing my name to Carson. *Or* will it be—"

"*Son,* would you knock it off?" Roxanne cried, trying her best to shut him up and change the subject. "How many times in one year do you think you can go swimming in the *wintertime* fully clothed and get away *without* catching your death from pneumonia? Where *is* your head?"

Cory shrugged his shoulders and glanced around at the rest of the crowd. "Maybe it's still in the pond ... with the others."

Roxanne made like she'd ignored his statement as she threw her arms up in defeat, a reaction he felt sure he'd never see again. "Guess there's no point in making you change into dry clothes, so sit your tail down there and eat your dinner. And don't come complaining to me when your head starts feeling all stuffed up!"

"Ah, Mom, my standing here like this gives these guys something to laugh about. In fact... it gives *me* something to laugh about," he said with a grin. "Anyway, it sure beats having them complaining. Now, how can I take that away from them?"

But the men weren't laughing, not now. Samantha wasn't laughing, and neither were LaKeisha and Purl. And their strained silence told Cory that Roxanne's blunder had gotten through.

With one eye trained on Zach and Roxanne, Cory sat himself down across the table with the children, fascinated that he was finally able to actually see God at work. His mind raced as he nibbled on a piece of pepperoni pizza. In the excitement, he hadn't noticed Frank's absence, nor had he seen him as he slipped in through the back door.

It wasn't long before the food was gone, and Bo came and sat next to Cory and the children.

When the Taylors looked away, Cory whispered to Bo, "Listen, there's an exit on the other side of the—" He nearly jumped out of his skin when out of the blue, Jason came up behind him and placed his hands on his shoulders. "When was the last time you youngins' got to visit us here? What, about a year ago? How about I take you chillin' on a tour?"

Dylan started bouncing in his seat. "Can we, Mom? Can Miss'er Jason take us on a t'er?"

When Julia dropped her gaze and said, "Mommy won't let us go on a t'er. She don't like t'ers," all eyes again became fixated on the woman.

The air in the room had again grown sickeningly tense.

Red faced, Roxanne glared down at Cory and then over to Bo. She thought hard for a moment, and to everyone's surprise, finally nodded her approval. "Okay. But only long enough for us to get our mess cleaned up. We don't want to hold these boys up any longer than we already have.

"But you, Carson Junior, you see those trucks all the time. You'll stay right here and help me clean up."

"Mom, don't you think C. J. would be the best one to show us around?" Bo asked as he momentarily cut his eyes over to Cory who in turn, shot him a reassuring glance.

"Not *this* time," the woman answered with an evil hiss.

Standing back away from the table, Samantha turned to Frank and whispered, "What is wrong with this picture?" They silently watched Jason alone pick up Julia, take Dylan by the hand, and lead Bo out into the engine bay.

While the Taylors focused their attention on the clean-up, Frank came from behind and tapped several of the crewmembers on their shoulders, shaking his finger toward the kitchen door. "Get out of the building," he commanded in a whisper.

One-by-one the men readily complied in complete silence. Only Samantha turned and looked at him like he was crazy, thankfully holding her silence as Frank led her out by her arm.

Once the others were out of the building, and the children were out of the Taylors' line of sight, Cory breathed a silent prayer of thanks while he helped pick up. "Either I'm incredibly brave or I'm incredibly stupid," he whispered under his breath as he watched Jason lead the children out past the ladder truck. He could only hope that at this point, he'd done the right thing.

Chapter 24

It took only a few minutes to pick up the garbage. Cory dragged it out as long as he could to give the others as much time as possible to get away. But when Roxanne suddenly noticed the silence, she flew into a rage. Slamming a garbage can down onto the floor, she hollered, "Where are the children?" She looked over at Cory. "What have you done with my children?"

Standing at the other end of the table, Cory looked around. Other than Zach, Roxanne, and himself, the room was empty. He glanced down at himself and held out his hands. "Mom, are you practicing for a senior moment? It looks very much to me as though I'm still standing here, right where I was the last time I looked. I haven't done anything with the children … short of praying for them, that is. *Jason* took them out to see the trucks. Don't you remember? You insisted I help you clean up, or don't you remember that either?"

Roxanne shot him the evil eye. "If anything happens to my children, you're dead meat!"

"Yeah? Do you mean like *C. J.?*"

"You're out of your mind!" the woman cried.

Cory sighed heavily and stared at the pair with

deep sadness in his eyes. He was totally helpless. He had no weapons. There was nowhere to hide, and running was sure to prove deadly. "No, ma'am, not anymore." And then he simply sat down at the table and rested his chin on his hands. "Your blunder wasn't a blunder at all, was it? My name is not Carson Junior, it's Cory Richardson. And today is not really my birthday. That's not until next October. I'm not twenty-two, I'm just barely eighteen." He then shifted his gaze to Zach. "Four bodies were pulled from that house fire today. Your friend Rayford, my friend Shane, the girl from the mall, and one Carson Zachary Taylor, *Junior,* the *real* C. J. Taylor."

"Enough!" Roxanne cried. "You're crazy!"

Cory shifted his gaze to the woman and laughed. "Why, yes ma'am, you told me that just this morning. That's why you've been forcing me to drink the poisoned hot chocolate.

"The sun has gone down outside. It's dark now. I'm sure you'll find the children having a good time out there. Maybe they're playing hide and seek."

Just then, Zach rushed into his office and came back wielding a gun and trained it between his eyes. "Do you think your mother's joking?"

All of a sudden, to Cory's bewilderment, the woman reached over and grabbed her husband's hand. "He's *still* my son!" she screamed as she struggled to wrestle the gun away from him. "*Don't you dare* hurt him!"

Out of pure instinct, Cory dove under the table and crawled toward the other end until all of a sudden the gun went off.

•

Outside the building, the Taylor children had been ushered into a waiting patrol car.

"Why didn't C. J. come with us?" Julia asked as a silent tear began to trickle down her soft, China-doll cheek.

Sitting in the backseat between the two, Bo uncharacteristically wrapped his arms around them. He knew he had to be strong for them. But how? C. J. had always been the strong one. And now Cory. Bo didn't know how to answer his little sister.

"I don't know why C. J. didn't come with us, baby girl. I don't know. But we'll wait right here for him, okay?"

The little girl seemed satisfied with Bo's answer. But then she changed her tone of voice. "Is Mommy going to make our new C. J. go away too?"

Her emotionless tone sent a chill down Bo's spine. The child was only five. How could a child as young as five appear so detached from her mother? And how could he tell her anything she would understand when he didn't know the whole story himself? "I hope not."

All of a sudden, outside the vehicle, a commotion arose and dozens of uniformed officers began scurrying toward the fire station. Bo overheard someone holler, "Shots fired!" And then he heard another yell, "Get those kids out of here!" And before he knew it, a female officer jumped into the front seat and hit the gas, whisking them out of the line of fire.

"Where are you taking us?" Bo cried. "Did somebody get shot?"

"I'm taking you someplace safe."

"Who got shot?"

"I don't know!"

"But we're waiting for Cory! We can't leave him back there!"

Sitting over on Bo's left, Dylan became puzzled. "Who's Co'y?"

On Bo's right, Julia looked over at Dylan. "Cory is our new C. J., silly."

"Oh."

Puzzled, Bo glanced down at his little sister. "How'd you know that?"

The little girl shrugged her shoulders. "I don't know."

•

Back inside the fire station, Cory remained crouched under the table while a highly agitated Zach rushed over and pressed his back against the wall near the window. He ranted and raved as he peeked out through the blinds. "I've got to get out of here!" But to his dismay, he found the building had been surrounded by police vehicles and officers who crouched behind them, readied with their guns drawn.

Across the room, sitting on the floor and leaning against a wall near Zach's office door with blood trickling from her abdomen, Roxanne was silently weeping and reaching out toward her son.

Under the table, Cory faced a grave decision. He could make a break for the door in hopes that Zach wouldn't see him in time to get off another round, or he could stay and help the woman with what little bit of first-aid knowledge he'd gained in the last twenty-one days. Either choice would more than likely prove deadly. *How do things like this happen to regular guys like me?*

Although his insides were trembling out of control, Cory crawled out from under the table and to the woman. While Zach had focused his attention on the window and to the commands being voiced through a megaphone from outside, Cory reached up and grabbed a handful of napkins from off the table and pressed them against Roxanne's wound.

To his utter shock, Roxanne reached up and gently stroked the side of his face. "So handsome," she whispered. "Just like your father."

"How would you know anything about my father?"

"I know him because . . . I am your mother, the woman who gave birth to you."

Cory didn't believe her. "You're lying to me again."

Roxanne was growing weaker as the anxious moments passed. She looked into his eyes and slowly shook her head. "No, Cory, it's true. Your father is a man by the name of Kerry Cantrella. And you are a perfect duplicate of him."

Suddenly overcome by anger, Cory whispered, "Why did you do this to me? And if you're my mother, then why did you give me up?"

"I fell in love with the man," she continued, "and wanted a part of him that would last forever. But your existence proved he was a liar and could not be trusted. Your existence caused him to lose a family fortune. He grew angry and wanted you dead." She stopped to take a breath and winced against the pain. And then she shook her head. "I refused the abortion, and for two years, I tried raising you as if nothing was wrong." Again she winced. "But he kept coming back. He kept insisting. With you out of the picture, he might regain his inheritance. So I tried to comply, and on your second birthday—"

Over on the other side of the room, Zach had begun pacing. "I've got to get out of here. Got to find a way—" All of a sudden, he rushed around the table, yanked Cory up by his neck, and pressed the barrel of the gun against his temple. "Make one wrong move and you're history."

Cory snickered. "Give me a break. What do you think I was doing in that pond last night?"

"You would be wise to keep your mouth shut!"

"I didn't go to that pond to go swimming, nor did I expect to find that ambulance or the two dead paramedics."

"I *said*, keep it shut!" Zach hollered with a swing of his fist.

"No!" Roxanne squealed from the floor. "Zachary, don't hurt him!"

For a moment, Cory reeled, nearly causing them both to fall. A drizzle of blood left thin red streaks trailing down the right side of his face. "Last night, all I wanted was to end this miserable war. But today, I gave my heart and my life over to Jesus. Now, when you kill me like you did Shane, Keeli, and C. J., I'll go to heaven with them. My friends are in heaven, the kids are in safe hands. Go ahead and finish me. Now I'm ready to go."

Cory's matter-of-fact attitude made Zach's skin crawl. "I gave that man way too much money for you!" he hollered as he dragged him to the door.

"You talking about the man in the silver beemer ... Cantrella ... my *father?* What do you plan to do? Ask him for a refund?"

"Cantrella bought a knife for a hundred grand and gave me my ticket to freedom."

Puzzled, Cory cried, "What?" All of a sudden, pieces of his nightmares were beginning to fall perfectly in order. The swinging knife blade, the flesh wound, the faceless man in the mirror. The ambulance in the pond, and the pair of dead paramedics. Finally something was beginning to make sense. "It was *him,* wasn't it? The man who cut me was my own *father.*"

"Shut it!"

"They'll gun you down."

"Not with you standing in front of me, they won't!"

"The scar!" Roxanne cried. Her voice was becoming less audible while her bleeding was becoming more profuse. Cory could barely hear her now. "Son, the scar—your brother—find him."

Those would be the last and by far the most puzzling words he would ever hear his birth mother say.

Outside, with the building surrounded by police officers holding rifles, the command was given to hold fire when Taylor came out of the door with a chokehold on a bleeding Cory. "Back off and don't follow me or I'll finish him!" Taylor hollered. Sweating bullets, he made his way to his truck and shoved Cory into the cab through the driver's door. After sliding in beside Cory, he burned rubber as he tore out of the parking lot, through downtown, and toward the interstate. Zach had only one thing on his mind: getting out of town as fast as possible.

Whipping his truck in and out of interstate traffic, Zach's wild eyes darted back and forth from the highway to the rearview. Had the police department taken his command seriously? Would he be forced to shoot his hostage in cold blood because they couldn't follow a simple command? Questions. Always questions. And as they sped along, he saw nothing out of the ordinary in the rearview; that is, nothing more out of the ordinary than a pair of headlights whipping in and out of traffic at speeds equal to his own. He thought nothing of it.

Over on the passenger side, Cory rested his wounded right temple on the palm of his hand and leaned against the door, fighting to keep himself alert. His head was throbbing, and a trickle of warm blood leaked through his fingers and down the back of his hand and wrist. He closed his eyes. "Don't you know they're going to plaster your face in every post office in the United States? Don't you realize you'll be profiled on Fox's *America's Most Wanted*... your *fifteen seconds of shame?* It won't be long before they find you and take you down. Why don't you just give it up?"

"Keep your trap shut!"

Ignoring Zach's warning, Cory asked, "You paid him to do it, didn't you? You paid Cantrella to cut me and then you sent the ambulance, not to take me to a hospital, but to bring me here where *she* could stitch me up."

Zach took another swing but missed. "

"Why don't you just tell me the truth?" Cory cried. "You're just going to kill me! What's it going to hurt if I finally know why? It's not like it's going to go anywhere else!"

"It was *her* fault! *She* did this! She lied to Cantrella!"

Amazing how fast we play the blame game when something isn't going quite right. "She told me my father wanted me dead."

"Yes, he did! But it was that big-mouth brother of yours who found out she'd just given you up for adoption and that you were alive and living in the public eye. That made her crazy! When C. J. questioned her about it, she panicked! She hired Vargas and Rayford to kill him off and then hatched a plan with Cantrella to bring you home. He would be satisfied and you could take C. J.'s place. Now, you know the whole story! Are you happy?"

All of a sudden, faces of familiar people and blessed memories of his past began invading Cory's mind, bringing a sad, albeit pleasant smile to his face. Again, he rested his head against the door. "I remember now. I remember. I told you I wasn't a fireman. I'm a pianist by profession." He laughed. "That's why she laughed at me when I asked for a piano. She didn't dare let me rediscover that talent."

Taylor kept his eyes focused between the road ahead and the rearview mirror. Still nothing out of the ordinary was going on ... no blue lights, no sirens, nothing but the same set of headlights keeping the same pace about a quarter mile back.

Cory knew that his only chance at life at this point would be to get Taylor driven over the edge and bring it all to an end. It wouldn't take much more. "Chief, do you believe in God?" he asked when the thought occurred to him.

"If you plan on praying, you'd better be praying to *me! I'm* the god in control of your life now!"

Cory snickered under his breath and opened his eyes. Up ahead, he noticed the well-lit, two and a half-mile long bridge spanning Escambia Bay. And just as they entered the westbound span of the bridge, he breathed a silent prayer, and then looked out over the moonlight glimmers off the green-gray water. "You know, Chief, this truck can only reach as far as the bottom of the—"

All of a sudden, the truck began to lurch and lose power. Zach pumped hard on the gas pedal all the while yelling obscenities. But to no avail. He managed to pull it off into the narrow emergency lane just as the vehicle coughed its last time and gave up the ghost.

Angry, Zach hollered, "You asked your God to do that, didn't you?"

Cory looked forward. So much of the bridge lay

ahead before they would reach the Pensacola city limits. He looked back and saw that they'd already come so far that the end of the bridge disappeared into the night. With a gun-wielding assailant directly on his heels, it would be much too far and much too dangerous to try to run back. The way he saw it, there was only one way out. He took hold of the door handle and turned to Zach. "In a word ... yes," then was out of the door and over the guardrail in a flash, all the while hearing what sounded like a popgun shooting off in rapid fire succession.

Chapter 25

Carson Zachary Taylor, Senior, was not the most intelligent cookie in the cookie jar. No, he'd made many mistakes in his life, mistakes that would include kicking God completely out of his life and marrying a Jezebel. Mistakes that would include hiring crooked cops to murder his own flesh and blood. And mistakes that would include kidnapping, not just the average kid from the house next door but a musician—a well-known, most deliciously handsome, unattached bachelor with thousands of adoring and perhaps a bit overprotective fans. Zach might as well have snatched Cory from center stage.

Yes, Zach Taylor had made many a bad decision throughout the years, but none would prove as minute or as devastating as slinging open his driver's door and stepping down out of his truck directly into the path of an oncoming tractor-trailer.

•

Down in the very cold water, with his arms tightly wrapped around one of the bridge's support legs, Cory leaned his aching, bleeding head against the support and closed his eyes. His body temperature was dropping quickly, and he shivered unmercifully. His breathing was quickly becoming difficult. From above, he could hear the whine of tire after tire as they crossed the massive bridge, and he could feel the vibration through the support. The drone might have lulled him to a deadly sleep, but all of a sudden the world above him exploded in a flurry of screeching tires, honking horns, and crunching metal. Glass rained down into the water as though it was salt falling from a shaker.

Cory slowly lifted his head. "God ... p-p-please ... don't let ... any-body else—" But his plea was interrupted when off in the distance, he thought he heard someone calling his name—his real name.

"Cory! Where are you?"

Hearing his real name gave him hope. He strained his eyes to peer through the darkness, hoping to find the voice. "Here ... I'm r-r-right here." Cory heard himself speaking, but it came out of him as barely a whisper. "T-T-Tired ... too t-t-tired."

"I can't see you!" the voice cried. "Do something! Make some noise so I can hear you!"

Under the surface of the water, green moss had grown on each of the bridge supports, making them dangerously slippery. Cory didn't dare let go for fear of losing what little grip he had, slipping under, and not being able to bring himself up again. He'd grown much too weak.

"Come on, Bubba! It's Brandon! I've come to take you home! Show me where you are!" the voice hollered.

Raspy and broken, even Cory's voice was succumbing to the cold. "T-T-Too ... t-t-tired." The words were inside of his head but were unable to reach his vocal cords. Again, he leaned his head against the support and shut his eyes. The water no longer felt cold or threatening. He felt himself slipping under. "J-J-Jesus ... I'm r-r-ready," he whispered just as he released his grip.

Chapter 26

Christmas Day, early evening

Filling a corner of the living room, a huge Christmas tree reached up and tickled the ceiling. It had been decorated in a most non-traditional fashion: white lights, homemade bows, and matching ribbon garland. And rather than the traditional ornaments, the tree was filled with a myriad of artificial poinsettias and red berry sprays. The fake poinsettias boasted a display of non-traditional colors, from blues and purples to golds, silvers, and pinks. But the flowers that drew the most attention were the burgundy ones. Year after year, Rhea Richardson had fashioned them into a cross formation on the front of the tree and used berry sprays to mimic droplets of blood that pooled at the foot of the cross.

The poinsettia cross had become a conversation piece, a real favorite—not an expectation, but somehow perfectly suited to the home of a Southern Baptist pastor and his family. But while the floral cross had become a favorite to most of those who laid eyes on it, it wasn't suited to everyone. Year after year, Cory would voice his personal opinion. "Crosses are Easter things, aren't they? Whatever happened to Santa Clause and Rudolph? Where's the sleigh, the candy canes, and the ornaments?"

This year, there would be no complaining. This year, the house had fallen sadly silent… other than whispers from the kitchen.

"Don't you remember," Jackie Richardson began in his lowest voice, "the doctor said he'd struggle with some depression. He's been through a lot."

"I know, but—"

Around the corner, in the living room, Brandon sat in the glider/rocker simply watching his brother.

Across the room, sitting on the edge of the couch with an official-looking piece of paper in his hand, Cory stared up at the poinsettia cross. His left eye had turned dark purple, and his right temple had been covered with a white bandage. Yes, he had been through a lot. How he survived, he might never know. He took in a deep breath. The air in the house smelled wonderfully delicious… of turkey and ham, sweet potatoes, and dinner rolls. And he felt certain he could distinguish the scent of his mother's homemade apple pie. But it seemed totally unfair, and he couldn't shake the feelings of guilt.

Cory half smiled when he overheard his parents' conversation. "Mom, I just need some time to sort it all out. I'm really… don't worry so much, okay?" he said loud enough to be heard in the kitchen.

Drying her hands on a towel, Rhea, a petite size six, came in from the kitchen and sat down next to her son. She wrapped her arm around him. "Honey, I know you went through a lot, but do you think it was easy for the rest of us?"

For a moment, Cory looked deep into her tearful green eyes. He could see the desperation his assault and kidnapping had brought to her. But he could also sense the joy his return had brought. He brushed back a lock of her blonde hair, wrapped his arms around her, and held her tightly. "No, ma'am. I know it couldn't have been easy for you either."

Just then, Jackie, a tall and slender man with dark hair and dark eyes, came in, patted his boy on the back, and then sat down on the loveseat.

Rhea sniffled the tears back and straightened her back. "But you're home now, and we're not going to lose you again. Your being home is the best Christmas present anyone could have given us. This will be a Christmas we'll never forget."

It seemed like forever as the complete family sat in the darkened living room and watched the tree lights flicker. But it was only a moment later when Cory said, "She told me she was my birth mother, but I just couldn't bring myself to believe her."

"What does that certificate say?" Brandon asked.

Cory laid the paper down on the coffee table and sighed. "It says—that was the only thing she said to me that was actually true. She was my mother and that Cantrella guy was my father. But it was the last thing she said to me, the last thing she said before she died, that really has me puzzled."

"What was that?" Rhea asked.

"She mentioned the scar on my side. She said

something about a brother, and told me to find him." And then Cory turned to his father. "Dad, you're a pastor. Maybe you can help me understand."

"What is it you don't understand?" his father asked.

"I don't understand why so many innocent people had to die when I should have been the one. *I* was the one who wasn't too keen on trusting in Jesus at the time. It would have been the perfect opportunity for him to wipe me out! So why did he take them and not me?"

All of a sudden, the doorbell interrupted him.

Rhea hopped to her feet, turned, and peered out through the living room window. "Our guests have arrived. Cory, will you do us the honor of answering the door?"

That was something else he didn't understand. She acted as though she hadn't heard a word. But without a complaint, Cory went and opened the door to a crowd of people, flashing cameras, and Christmas carols.

It was dark outside. The air felt chilly. Although the porch light was on, all Cory could see were spots made by the flashing cameras. He couldn't make out their faces. Yet, the simple music brought a sad smile to his handsome face. But when the two smallest members of the crowd came running up to him and wrapped him in hugs, he was taken by total surprise.

"Hi, my favorite Cory in the *whole* world! I brought you a Christmas present," little Julia Taylor whispered as she handed him a small gift.

"Me, too! Me, too!" Dylan cried.

With a host of tears streaming down his face, Cory knelt down and hugged the children back. "I didn't need a gift. All I needed ... was to see you both again, and to know you're okay."

"We're fine!" Julia answered. "Your *real* mommy and daddy invited us to eat Christmas dinner with you tonight. Is that okay with you?"

Cory turned and found his parents and his brother had come and gathered around behind him. And when he glanced up at his teary-eyed mother with a smile on his face and a sparkle in his eye, he felt too choked up to answer.

Rhea took the children by their hands, and said, "Yes, sweetheart, it's okay with him. And do you know how I know that?"

"No, ma'am," Julia answered.

"Do you see that handsome smile on his face?"

The children turned and looked at Cory again. "Yes, ma'am."

"That's all the proof I need," Rhea answered. And then she invited all the others in as well.

Cory was stunned when he saw the people who made up the crowd; Samantha, LaKeisha, and Purl who were flanked by Bo and then the members of his band, Spirit of Peace.

With tears, Cory gave each of the ladies a hug. But when it came Samantha's turn, he whispered, "Now do you understand? I'm not the guy you thought you fell in love with."

"Oh, honey, if only you knew—" the gorgeous blonde said with a silly wide-eyed grin.

Confused, Cory looked strangely at her as if to ask, but he was interrupted by those who came up next in line. Jason Cruz shook Cory's hand and went on inside, but Frank White stopped and handed Cory a piece of candy and a roll of duct tape. "Merry Christmas!" he cried.

Immediately, visions began to dance in Cory's head, visions of the burned trio in the closet, and his expression changed once again. Time may heal wounds, but no one has ever said how much time it takes. For Cory, it had only been forty-eight hours—nowhere near long enough. This one might never heal. Trying to be polite, Cory handed the tape and the candy back to Frank. "I'm not ready to laugh about this yet."

"Then let me ask you a question. What do you think would have happened had Vargas seen any of the three of them just get up and walk out of that closet?"

Cory sighed. "If you're trying to make this into a God-thing, forget it. I just don't think he'd be that cruel."

"Then, answer my question."

"Vargas *wasn't* there, Frank!"

Curious, the big man leaned against the wall, crossed his ankles, crossed his arms, and studied Cory's emotional reaction. The boy again had tears building in his eyes.

"You're trained to keep your emotions separate from your job," Cory said. "It's got to be that way. But how do you keep from falling apart when it's a friend? Or don't you have any friends?"

The house had once again grown strangely quiet and tense. Everyone else was listening intently.

To everyone's surprise, Frank pulled a wallet-like case from his back pocket, flipped it open, and came and showed it to Cory. "The name's Gabe Winstead. My bud here," he pointed to Jason, "is Jose Gonzalez. We're police officers, undercover."

Confused, Cory said, "I don't get it."

"Well then, let me explain. Zach and Roxanne Taylor, Billy Rayford, and Al Vargas have a history. Money laundering, murder for hire—and added to that, assault and kidnapping. They've been under surveillance for a while now. The Taylors called the shots. Rayford and Vargas provided the muscle."

"How long?"

"Months. But it wasn't until you showed up on the scene that we were able to confirm our suspicions."

"You *knew* from the beginning that I wasn't C. J. Taylor?"

Gabe nodded with a strange smirk on his face. "*Everybody* knew you weren't C. J. Taylor! What'd you think we were? Morons? Nevermind! Don't answer that."

Cory's face flushed a deep red. "What took you guys so long to get them stopped and thrown in jail? Shane, Keeli, and the real C. J. might have had a chance had you guys stopped them before it got that far!"

"Proof is everything, and sometimes evidence comes at a cost. But your safety, and the safety of the other Taylor children, became paramount."

Cory understood that. The safety and well being of the children had been his own concern. "But that doesn't mean Vargas was at that house when it burned!"

"How quickly you forget. The other morning, on your way in to the station, Taylor confirmed your suspicions about your not being who they said you were. Once you got there, he contacted Vargas by cell and gave him the order. Vargas was not only on the scene, he *started* the fire and then hid in the woods—complete with binoculars and a high-powered rifle, waiting for you to arrive."

Cory sat down on the floor and rubbed his aching temples. "Why?"

Frank sat down on the floor across from him. "We knew Vargas intended to finish the job. So when you ran, we had no choice but to stop you before you could get within range of his rifle. That's why the tape.

"And as for the candy, it was laced with the antidote to the Triptazine. That's why we shoved it in your mouth and then taped your mouth shut. You couldn't spit it out. It also made you a bit groggy—that's why the blast of cold water."

For a moment, Cory lost himself in thought. "I guess that would explain how I suddenly seem to be able to remember everything. But ... I just wish that Shane and Keeli, and the real C. J. Taylor ... they were good Christian people! They cared enough about me ... they didn't deserve to *die* for trying to help me! They didn't have to *die* to prove to me who Jesus was. And they didn't have to *die* so that *I* could be saved.

How can my one miserable life be worth all three of theirs?"

Gabe stood to his feet and helped Cory up. "Cheer up, Hollyweird. This story's not over. You still haven't answered my question."

Cory's face had turned an even darker red. His distress brought tears to the eyes of the others, but they held their peace. "I guess ... *if* any of the three of them had been able to get up and walk out of that burned out closet, Vargas probably would have shot them down."

"That's it. That's the answer. He would have shot us all down, you, me, Jose ... the casualty count would have continued to increase. However—"

Confused, Cory said, "However, *what?*"

"Just remember this one thing. I told you we'd been on this case a while—a long while. Don't forget that."

Just then, the doorbell rang again. When Cory opened the door, on the porch stood Officer Deanna Clark, holding the small black-and-white puppy Shane had brought home from the pet store. She handed it over to Cory.

"Is this—" Cory couldn't finish his question. The very sight of the puppy brought too much pain to his heart ... pain that Deanna could sense."

With a smile on her pretty face, Deanna said, "Shane Westbrook was a good man. He left us gifts. The puppy's name is Shelly. But Cory, there's more. Jesus rose from the grave on the third day. And for Shane, Keeli McKenzie, and C. J. Taylor, today would be the third day." And then she moved back away from the door.

When Cory looked up, he stumbled backwards into a wall and dropped to his knees. Shane, Keeli, and C. J. stood on the porch, fresh from the grave, and waiting to be invited in. "*No way!*" Cory hollered. "But ... *how?*"

With huge smiles on their faces, the trio came up to the door. Shane said, "Aren't you going to ask us in?"

Stunned, Cory stared wide-eyed at his friends. He couldn't believe it. Keeli was even more beautiful than he remembered. "But ... I don't get it! *How?* I mean ... you were all like ... *dead!* Like ... *real* dead! I saw your bodies ... all burned up! That house had been totally gutted ... burned to the ground! There's no way anyone would have been able to survive the inferno."

Frank came over and looked Cory in the eye. "Remember what I said. We'd been on it a while. Rag-filled pillowcases, wigs, it don't take a lot of effort to make homemade dummies."

"I can explain it like this," the soft-spoken Keeli began as she came in and wrapped her arms around his. "It all happened several years ago, back in the days of Daniel. In Daniel, chapter three, it says—"

Epilogue

Cory's question haunted everyone's mind. *Why?*

Sitting amongst the crowd, C. J. felt humbled. Not dressed in his usual costume, he wore a shirt and tie. His face was not covered in black paint. He was washed and clean shaven. His hair was not spiked. Rather, others envied the perfect natural wave that made it lay in soft, natural feathers on either side of his head. He and Cory looked so very much alike that the question reared its ugly head over and over again.

Holding tightly onto Samantha's hand, C. J. brought his gaze up from the floor and looked into the faces that surrounded him. He sighed heavily. "I have to take the blame."

Sitting on the floor over in front of the Christmas tree with Keeli sitting next to him, Cory looked up at C. J. and said, "In the last twenty-one days, I probably learned more about you than you knew about yourself. None of this was *your* fault."

"Hear me out … please."

"Okay."

C. J. again sighed heavily. His mind seemed to disappear momentarily. "I suppose that when a child is traumatized, they never forget. I can still remember the incident as though it happened only yesterday.

"It was your second birthday. Cantrella had been there again … made her cry as usual. After he left that day, she rushed in, drew a bathtub full of water, and then snatched you up from a perfectly good nap and sat you down in the middle of the tub … clothes and all. It's still so vivid in my memory that I can still remember the denim overalls you were wearing. There was a picture of a train on the front."

C. J. paused. The memory had been difficult for him.

"When she shoved your head under the water and held you down, I knew I had to stop her. I hit and hit. I screamed, hollered, and kicked until she finally pulled you up out of the water, wrapped you in a towel, and ran out of the house with you in her arms." Again, he was forced to catch his breath.

"Dad was on duty that day. I was left at home all alone. Mom had been gone for hours, but in my five-year-old mind, it might as well have been days."

Overwhelmed, tears filled his pale-blue eyes. "I never saw you again. And she never talked about you again. I grew terrified of her, my own mother, because I became convinced she'd taken you out and buried you in the woods somewhere. I just knew you were dead. And I honestly believed she would do the same thing to me.

"But Cantrella stopped badgering her. He didn't come around much after that. He didn't call. And then years later, Bo came along. And then Dylan and finally Julia. I was afraid for myself… but I was more afraid for them. That's why the costume. That's why the posters. That's why the trips to the children's hospital in Pensacola. I was much too young to help you back then, but I determined then that I wouldn't let it happen to another innocent child."

By now, there was not a single dry eye in the

house. Samantha took C. J.'s arm in hers and held him tight.

"It was by accident that I finally learned the truth when one day, I picked up your CD and found your face on the inside. I was thrilled when I learned that she hadn't killed you after all but that she'd given you up for adoption. And I was thrilled when I found that you'd become famous, playing the type of music I love the most. I became so blown away that I finally confronted her about the drowning, or what I thought had been a drowning. She became enraged, not only that I brought it up, but more so because you'd become famous. Maybe it was because if Cantrella found out that you were still alive—man, if only I'd kept my mouth shut! I'm sorry! I'm really—"

Cory hushed him with a wave of his hand. "No, C. J., don't apologize to me because," with a tear trickling down his cheek, he stood to his feet, and reached up to touch the velvety petals of the burgundy poinsettias, "if you hadn't opened your mouth, I might never have understood Mom's reason for putting this blood red poinsettia cross on the Christmas tree. I now fully understand that Jesus willingly gave up his throne in heaven to become a man. He was born on this earth ... born of a virgin ... only to willingly sacrifice his life on a cruel and bloody cross ... for us." He then turned and glanced at his teary-eyed father. "He did it for me.

"Even after hearing it a thousand times, you might have thought that the words of our music and the testimonies of our band members would have smacked me like a flying 2x4, or like the proverbial ton of bricks. But I'm a little slow. I'm a little dense at times, and maybe a little stubborn."

Everyone laughed. "A *little?*" most of them cried at the same time.

Cory grinned. "Well, okay then. Maybe I'm a lot stubborn. But I felt absolutely certain I could handle life on my own. I didn't need any help, especially from a God I couldn't see with my own eyes.

"However—"

The talent Cory had been known for had been in his fingers. He had a most awesome ability to play a keyed instrument such as a piano or a keyboard. But his voicing ability had remained untapped until all of a sudden, he turned to face the poinsettia cross and broke out in a verse of "Silent Night."

"All is calm, all is bright—" Never had those words held such deep meaning as they did that Christmas night. "All is calm, all is bright. Thank You, Lord Jesus," he finished in a whisper.

•

"We just lack one thing," Gabe added.

"What's that?" Cory asked.

"One high profile fugitive by the name of Kerry Cantrella."